Erin Go Bloody

A Sebastian McCabe – Jeff Cody Mystery

Dan Andriacco

Paperback ISBN 978-1-78705-011-2
ePub ISBN 978-1-78705-012-9
PDF ISBN 978-1-78705-013-6

Published in the UK by MX Publishing
335 Princess Park Manor, Royal Drive,
London, N11 3GX
www.mxpublishing.com
Cover design by Brian Belanger

This book is dedicated to

Steven Doyle, BSI

of Doyle's Irish Pub

CONTENTS

Chapter One
"Everything but the Grudges"

"I have the Irish Alzheimer's," Walter Ellicott declared. "I forget everything but the grudges."

Later I would remember that comment because it was a kind of prologue to murder and suicide. Even at the time it struck me as out of character for a corporate legal eagle like Walter. And yet he was talking loud enough that I could hear him over the low mumble of the soft jazz band a few yards away.

I'm not above eavesdropping at a crowded cocktail reception, so I moved a little closer. Walter was conversing with the stylish and refined Lesley Saylor-Mackie, who was slightly older and grayer but could match him crease by crease in the spit-and-polish department. They both wore blue pinstripes, but hers were softened with a red silk scarf. She's been known to wear dresses in off-hours, but apparently she considered this business, maybe even double business, given her two jobs.

"Of course he's my brother," Walter told her, "and blood is thicker than water and all that, so I guess I'm supposed to forgive him. But that's not happening." Walter stared down at his dark amber beverage, which I strongly suspected was not tea. His thick mustache appeared freshly trimmed. "When Jamie left town he gave the whole family one big digital salute. He didn't even come home for Mom's funeral. But now that Dad's not doing well, he's moved back. I think he just wants to make sure he's in the will."

Saylor-Mackie looked sympathetic. "And what does your father think?" I couldn't tell whether she was really interested in this soap opera or just wanted to keep the conversational ball rolling.

"All is forgiven." The expression on Walter's face matched the bitterness in his voice.

As he paused to take a healthy slug of liquid refreshment, his eyes landed on me just behind Saylor-Mackie's elbow. *Hey, I didn't hear a word about your family feud, Walter!* Trying not to look like a deer caught in the headlights, I nodded as acquaintances do. He nodded back and I quickly moved on toward the closest of the four bars set up around the Weiss Gallery of Art.

Accessing the Cody memory banks, I mentally reviewed what I knew about the Ellicott clan: Walter's father, Samson I. Ellicott, Jr., age seventy-six, had founded the company now known as Samson Microcircuits more than forty years ago. It's very high-tech stuff, microcircuits and semiconductors and whatnot for the defense industry. I'd heard that Ellicott had largely withdrawn from the day-to-day management after the death of his wife, Gladys. Samson I. Ellicott III, familiarly known as "Trey," now ran the company as president. Apparently he'd been doing a bang-up job, boosting revenues nicely after the Great Recession. Walter, just slightly older than me, was the corporation's lead attorney. I'd been vaguely aware that there was also a sister, but I hadn't known of a third brother. Unlike some people, I can't keep up on all the local gossip. Erin is a small town, but it's not St. Mary Mead.

Besides, I don't normally socialize with the likes of the Ellicott family. What had brought me into Walter's orbit that evening was a staff, faculty, and board soirée following the news conference announcing that St. Benignus College, where I slave away night and day as director of communications, would become St. Benignus University with the fall semester. Walter Ellicott was a long-time St.

Benignus board member. We'd had enough interactions in that capacity to be on a first-name basis.

His conversation partner at the reception, Ms. Saylor-Mackie, is head of the history department at St. Benignus and mayor of Erin in her spare time—or maybe vice versa, depending on your viewpoint. Whether her larger ambitions involved city or college (make that university!) politics I hadn't figured out yet. I usually call her Mayor or Professor, depending on the context.

"So what's the difference between a college and a university?"

That's the question Lynda had tossed me over dinner one night almost a year previously. She'd done some wordsmithing that day on a story about a state college no bigger than St. Benignus that branded itself a university in a bid to get more out-of-state and international students. If you're married to a journalist, as I am, you have to expect a few questions from time to time. But I didn't know how to answer that one. So I booted it the next day to my indispensable aide-de-camp, Aneliese "Popcorn" Pokorny. She poked around and found out that there is no hard-and-fast rule on that. And university sounds so much better. So why not rebrand?

It took me months to kick the idea up the food chain at work, fighting tooth and toenail for my brainstorm all the way. But after it had been high-fived by Father Joe Pirelli, our fearless leader, and the entire board of trustees, everybody else agreed that they'd always thought it was a swell move, and long overdue. Even Ralph Pendergast, our provost and academic vice president. You can say what you like about Ralph (as long as it's bad), but he does have a head for marketing. Under his direction, we had recently added five graduate programs and online courses aimed at military personnel. That made a good rationale for the name change.

The announcement of our new name and status was a watershed for the institution and a triumph for Father Joe, a white-haired, grandfatherly figure who worked the room at the reception with a glass of red wine in his hand. He had been president of St. Benignus and the face of the school for decades. Watching him, I couldn't help wondering whether he might decide to retire soon and spend more time on the golf course with his legacy firmly established.

But he wasn't retired yet. I knew that because I spotted him talking to Ralph. That had to be work.

I bellied up to the bar right behind the gnomish Gene Pfannenstiel, head librarian of the Lee J. Bennish Memorial Library on campus and curator of its Woollcott Chalmers Sherlock Holmes Collection. Grace Pendergast, Ralph's pleasant wife, was in the other line. We exchanged waves. If I were married to Ralph, I'd be getting ready to order myself a double of something alcoholic—and I don't even drink adult beverages much.

Well, usually I don't. Tonight I was not usual because Lynda was two months pregnant. Though not even showing yet in her standout red cocktail dress, she refused to indulge in her fondness for Kentucky bourbon while our first child was *in utero*. So I had to fill in.

"Have a drink for me, Jeff, will you?" she'd said in her throaty voice by way of sending me off to the bar.

"Uh, sure. I'll grab a Hudy DeLight."

"Make it a Manhattan."

"But I don't—"

"I know what I want, all right?"

Never argue with a pregnant woman, especially if she's your wife.

The gallery was packed with fellow St. Benignus staffers, interspersed with a number of freeloading politicos whom Saylor-Mackie had insisted on inviting. I spotted Lynda's pal, and mine, Sister Mary Margaret Malone craning her neck to chat with Lt. Ed Decker of Campus Security.

An oak tree in a brown suit, Ed is two heads taller than Triple M—two big heads. Reporter Maggie Barton, who has been covering St. Benignus for the *Erin Observer* & *News-Ledger* since the Bronze Age, made it a trio.

On the way back to Lynda from the bar, I nodded at Dr. Dante Peter O'Neill, head of the art department at St. Benignus. As usual, he was dressed like a *GQ* model in horn-rimmed glasses. At six-five, four inches taller than me, he looked around the room like a cop afraid somebody was going to steal one of the gallery's paintings. Spoiler alert: Nobody did. O'Neill should have relaxed and let Decker worry about the non-existent art thieves.

"Nice party," O'Neill said.

"Everybody seems happy." *Except Walter Ellicott.*

O'Neill and I had both been involved in planning the logistics for the reception, so this commentary was by way of patting ourselves on the back. Who else was going to do it?

When I got back to where I had started from, I found that in my absence my spouse had gathered family around her—my sister, Kate; my brother-in-law and best friend, Sebastian McCabe; and Popcorn, without whom I would get nothing done at work.

"Thank you, darling," Lynda said when I handed her a Diet Coke, usually my drink of choice in its caffeine-free variety. Her curly, honey-blond hair was done up in a French braid, one of my favorite styles.

"Hey, did you know that there's a third Ellicott brother?" I asked at large.

"Yes," all four of my companions said at the same time.

"Baaa," Popcorn added. At the same time, with a shake of her head, she refused a salami and cream cheese canapé that a waiter offered her. Weight-watching now that she was dating Oscar Hummel, was she? That sounded serious.

"What's that supposed to mean—baaa?" I asked.

"Black sheep of the family," Lynda translated. Eating for two, she accepted the calorie-laden canapé that Popcorn had refused.

"Jamie left Erin years ago, cursing the whole family and the horses they rode in on," Popcorn said, "except for his sister, Karen."

"I just got a hint of that from Walter Ellicott," I said. "I overheard him venting to the mayor. Daddy Samson apparently welcomed Jamie back to town with open arms, but Walter not so much. He claims his long lost brother's interest is more financial than familial. With Trey and Walter running the family business, I don't suppose that Jamie will be asked to join the executive suite."

"Hardly, old boy," Mac said with a chuckle. That's my brother-in-law—huge, bearded, and damned near always ebullient. "For one thing, he has created a public persona as a nouveau Luddite. That puts him squarely at odds with the technological basis of Samson Industries—perhaps not coincidentally. And besides, James Ivanhoe makes his living as a novelist."

"His name is Ivanhoe, not Ellicott? So he has a different father?"

"By no means. He adopted the Ivanhoe pseudonym for his fiction writing. I understand that he now uses it in daily life as well. If one were given to amateur psychoanalysis"—*as if you aren't*—"one might speculate that in choosing his *nom-de-plum* he rejected his family and embraced it at the same time. Ivanhoe is his paternal great-grandmother's maiden name, and the 'I' in Samson I. Ellicott—all three of them. However, the surname is also redolent of the hero in the eponymous historical romance by Sir Walter Scott, so perhaps that was a reason for the choice as well."

Whatever. I'll just call the man Ivanhoe from now on. There are enough Ellicotts in this account already.

"I've heard about him and his books from his sister-in-law, Cassandra Ellicott, but that's the only place," Lynda said.

"James Ivanhoe has a relatively small but devoted readership," Mac said. "He writes historical mystery novels rather in the manner of John Dickson Carr, strong on atmospherics and the use of the 'impossible crime' trope. Many of them involve some of the more colorful characters from the pages of history, such as Queen Elizabeth I's court astrologer, John Dee, and the mysterious eighteenth-century alchemist, Comte Saint-Germain. They would be better if they were shorter, in my opinion."

"So, do you know this dude?" I asked.

"Our paths have crossed. He is not a gregarious man, still less a sociable one. I understand that he has talked of building a log cabin in the woods for his residence in Erin."

That sounded cool. As the son of a Realtor, I've always been interested in houses, and a log cabin surrounded by flora and fauna has always been a secret dream of mine. (Which I guess is no longer secret.)

"Walter's wife despises Ivanhoe even more than Walter does," Lynda said.

"How do you know that?" I asked. This was the kind of local intelligence, i.e., who hates whom, that I usually pick up from Popcorn.

Lynda eyed the Manhattan in my hand longingly. I sipped at it, unexpectedly enjoying the taste.

"Cassandra Ellicott volunteers with me at Serenity House." That's Erin's leading social service agency, which helps the helpless in numerous ways. "She's been unloading on Ivanhoe—'Jamie,' as the family members still call him—ever since he got back to town. Obviously, those two must have a history. She wouldn't hate him so much if she hadn't loved him once. Also, he's more her type than her stodgy lawyer husband."

Mac raised an eyebrow at that. He said nothing, but my wife had probably just inspired his next mystery novel.

"I've never met the woman," I said, "but I know she's Lincoln Todd's daughter." I'd worked with Todd, executive director of the Sussex County Convention & Visitors Bureau, on a number of civic projects. There are more conventions and more visitors to our community than you might think, drawn by the race track, the minor league baseball team, and the small town charm just forty miles upriver from Cincinnati. Todd was a friend of Ralph's, but I tried not to hold that against him. At least he had good taste in literature, being fond of some of the same hard-boiled detective novels that I hold dear.

"Turn around slowly," Lynda said. "Cassandra's the one in the dress that looks like a Mondrian painting." I don't know Mondrian from Monet. Or is it Manet? Kate's the artist in the family. But somehow I instinctively knew that Cassandra Todd Ellicott was the blonde in the multi-colored frock, lots of bright rectangles, yakking it up with Tony Lampwicke from our campus radio station, WIJC-FM. I pegged her age at early thirties, maybe a decade younger than her husband. She had a large tattoo of the sun on her well-formed right leg. When she ran her hand through her hair I saw that she wore gold earrings matching the tattoo.

"She has expensive taste," Kate observed, "but not good taste."

What was a guy to say to that? I looked down at the empty glass in my hand.

"That Manhattan wasn't bad," I said.

"Have another," Lynda ordered.

I shouldn't. Well, okay. The things I do for you.

"Does the Ellicott family story remind you of anything?" Mac asked on the way to the bar.

"Yeah. That TV game show, *Family Feud.*"

"I was thinking more along the lines of the New Testament. The Ellicotts call to my mind the Parable of the Prodigal Son, which some Scripture scholars have suggested might better be called the Parable of the Loving Father. While I am touched by the unconditional love of the father in that story, I have always had some empathy for the good son who stayed home and did everything right. The Ellicott family appears to have two such 'good sons,' plus a good daughter. If they resent the returning prodigal, that could create an explosive situation."

I handed two empty glasses to the bartender, who looked about twelve years old except for the handlebar mustache, and ordered up a fresh Manhattan and another Diet Coke.

"Walter did seem to have his shorts in a bunch about Ivanhoe," I acknowledged to Mac, "but I'm sure it will all work out."

I should have known better.

Chapter Two
The St. Patrick's Day Charade

I don't remember much of the reception after that, although I vividly recall the next day's Manhattan-sized hangover.

That was in late May. Over the next several months, during which the only alcohol that passed my lips was in mouthwash (despite my wife's pleading), James Ivanhoe's name kept popping up.

For example, there was a section-front feature story in a Sunday edition of the *Erin Observer & News-Ledger* in early summer. Lynda commented favorably on the headline, **HISTORY IS NO MYSTERY FOR LOCAL WRITER**. The accompanying photo showed the author looking very Byronic, with long dark hair, and surrounded by stacks of his own books. Interested in the subject, I read every word of the article. I reprint it here with permission:

By Henry Knox Wilcox
Observer & News-Ledger contributor

Many writers turn to exotic locales for mystery, romance, and adventure. Erin novelist James Ivanhoe looks to earlier times.

"I have always been fascinated with the past in all periods," said Ivanhoe, 35. "Maybe that's because I'm so dissatisfied with the present and so pessimistic about the future."

Ivanhoe's latest novel, *The Whirligig of Time*, is about a burnt-out American private eye named Peter Schiller who sells his soul to the devil in exchange for the opportunity to travel back to Victorian England and solve the Jack the Ripper murders.

With the help of Arthur Conan Doyle and Doyle's mentor, Dr. Joseph Bell, the detective learns the shocking truth about the connection between the Ripper murders and the Hermetic Order of the Golden Dawn, an occult society founded the same year as the Whitechapel killings. It is a truth with profound implications for the detective's family and for the twentieth century.

Schiller's daunting challenge then becomes to change history—and save his soul in the process.

The book, Ivanhoe's seventh, has been climbing steadily in the Amazon rankings since its release three weeks ago. His previous novels include *Blood Moon*, *Fire and Ice*, *Black Magic*, and *The Queen of Hearts*.

"I love that Faulkner quote that the past is never dead, it's not even past," Ivanhoe said as he signed books at Mo's Mysteries and Marvels bookstore in downtown Erin. "Most of my books reflect that, I suppose.

"I'm also intrigued by the Faust legend of the man who sold his soul to the devil, or rather, traded it. Our culture has done the same thing in a way, made a kind of Faustian bargain with technology. We've gained a lot by buying into every new gizmo that's offered to us, but we've also lost a lot in terms of our humanity."

Fittingly, Ivanhoe, who grew up in Erin and recently moved back after a thirteen-year absence, writes on a typewriter rather than a computer.

He's also the president of the Ned Ludd Society. Don't expect to find a website for it. The group eschews almost every hallmark of the computer age, including the Internet and social media. Such technologies are not only unnecessary, Ivanhoe argued, they are actually harmful.

"Social media are anti-social," he said. "They pull people apart as much as they bring them together. People say mean-spirited things on Facebook or Twitter that they would never say to a person's face. In cyberspace, differences of opinion often escalate into nastiness with unbelievable speed.

"Social media magnify the trivial, and therefore trivialize the important," he continued. "People who know nothing but have a lot of Twitter followers are treated as sages. News stories often rely on Twitter and Facebook as sources of information. When a celebrity dies the obituary often includes his or her last tweet. This is mass insanity."

Ivanhoe acknowledged that he "may sound like a young curmudgeon."

"But don't call me a technophobe," he pleaded. "I'm kind of a techno-selective. I don't reject all technology. I mean, the wheel is a technology and my bicycle has two of those."

So, he was a fellow bike rider! Ivanhoe couldn't be as bad as Walter Ellicott seemed to think.

The long story included some background on the name Ned Ludd. General Ludd was a semi-legendary character whose name was appropriated in early nineteenth century England by a group of people who destroyed knitting frames—the high-tech of the day—to preserve jobs. The name of the society was "something of a joke," Ivanhoe was quoted as saying. "We don't plan to break anything."

What the story did not include was any reference to the Ellicotts.

Lynda, whose job as editorial director at the *Observer & News-Ledger*'s parent company makes her a circuit rider for quality journalism at its various Ohio outlets, agreed with Ivanhoe that reporters rely too much on social media. "Lazy journalism," she complained.

"He does offer some points worth pondering," Mac said the next day when I pressed him for a reaction. "I myself am worried about the addictive nature of digital technology. How is it that we can no longer function without devices that did not exist for most of our lives? I have observed elderly individuals accessing their smartphones during a film."

"You're a fine one to talk!" I retorted. "You once took your laptop along on a fishing trip so you could work on a novel while Oscar and I were catching fish."

"An excellent example, Jefferson! You have made my point for me. Of course, I would never do that today. I now have an iPad." He also owns the latest version of every other techno-toy. I expect his wristwear to change as soon as the iWatch comes out in a Sherlock Holmes model. "And yet, I am not in any true sense a modern man. I would feel much more at home in an earlier century."

"So how about *The Whirligig of Time*?" I asked. "Is it worth *my* valuable time?"

Mac proclaimed the novel to be an ingenious foray into speculative history, although he judged it not as good as some of Ivanhoe's earlier works. "I had never noticed that the Order of the Golden Dawn and the Ripper appeared on the British scene contemporaneously in 1888. Perhaps James is onto something with that as well. He is a meticulous researcher. The title, of course, comes from Shakespeare's *Twelfth Night*, Act Five, Scene One: 'The whirligig of time brings in his revenges.'" *Of course.*

I made a mental note to borrow the book from the library—*The Whirligig of Time*, not *The Twelfth Night*.

Popcorn didn't have much to say about the story, but she thought Ivanhoe looked "luscious." Her taste in fiction still leans more to the steamy romance novels of one Rosamund DeLacey, even though she now knows the pseudonymous author's true identity.[1]

Myself, I watched *The Whirligig of Time* climb in the Amazon ratings and even make its way to the bottom of the *New York Times* best-seller list for a few weeks. All the while I wondered how much of what Ivanhoe prattled on about in the interview he really believed and how much was as phony as his last name. I got a partial answer to that a few weeks later in the summer when I ran into Amos Yoder, an Amish craftsman who'd built some bookcases for Lynda and me not long before.

The Amish are a visible presence in our part of Ohio. I'd always been intrigued by them. They don't have credit cards and they don't borrow money. How could I not like a subculture of people who make me look like a spendthrift—and my seldom-driven car is eighteen years old? And although they constitute a separate society from everyone else, whom they call "*Englishers*" or "the English," the Amish are also friendly and welcoming.

"What's new?" I asked Amos, as usual. I think that's a funny line to throw a guy who drives a horse and buggy

---

[1] See *Bookmarked for Murder*, MX Publishing, 2015.

and wears clothes that went out of style about 1836, but he never gets the joke.

"I'm building a log cabin for a customer," he said. "That's new because I haven't done one of those in a while."

This struck a chord of memory.

"Let me see if I can read your mind." I closed my eyes and put my right hand up to my forehead in a dramatic gesture that I hoped was evocative of a stage mentalist. "The customer is . . . James Ivanhoe."

He thought a moment. "You didn't read my mind."

"The customer isn't Ivanhoe?"

"Oh, it's Mr. Ivanhoe for sure, yeah, but you didn't read my mind because nobody can read minds. Somebody must have told you."

I gave up. He was no fun. "Does the cabin have all the modern conveniences—for this century, I mean?"

"It has everything a person needs, but he told me he wasn't getting a phone or a cable hookup."

No Internet, then. So Ivanhoe's persona as a "techno-selective" wasn't just a façade to set him apart from other authors on the interview circuit. I filed that away as an interesting factoid and didn't think much more about it until early September.

Mac and I were dining at Bobbie McGee's Sports Bar one night a couple of weeks before my forty-second birthday. (How can I be so old?) Our wives, who sometimes seem more like sisters to each other than sisters-in-law, had abandoned us for some chick flick.

"Remember what this place was like when we were students?" I said, waxing nostalgic. In those days the bar had been known as Doyle's Irish Pub, and it was owned by a former boxer named Schmitz. Go figure. Of course, that was back in the days when I was smarter than my phone, which I didn't carry in my pocket or use to take pictures. In other words, it was a long time ago and sometimes seemed even longer.

"I remember it quite well, Jefferson. The food was not as good then and only three brands of beer were available on tap, none of them exceptional. Also, there was but one television in the establishment, mounted in a corner, and it had approximately a twenty-one-inch screen."

Mac didn't seem to get it that things were always better in the past, even when they weren't. But before I could wise him up on that score, Brett McGee plunked down at our table in a state of high dudgeon that was out of character for him. His signature grin had taken a sabbatical.

"We're screwed," he announced.

"That sounds like the theme of a *film noir* movie," Mac said, pouring from the pitcher of beer in front of him.

Brett looked blank. "If you say so."

You no doubt remember Brett McGee as the curly-haired Cincinnati Reds slugger, more than twenty years at the plate for his hometown team. But around Erin, he's Mr. Bobbie McGee. His wife wears the cowboy hat and balances the books at her restaurant; Brett eats there. He also owns a car dealership in Cincinnati. In five or six years, I may see him about a replacement for my not-so-new New Volkswagen.

"So what's the problem?" I asked.

"It's the parade. It's turning into a damned charade."

I didn't need to ask which parade. Erin's St. Patrick's Day celebration is the third or fourth largest in the country, depending on which list you believe. Planning for it was well under way half a year before the event. Brett was president of the St. Patrick's Day Parade Committee, the Ancient Order of Hibernians having given up sponsorship long ago. I was a member of the committee as well, and not because the surname "Cody" comes from the Gaelic "ÓCuidighthigh." I represented St. Benignus University, as it was now branded. We always have a major float in the parade, St. Benignus having been St. Patrick's disciple and the second bishop of Ireland.

"Please elaborate," Mac said, pouring Brett a Rivertown Roebling Porter from his pitcher into a glass that an observant server had added to our table upon Brett's arrival.

"Some guy named Ivanhoe—a book writer—filed an application to march in the parade under the name of something called the Ned Ludd Society."

Mac arched an eyebrow.

"And why is that a problem?" I asked.

Brett downed some of his beer, and then answered: "Because it's not the Holy Name Society or the St. Vincent de Paul Society, that's why. It's a different kind of society. I'm not sure that I entirely get it, but from what Linc Todd tells me, it's some kind of looney-tunes anti-technology group. They hate computers or something. That means it's a cause, and we don't do causes. You know that, Jeff. It's one of our rules. Because if we let one cause in, we'd have to let them all in and it would be a mess."

I nodded sympathetically. St. Patrick's Day parades in other cities had been marred over the years by disputes over including or not including gay rights groups. No matter how the organizers handled these situations, I'm sure they also wound up saying "we're screwed" or the more emphatic equivalent.

"Besides," Brett added in a lower voice as he leaned forward, "it doesn't take a Stephen Hawking to figure out that Samson Microcircuits wouldn't like it, and that's one of our major corporate sponsors."

"Ah, yes, the prodigal son's siblings," Mac said.

"But it's partly Ivanhoe's company, too," I protested. "He inherited a share."

"I have heard rumblings, Jefferson."

So had I. Samson Ivanhoe Ellicott, Jr., the patriarch of the Ellicott clan and founder of Samson Microcircuits, had died over the summer. The end was not a surprise, and all of his progeny were gathered at his bedside when it happened. That rare moment of sibling harmony apparently lasted less time than it took for the old man's body to cool. I'd heard that Trey and Walter left the hospital headed in one direction, James and Karen in another. But the estate, including the ownership of the company, had been split among all four. The Erin rumor mill, to which I'd kept a close ear after that reception in May, was buzzing that Trey and Walter planned to challenge the will in court. *"I have the Irish Alzheimer's. I forget everything but the grudges."*

"What are you guys talking about?" Brett asked.

"James Ivanhoe is actually an Ellicott, and one of the old man's heirs." I gave him the CliffsNotes version of the family saga, ending with the business of the will.

The stunned look on Brett's still-handsome face surprised me. The future Hall of Famer wasn't an Erin native, but didn't everybody in town know about this fractious family by now?

"I had no idea," Brett said. "All I knew about Ivanhoe was that he was a writer, and doing pretty well for himself. Why the different last name?"

"Undoubtedly he wishes to distance himself from a family that he largely disdains," Mac opined.

"But not from their money," I quipped.

"Touché, Jefferson!"

Brett gulped again from his glass of dark brew. "So you're telling me that this Ivanhoe may wind up with a fourth of Samson Microcircuits. But even if he does, that's not control. We'd still have one of our major sponsors unhappy about an entry in the parade that I don't want in anyway. You're the PR guy, Jeff. How do we keep this Ned Ludd Society out of the parade without causing a big brouhaha in the media?"

"You can't, that's all. It's as simple as that."

I gave the answer without a second's thought. Mac can pontificate all day long on mysteries and magic and so forth, but we were in my zone now. Handling controversies is a big part of what I do.

"If you turn down his application," I continued, "Ivanhoe will raise holy hell for sure. He'll pit himself against you. Think of what that fight looks like from the media's ringside seat: On one side you have a guy who can call himself a *New York Times* bestselling author, and on the other a legend of baseball. You can't expect the media to ignore that. It'll be a journalistic free-for-all! Even the sports columnists will be weighing in."

"So, should we let the Ned Ludd Society in?"

"I know what my father would say: What would you do if you weren't afraid?"

"A very astute question," Mac muttered.

"Afraid?" Brett didn't seem familiar with the concept.

"Yeah. If you weren't afraid of losing a sponsor and if you weren't afraid of setting off a big controversy, what would you do about Ivanhoe's group being in the parade?"

Brett didn't hesitate. "I'd go to the rest of the parade committee and say, 'Let's stick to the rule. The parade is a fun, family event to celebrate the day when everybody is Irish. Save the pet causes for another day.'"

"Then that's your answer. Don't worry about making everybody happy—because that's not possible. Whatever you decide is going to piss people off, so you might as well do what you think is the right thing."

Brett looked bleak. "People will take sides."

I nodded. "I'm afraid so. And maybe not just in Erin, at least for a few days. Things could get a bit bumpy. But don't lose any of your curly hair over it. It's not life and death."

Chapter Three
St. Patrick the Luddite

So Brett McGee took his set-in-concrete position to the parade committee via conference call and we all concurred: No banner of the Ned Ludd Society would be permitted in the parade, as per the long-standing rules. James Ivanhoe would be welcome to march as a celebrity author, but sans the Ludd propaganda.

Not surprisingly, Ivanhoe didn't roll over. Instead, he chose to take it outside by going to the media, just as I had feared (but kept mostly to myself).

What would eventually become a minor tsunami of news coverage began with a ten-inch story in the local section of the *Erin Observer & News-Ledger* under the top-of-the-page headline **NO SHAMROCKS FOR ANTI-TECH GROUP**. ("Not a bad head," Lynda judged.) The headshots accompanying it were of Ivanhoe, cropped down from the photo of his book signing, and of Brett McGee in a Cincinnati Reds cap.

Reporter Johanna Rawls gave a balanced account with quotes from both the author and the athlete. Brett pounded on the rulebook: "There have always been restrictions on what kind of groups can be in the parade, and they have served us well." Ivanhoe played to the emotions, tossing logic out the door: "I don't think St. Patrick would have any objection to our group. He did perfectly well in the fifth century without the problematic technologies that the Ned Ludd Society is trying to highlight."

Johanna's story—one of three in the paper with her byline that day—also had Lincoln Todd, from the Convention & Visitors Bureau, weighing in to say, "St. Patrick's Day is not a time to parade our social values or political beliefs." I thought that was a rather good quote when I wrote it for him.

Veteran reporter Morris Kindle in the Cincinnati bureau of the Associated Press picked up the story and rewrote it to emphasize the Brett McGee angle. Johanna's lead sentence had been: "The St. Patrick's Day Parade Committee has banned a group skeptical of most digital technology from marching in the parade." The rewrite became: "Six months before the event, legendary Reds slugger Brett McGee is in a dustup over a St. Patrick's Day Parade in his adopted hometown."

That six-month lag between Brett putting the kibosh on the Ned Ludd Society and the date of the parade gave lots of opportunities for different media to keep discovering the story. It was death by a thousand cuts as stories varying in tone from smirking to sneering trickled out over the months in *Tick* magazine, *Sports Illustrated, Us,* Prime News Network, *USA Today, The Irish Echo,* and even NPR. Somewhat lacking in originality of presentation, the stories invariably referred to "the growing controversy around this time-honored small-town tradition," or similar words. Why are controversies always described in the news media as "growing"? (And why are majorities are always "vast," for that matter?)

In every story, Ivanhoe made it clear that he wasn't giving up. Neither did the folks who felt compelled to hoist the flag for the digital age. Defenders defended the writer and opponents opposed him in letters to the editor (online as well as in print) and in tweets and other social media postings. Of course they had hashtags—*#goludd* and *#noludd* memorably among them. The irony of this high-tech face-off over the Ned Ludd Society was not lost on me. But after a while the amusement paled and I stopped keeping track of the stuff I discovered through Google Alert.

In Erin, people were talking and, as Brett had predicted, taking sides.

"It's a parade, for crying out loud!" I complained to Mac late one autumn afternoon before the comfort of a fire in his man cave. "Western civilization doesn't hang in the balance! Since when did marching in a parade become a human right? And since when did every difference of opinion cause people to explode into digital road rage on the information superhighway?"

"As to the latter," Mac mused from the depths of his leather wingback chair, "I believe that the seeds for it were sown with the development of the first blogs in the late 1990s. Blogs and social media give everyone a voice, and most people feel that their voice is as important and valid as everyone else's—whether they know anything about the subject at hand or not. That does seem to escalate tensions, making all issues big issues. James Ivanhoe said something of the sort in an interview, did he not?"

Even a stopped clock is right twice a day.

If Ivanhoe's Ned Ludd Society gig was in any measure a publicity stunt, it worked—at least at the Sussex County Public Library. I was on the waiting list for *The Whirligig of Time* for weeks before I finally got my hands on it. Lynda waited almost as long to take out an e-copy. Whatever his personal flaws and foibles might be, Lynda and I agreed that the man could sure write a page-turner. The fantasy aspects of the book appealed to her, and I was drawn in by the hard-boiled prose style.

By the holiday season, the controversy about an event that was still months away had faded. Or maybe I just wasn't paying attention anymore because I had more important things on my mind. Like fatherhood.

Lynda delivered our first child, Donata Marie, on December 25—the greatest Christmas present ever. She was named for Lynda's late *nonna*—grandmother—to whom my wife was very close. Our baby had Lynda's dark complexion and an impressive head of curly hair in a color that couldn't quite make up its mind between blond and red. Her eyes were blue, like mine, but don't all infants have blue eyes?

"She looks just like—" Lynda began.

"A baby," I said.

Let's face it, all babies look like Winston Churchill, but I was smart enough not to voice that.

Erin didn't have a white Christmas that year, but we were hit with a near-blizzard in the first week of January. With Lynda and I both on parental leave, being snowed in was never so much fun. We cuddled up in front of the fire and watched Donata have a hard day of being cute—day after day. Occasionally her cousins, the three McCabe kids, would come over to hold her. Friends dropped by and/or sent flowers. I didn't even mind the lack of sleep.

One evening, while Lynda was nursing the baby, a task for which she is quite well endowed, I surfed into an author-interview show called *Bookmarks* on PBS. All of a sudden my TV screen was filled with the Byronic image of James Ivanhoe, looking like he could pose for the male lead on the cover of one of those paperback bodice rippers that Popcorn reads. The middle-aged woman in magenta glasses who interviewed him didn't giggle or drool, however; this was PBS, after all. We joined her in mid-sentence.

"—a computer?" she finished.

"No, I've never felt the need to. I use a manual typewriter, just like Loren D. Estleman. Loren's a fine writer and a prolific one—more than eighty books, all turned out on his typewriter."

Okay, that hooked me. Estleman is a terrific private eye writer, although he plays in other playgrounds as well.

The interviewer looked earnestly quizzical. "How does that work? Don't writers today have to submit their manuscripts electronically? And what about having a website, a Facebook page, a Twitter account?"

Ivanhoe chuckled. "All of those things get done. I just don't do them. My agent is very good at that sort of thing."

"I like his hair," Lynda informed me. "Maybe you should let yours grow long like that."

I threw a plush pillow at her.

"Just trying to help, darling."

The camera shifted back to the interviewer, who was now helpfully identified at the bottom of the screen as Marianna Hudson-Klein. She shifted in her seat, body language that told me she was going to change the direction of her questions. "We've talked about the way you treat the Victorian era in *The Whirligig of Time*. All of your novels are set at least partially in the past, when computers didn't exist—or even typewriters, in some cases. In your stories, the past is often in tension with the present. Do you think that past times were better times?"

Not a bad question, I thought, having by this time worked my way backwards through the entire James Ivanhoe *oeuvre*. My favorite was *Black Magic*, in which the eighteenth-century occultist Cagliostro has to prove that he *doesn't* have magic powers after being accused of a murder that couldn't have been committed any other way—by him or by anyone else. Along the way, Cagliostro solves the ingenious crime as a side effect.

Ivanhoe's smile was just short of condescending. "That's way too broad a question. A little over a hundred and fifty years ago we had slavery in this country. That wasn't better. Women couldn't vote in the United States a hundred years ago. That wasn't better. So, obviously, the twenty-first century is a good place to be in a lot of ways.

And technology has helped. I rather like electricity and central heating, for example."

The smile faded. "But the digital technology that's been embraced without a second thought by most people over the past few decades is unhealthy in several ways, for individuals and for our culture as a whole. Smartphones and tablets can cause their users to suffer text-neck syndrome, obesity, trouble sleeping, depression, radiation, and addiction. I didn't make that up." *Who said you did? A little paranoid, are you?* "The studies that consistently verify these problems are usually given some ink in *USA Today* or *The Telegraph* and then promptly ignored, but they exist. And I haven't even mentioned the car deaths related to texting while driving, the careers ruined because of an imprudent tweet intended as a lame joke, or the threats to privacy posed by the ability to track text messages, e-mails, and even the location of mobile phones."

That last was a big help to law enforcement, I knew, although I suppose that would be cold comfort to someone of a libertarian bent.

"Then I assume you haven't cut your landline," Ms. Hudson-Klein quipped with a smile.

"I don't even have a landline at the moment, Marianna. I've decided to do without one in my new home, at least for a few months. And I must say I'm enjoying the quiet."

Ivanhoe was going further than he had in the *Observer & News Ledger* interview, in which he had limited his assault to social media. (And after a few weeks of following the Facebook and Twitter rage over the St. Patrick's Day Parade, I wasn't so sure he was wrong on that score.) But his greater concern about computer technology was no surprise, coming as it did from the president of the Ned Ludd Society.

"I've heard that you live in a log cabin," Ms. Hudson-Klein said.

The writer seemed to relax at the very thought of it. "That's true—a cabin in the woods, built by an Amish builder."

"You sound a little Amish yourself."

He shook his head slightly. "I'm not a religious man. But I do agree with the Amish approach to technology—which isn't what you probably think. They ride in buggies instead of cars and they use natural gas instead of electricity, but that doesn't mean they shun all technology. From what I've learned by talking to my Amish friends, the local bishop decides what's allowed. In general, the principle is this: Don't use technology that divides the community. So even though they don't usually have telephones, they might be allowed one community phone to serve a number of families and to do business. Some Amish bishops even permit cell phones for use in business.

"By the way, some Amish use hydro-electric, wind, and solar power, and there are quite a few energy-based Amish businesses, especially solar. Obviously, that's high-tech, not no-tech. So the Amish are very discerning about this."

Marianna Hudson-Klein looked fascinated. "I guess we could all learn something from that example. Of all of the dangers of technology that you cited a few minutes ago, which do you think is the greatest?"

Ivanhoe didn't even pause. "The biggest technological danger, both for our culture and for individuals, is the addictive nature of digital media—what some have even called digital drugs. So many people today feel that they have to be connected all the time. They look at their work e-mail while they're on vacation, they check posts on Facebook and send tweets while they're in a theater, and they can't walk down the street or drive without talking on the phone.

"And what's the bottom line on all of this 24/7 connectedness? Smartphones and tablets and all of those pricey techno-toys haven't made us any happier as individuals or collectively as a society. It's just the opposite, in fact—they've made us more anxious."

"You raise some interesting issues, but not everyone would agree with you."

"Of course not. I'm pretty sure that Tim Cook at Apple isn't in my corner, for instance. What does he make—about $65 million a year for running a company with highly questionable labor and environmental practices?"

Ouch.

The expression on Hudson-Klein's face said she was offended by this indelicate low blow. "I was thinking of your own hometown, Mr. Ivanhoe. You've been banned from the St. Patrick's Day Parade in Erin, Ohio, because of your Luddite views, haven't you?"

No, no, no, Marianna! The guy can march in a kilt without underwear for all we care—he just can't carry a Ned Ludd Society banner while he's doing it Sheesh!.

The superior Ivanhoe smile returned in triumph. "It's a long way to the middle of March. I'm sure we can work things out. You know, St. Patrick lived in the fifth century and he . . ."

"Time for Mommy to take a potty break," Lynda told Donata, carefully handing her over to me. "You be a good girl."

"No burping," I said sternly, arranging her on my left arm.

She burped, then smiled adorably.

As Lynda left the room, I slipped the smartphone out of my front pocket and checked my e-mail.

Chapter Four
"This Isn't Over!"

The parade issue simmered on low boil for a couple more months. The national media moved on to other controversies *du jour* and the denizens of Erin seemed to have largely forgotten about a topic that had been so tweet-worthy in the fall.

So I was a little surprised when social media started buzzing about it again a few weeks before the parade. Both sides were urging their partisans to attend the Wednesday, February 24, Erin City Council meeting. The St. Patrick's Day Parade was on the agenda, which puzzled me.

"The parade is privately run and doesn't get a dime from the city coffers," I reminded Mac, no doubt unnecessarily. "What does City Council have to do with it?"

"Nothing, old boy! That is what will make this afternoon's meeting such good sport. We must attend."

"You mean I'm supposed to just drop everything and leave work to go with you?"

He chuckled. "You usually do."

Fair point.

"Well, I suppose I should be there," I mused. "I do represent the university on the parade committee. So I wouldn't *really* be leaving work by hoofing it over to City Hall; I'd just be working out of the office."

Nobody can out-rationalize Jeff Cody.

The City Council chambers on the second floor of City Hall, an antebellum brick pile on Main Street, were filled with more people and more chatter than I'd ever experienced. Maybe that's because my previous trips had all involved some smile-worthy event like an award for Father Joe or the official renaming of Fort Hogue Way to St. Benignus Boulevard.

Mac and I squeezed in at the back left of the room. The eight Council members sat at handsome wood desks on a dais at the front of the room, facing us rabble. While the guardians of our local democracy argued about a plan to share some city services with the county as a cost-saving measure, I studied the audience.

Bernard J. Silverstein, of the *Erin Observer & News-Ledger*, sat in a front row scribbling away. He also had his smartphone next to him, ready to tweet out important developments. Ben had given up police and most of his other beats (courts, aviation, and the garden column) upon succeeding Lynda as news editor, but he'd kept the local government portfolio. On a paper that small, even the boss has to do some work.

In an era in which few journalists even bother to wear ties, Ben was always well suited. Gray-haired and stocky, he was also one of the few men I knew who smoked a pipe, a gnarled wood number, although only where permitted.

Just a few rows in front of us, James Ivanhoe sat with his jeans-clad legs crossed in a casual attitude. He was talking to a slim, athletic woman in her early thirties with neck-length chestnut hair tucked behind her ears. A few rows up and across an aisle I spotted Cassandra Ellicott by her piled-up blond hair. She occasionally mouthed a few words to her husband, who was sitting next to her. Walter muttered his responses without looking up from the tablet on his lap.

Other partisans in the chambers babbled at a low rumble through most of the Council meeting, occasionally holding up their hand-painted cardboard signs (**Against the**

Machine and the opposing **#NoLudd**, for example). Mundane stuff like who was going to put out fires in the city of Erin and how that was going to be paid for seemed to hold little interest for them. The city-county proposal got tabled anyway. On to the agenda hot spot!

"The next item is a resolution from Mr. Gordon," Mayor Saylor-Mackie announced. I could almost see her temples throbbing beneath her distinguished gray hair. As an historian, she might enjoy reading Ivanhoe's books for recreation. But I knew from talking to her that she had little patience with Bruce Gordon's resolution, seeing it as an unwarranted and time-wasting interference in a private gig. As mayor, she only got to vote when there was a tie. That hardly ever happened with resolutions, which tended to be non-controversial. But this one might be different.

"*Pro-Ludd resolution introduced,*" Ben tweeted. I won't give you all of his blow-by-blow Twitter coverage, but it was comprehensive enough that when I got home that night Lynda knew most of what had happened just from following her Twitter feed. ("If it were a Shakespeare play," she said, "it would have been *Much Ado About Nothing.*" Everybody's a critic. But she was right.)

Councilman Gordon, his potbelly barely reined in by a pair of bright yellow suspenders, grabbed the microphone in front of him. "My resolution is so simple that even my fellow Council members should be able to understand it." That was classic Gordy. He fancies himself a straight-talking maverick. "It merely declares that this Council supports the right of Ned Ludd Society members to march under the banner of their organization in the St. Patrick's Day Parade."

Ivanhoe and a group of supporters clapped. Gordy glared at them, even though they were his claque. You might wonder how this misanthrope got elected. I credit stamina (he ran three times) and name recognition. He owns the biggest floral shop in town, and for my money the best. He's also been around Erin for seventy-one years, never mind that he apparently prefers plants to people.

"We have a rather large attendance here today," Saylor-Mackie observed. "So for the benefit of those who have never attended a City Council meeting, I will explain our procedures. Any resident of Erin who has registered to speak can now come up to the microphone, in an orderly fashion, and speak for up to three minutes. If you reach the three minutes, I will let you know. Please begin by clearly stating your name for the record."

The first person to the microphone was a young woman with curly black hair down to her shoulders. She seemed vaguely familiar to me, maybe from seeing her around campus. Also, I was pretty sure she wasn't wearing a bra.

"My name is Lani Alvarez and I represent the Young Socialist Brigade at St. Benignus University," she announced. *Wait a minute! That's not an official student group!* Ralph had taken away their campus recognition because the YSB's national charter is not only Trotskyist but atheist as well. "The St. Patrick's Day Parade is racist, sexist, homophobic, and a tool of the capitalist-imperialist state. The Young Socialist Brigade will be there to protest. City Council should condemn this farce, not try to fix it. But what can we expect from an elitist group in which female and minority members are so underrepresented. Where are the Latinas?"

"Where is the relevance to the resolution?" Mac whispered loudly in my ear. I didn't answer; I know a rhetorical question when I hear one.

Without waiting for an answer to her own rhetorical question, Alvarez bounced off in her two-hundred-dollar Nikes. She *definitely* wasn't wearing a bra.

Next up: "My name is James Ivanhoe. I'm a resident and a native of Erin." There was some scattered applause. His sister-in-law Cassandra seemed to be watching the handsome writer carefully. "I remember coming to the St. Patrick's Day Parade with my family when I was a kid. It was always a fun time. It doesn't seem to me such a big deal to be allowed to participate under the name of a group that's very important to me, the Ned Ludd Society. We have important issues to raise—too important to be just swept off the table by the archaic rules of the unelected parade committee. I'm grateful to City Council for taking up this issue, and I hope you will vote for this resolution."

I graded him an A-. The appeal to nostalgia and keeping it short were both good moves. Ben's tweet referred to him as "*returned native Jamie Ellicott cum-Ivanhoe.*"

Brett McGee was equally grateful to the eight men and women on the dais. "I want to first of all thank City Council for their support of the St. Patrick's Day Parade over the years. You've helped to make it one of the biggest such parades in the country by suspending the open container law for several city blocks so that participants can enjoy a few beers on the street. But, as chairman of the committee, I would like to point out that this is all we've ever asked from the city. We have never requested or received taxpayer money. That was a strategic choice on the committee's part. We like our independence from government and we plan to keep it."

Translation: Please butt out.

But since that wasn't going to happen, Brett moved on to the core issue:

"This isn't about whether an individual can march in the parade. It's about what banners can be carried. What we call our 'Parade Orders,' the rules we operate under, have always specified that the parade not be used to advance any political party, social movement, or cause. For that reason, we don't allow any groups to carry signs that would do so. In our judgment, a banner bearing the name of the Ned Ludd Society would fall into that category. With all respect, that will remain our position no matter how Council votes on this resolution, which—as you know—doesn't bind us in any way. Thank you."

"*Strong pitch from Brett McGee,*" Ben Silverstein tweeted too cutely. Brett had been a catcher. But I agreed with Ben's assessment that he had delivered the goods for our committee.

Brett walked briskly back to his seat, not the hustle of his baseball years but not dogging it either. It was as if he were making up for almost going over the time limit—the first speaker to get anywhere close. Bobbie McGee kissed him as he sat down, prompting the ex-athlete to break into his familiar boyish grin.

The Lincolnesque Lincoln Todd—tall, lean, and sporting a Great Emancipator-style beard without a mustache—stepped up to one of the other microphones and identified himself as a member of the St. Patrick's Day Parade Committee. "Speaking on behalf of the Convention & Visitors Bureau, we're very concerned that City Council is spending valuable time on this resolution offering unsolicited advice to the parade committee. Council's time would be much better spent on the legitimate functions of local government." I didn't write that one, but I liked it.

Harriet Ballou, president of the Erin Historical Society and at her age a bit of living history herself, had a different take. "I understand that Mr. Ivanhoe and the Ned Ludd Society plan to enter the parade with an antique vehicle recalling the founding of the parade in 1923. I think that would be very interesting." Looking at Brett's face, I could almost read his mind: "The car's okay, but not the sign he'd put on the car." Harriet claimed to be a descendant of Ulysses S. Grant, but I think she had probably been his babysitter.

The final speaker looked like a Junior Achievement graduate or a stockbroker in a movie—suit, vest, brown glasses, and neatly trimmed hair.

"My name is Neil Carboy," he announced, "and I am vice president of public affairs for Samson Microcircuits." *Ah, the plot thickens.* Walter Ellicott, I noticed, finally looked up from his tablet. Fireworks ahead? I doubted it. This Carboy fellow didn't look like the type to light the match. "Our company is a major sponsor of the St. Patrick's Day Parade. We would simply like to express our support of the St. Patrick's Day Parade Committee and our complete confidence in its ability to run the parade as it has for many years." He sat back down. Message sent.

"That was subtle but clear," Mac observed.

But I wondered: Why didn't one of the Ellicotts speak for the company? But then I realized that might have made the issue seem merely personal, given the expected lawsuit against Ivanhoe over the old man's will.

The citizens having had their say, Council members began debating the resolution.

"This is ridiculous on so many levels," said Loretta Danby. Bruce Gordon may have been twice as old as Danby, an engineer at the Altiora Corp. by profession, but he had nothing on her when it came to clear talk. "First of all, nobody has a right to march in a parade sponsored by a private entity, much less to carry a banner which, in effect, advocates a cause which might be anathema to the sponsors who are paying for that event. And secondly, there's that whole private entity thing. We have no legal authority as City Council to dictate to the parade committee what its policies should be."

"We aren't dictating," Gordy snapped back. "We're expressing an opinion. Everybody has a right to an opinion."

"A dubious proposition, at best," Mac whispered. I've heard him hold forth on this subject before. He's not sure that people who are completely ignorant about a subject have a right to an opinion about it. Most of us probably feel the same way without thinking about it. I've never heard somebody say, "You don't know what you're talking about, but you certainly have a right to that ill-informed opinion." But I digress.

"Loretta's right—this is a complete waste of Council's time," said Chad Hollings. His affirmation made her position non-partisan. "I'm sure the parade committee isn't going to listen to us anyway. And why should they?"

"This is a moral issue, Chad." Thus spoke the rotund Reverend Fred Sutterlee, who tended to see everything as a moral issue. Applause ensued. "It is imperative that City Council speak out on this issue, for when the rights of one minority are imperiled, the rights of all minorities are imperiled."

"Let me repeat," Danby said "There. Is. No. Right. Involved. Here."

Reverend Sutterlee and Loretta Danby, the two African-Americans on Council, hardly ever agreed on anything.

From where we sat in the rear, it was hard to tell how this was going over with the partisans because I couldn't see the expressions on their faces. Walter Ellicott spent most of the time with his nose in his tablet. Cassandra looked back at James Ivanhoe, but if she hissed I couldn't tell. For his part, Ivanhoe still looked relaxed. Did he have some ace in the hole? Or—and this just hit me then—would he prefer *not* to have the support of City Council? Maybe bolstering his image as a rebel standing alone in the arena was more valuable to him than a symbolic vote.

Two of the other four members of Council begged to differ with the ordinance, while carefully avoiding rights talk. Each expressed confidence in the parade committee's ability to put on a great parade, as it had for more than half a century. That left two Council members undeclared as the discussion limped to an end. If those two supported the resolution, the vote would be 4-4 and the mayor would get to break the tie.

But it wasn't.

The resolution failed, 6-2, bringing raspberries and cheers. *"Council says no to Ned,"* Ben tweeted. I was surprised by the bottom line, and even more so by the wide margin of the vote. Making an issue about "the right to (whatever)" is usually a winning strategy. That's why so many interest groups have "Right to" in their name.

Even though the Council meeting continued after the vote, about half the audience left. Ben Silverstein followed Ivanhoe and caught up to him before he left the chambers. They chatted for a minute.

"I wish I knew what Ivanhoe was saying," I told Mac.

"I read lips, old boy." *How could I forget?* "Ivanhoe just said, 'This isn't over.'"

Chapter Five
Bad Publicity

Mary Landfair, Lincoln Todd's fair and willowy administrative assistant, offered me a cup of coffee. Having been in those precincts before, I knew that Todd only drank high-test.

"No, thanks. I don't do caffeine."

"You don't? Then where do you get your energy?"

"From sleep, exercise, and good nutrition."

She shivered. "Wow! That's downright scary."

I settled for a bottle of water.

The other members of the St. Patrick's Day Parade Committee weren't on deck yet for our Friday afternoon meeting in the conference room of the Convention & Visitors Bureau.

"Mr. Todd just got back in his office," Mary informed me. "He seems very stressed today."

I'd always thought of Todd as a cool customer, but I figured the strain of the Luddite silliness must be getting to him. He had a personal stake in it as well as a professional one: His daughter was married to Walter Ellicott and was therefore the sister-in-law of the troublesome James Ivanhoe, whom she apparently couldn't stand.

And the beat went on. In the two days since the City Council meeting, Ivanhoe had launched a petition drive that had already gathered a few hundred names from the good citizens of Erin.

"Look at the bright side, old boy," Mac had said. "An online effort would have gathered many more electronic signatures."

"Don't worry," I'd replied gloomily. "Somebody will think of that, even though they're Luddites."

While I hydrated myself, other members of the committee drifted in. Our chairman, Brett McGee, came not far behind me. Sister Jacinta Harrington, president of St. Hildegarde Health, and Amy Quong, executive vice president of Gamble Bank, came in together a few minutes later. Their respective institutions are among the parade's long-time sponsors.

"I like what you've been doing with social media to promote the parade," the lovely Asian-American banker told me as she sipped her tea.

I tried to look modest. "Thanks. I have good help."

Actually, that was understating it a bit. My entire involvement in the social media campaign consisted of telling Popcorn I had a project for her.

"I don't suppose James Ivanhoe has been following us on Twitter, though," I added. *Hey, don't glower at me like that, Linc. Just trying to keep it light!*

"Well," Brett said, which is how he called a meeting to order. "Things have changed a little since our conference call." That was when the committee had agreed with Brett to bar the Ned Ludd Society from the parade, in line with long-established policy. "We knew we would ruffle a few feathers, but this is almost out of control."

"Your points at the City Council meeting on Wednesday were very well taken, Brett," said Sister Jacinta. I happen to know that she's a big fan of Brett, dating back to his baseball days. I also know that she has gray roots.

Amy Quong frowned. "I am a bit concerned by the letter to the editor in today's *Observer* calling for a boycott of parade sponsors if we don't change our policy with regard to the Ned Ludd Society. Frankly, I would hate for Gamble

Bank to lose any of our Amish customers over this. When they save, they save a lot. And when they borrow, they never miss a payment."

Getting tapped to run the day-to-day operations of a family-owned bank when you aren't part of the family is no easy task, but Ms. Quong had pulled it off. The Gambles were smart enough not to let all that brains and drive go out the door by denying her the promotion she deserved. I'm not saying that just because we once lived together. Lynda always rolls her eyes when I say that, but it's true, technically. Amy Quong and I were fellow guests at a bed and breakfast where I was exiled so that Lynda's father could stay in my apartment the week before the Cody-Teal wedding. The third guest didn't survive the experience.[2]

"I'm not sure the Amish read the *Observer*," I said. "They have their own newspaper, *The Budget*." And, oddly enough, it has a website.

"My experience of the Amish is that they mind their own business, and this is not part of their business," said Sister Jacinta, who had not endured thirty years in the ever-changing hospital world by wearing blinders. "It would be an understatement to say that they are not activists in civil society. I don't think you have to worry about losing any Amish customers over this."

That tracked. I didn't recall seeing any Amish at the City Council meeting, and I would have noticed. There are no stealth Amish, what with the black hats on the men and the prayer caps on the women. Do they even vote? (Editor's note: They are permitted to, but usually don't.)

"Boycotts lose their punch after a while anyway," Todd said with a distracted air. "That's not my biggest concern. Sponsors don't want to get mired down in a controversy, I appreciate that, but I'm more worried about the general impression this is giving of Erin. We're not in

_____

[2] See *The* 1895 *Murder*, MX Publishing, 2012.

the state or national news very often, but it seems like whenever we are, it's negative. This fight about who can march in a parade makes us look very small town and out of touch with the modern world."

"But Erin *is* a small town!" Brett objected. "That's why I like it."

"I mean we look narrow-minded and silly."

"Are you saying we should change the Parade Orders?" I asked. "I thought we closed the book on that question at our last meeting. And you didn't object then."

Todd shifted in his seat, glancing at his watch. Mary Landfair was right—he looked stressed, bordering on frazzled. "Maybe there's a compromise."

Compromise over controversy! Todd should have been a politician. I mean that in good way.

"There is no compromise," Brett snapped back. "We already said Ivanhoe and his troops can be in the parade as long as they follow the rules. They don't want to follow the rules. How can you compromise on that—follow half the rules?"

Todd sighed. "I'm sure they'll have their signs anyway, protesting on the sidewalk, and get twice the publicity than if we just let them in. I had a call yesterday from Prime News Network about setting up an interview in a couple of weeks for use on the day of the parade. Why are they doing that? This isn't news!"

The man was unraveling before my eyes.

"*Au contraire*, Linc." Did I really say that? I've been hanging around Sebastian McCabe too long. "It *is* news, because news is whatever an editor says it is. Take my advice: Never tell a journalist 'there's no story here.' If anything convinces reporters and editors that there's a story, it's being assured there's no story. Did you tell PNN you wouldn't talk?"

"No, I put them off. It was a producer who called me."

"Okay. Call the producer back and say you'll do the interview. But you need to take control of it and use it to your advantage." I thought fast, and a little out of the box. "Here's one idea: Make a joke out of the inane notion that Erin is some kind of no-tech zone. Parody it to the point of absurdity! Borrow an Amish buggy and use it to show the reporter around town. Take him to our one remaining phone booth."

"And that's supposed to help how?" Todd said.

"By showing that you don't take this seriously and neither should anybody else. You could also suggest the reporter visit the Altiora Corp. and Samson Microcircuits for the contrast."

He looked skeptical. Or sick. I wasn't sure which. "All right, I'll do it." Todd is a smart guy and a fast thinker. He doesn't take a long time to make decisions.

"They say any publicity is good publicity," Sister Jacinta said. She must have forgotten the time her head of cardiac surgery got caught in the woods with his clothes off. That old saw about any publicity is a lie, but sometimes it calms people down. So I didn't contradict the good sister.

Brett was going to say something, though. He had his mouth open. But a phone rang—a loud, jangling ring tone. Todd yanked the offending instrument out of his pocket.

"Yes!" he said tensely. His lean face fell, almost comically. "What! How? What happened?"

After a minute he said, "I'll be right there" in a wavering voice. He was standing up before he even had the phone disconnected.

"What's wrong?" Amy Quong asked.

"It's Cassie, my daughter. She's been shot. She's dead."

Chapter Six
A Death in the Family

By the time I read Johanna Rawls's story in the *Erin Observer & News-Ledger* over breakfast on Saturday morning, Lynda had already absorbed the details from the online version.

The body of Cassandra Todd Ellicott, 33, had been found in the family room of her Skylark Lane home on Friday afternoon by her husband, Walter Ellicott, 47. Walter had just returned from an out-of-town business trip. He had called his wife earlier in the day on their landline, but the phone was busy. He had then tried her cell phone, but she didn't answer.

Mrs. Ellicott had suffered one bullet to the head. Police Chief Oscar Hummel was quoted as saying the crime was being investigated as a home invasion robbery gone wrong. Mrs. Ellicott had owned and operated her own business, a high-end consignment shop called Cassandra Couture, but had taken the day off on Friday. She and her husband had no children. The story ended with:

> Friends say that Mrs. Ellicott was a vivacious, friendly woman who gave back to the community. She volunteered at Serenity House, helping homeless women to dress for job interviews.
>
> "This is like a death in the family," said Serena Mason, board chair of the non-profit organization. "Cassandra gave unselfishly of her

time to help people who were not as fortunate as she was."

"Johanna covered all the bases adequately enough, and the story reads okay," Lynda said as she fed Donata, "but I wish she'd been able to get a little more out of Walter." Apparently my beloved spouse had forgotten to flick the "off" switch on her journalism genes when she'd gone on maternity leave. Also, she took a special interest in anything written by Johanna, her protégé. "What do you think of Oscar's line about the home invasion?"

"In what way?"

"It sounds fishy to me. The husband just happened to come home and find his wife dead after he's been away establishing an alibi? If this were an episode of *20/20*, I know how it would turn out."

"Well, it's not, Lyn." *Yet.* "Walter Ellicott is a board member of St. Benignus, and therefore by definition as innocent as our sweet baby." *I hope.*

Lynda looked down at Donata, who was taking an after-breakfast nap. "I bet Lincoln Todd is really broken up."

"What father wouldn't be? And he looked like he was about twelve minutes from a nervous breakdown *before* he got the call." After finding his wife's body, Walter Ellicott had called 911 and then his father-in-law. I regarded Donata. Have I mentioned that she's the cutest baby in the world? "If somebody killed my daughter, or even broke her fingernail, he wouldn't have to worry about being arrested."

Just at that moment, Donata gleefully filled her diaper. How can she do that in her sleep?

"I'll get this one," Lynda said.

While she did so, I pulled out my smartphone to check the number of hits on my latest Dance Party Friday video, which had gone up on YouTube the day before. It may not be obvious in these chronicles of Sebastian

McCabe's adventures, but I do occasionally attend to my day job. Like all my best ideas, the Dance Party Friday series wasn't my idea. Popcorn had suggested it when she saw how many hits were generated by the infamous videos of our former faculty member James Gregory Talton, now professor emeritus and good riddance.[3] The idea was to present a fun image of our faculty dancing in the hallways. Ralph would hate it, if he ever found out about it.

I'd barely touched the YouTube app icon when my phone made that little ping that tells me I have a text. It was from Mac, just five words:

It was not a robbery.

I was in Mac's man cave—he calls it his study—within fifteen minutes. But first I'd had to promise Lynda I'd handle the next three changes of diapers required during my presence.

"Okay, give," I told Mac, settling into the chair by the fire with a Caffeine-Free Diet Coke (from the tap!) in my right hand.

"I have been talking to Oscar," he announced. The expression on his face was beatific, like that of a cat in a creamery. Getting the inside scoop on a murder case does that to him. "What follows is not for public consumption, Jefferson. Oscar confided to me that his original thesis of a housebreaker caught in the act did not stand up under scrutiny. Although the first floor of the Ellicott house, quote, 'looked like a tornado hit it,' thus giving credence to the robbery theory, further investigation established that that appearance was deceptive."

"Nothing was taken?"

"No. Cassandra's purse had been rifled and items of clothing and furniture scattered around. However, when asked about his wife's jewelry, Walter quickly took Assistant

---

[3] See *Bookmarked for Murder*, MX Publishing, 2015.

Chief Gibbons to a jewelry box on Cassandra's dresser. It was full. Even a scared intruder, one alarmed by an unexpectedly deadly turn of events, would have run through the house picking up anything light enough to lift in approximately ten minutes—most especially any jewelry. The heroin epidemic has unfortunately made Oscar quite familiar with that kind of crime."

"Okay, so it wasn't that kind of crime or that kind of killer. Did the Ellicotts have a maid or a weekly cleaning lady with a key to the house?"

I don't know where I was going with that question, but it didn't matter.

"No. Walter said his wife did not like the idea of someone in their home while they were gone."

I shifted gears.

"What was the means of entry? Johanna's story didn't say." I made a mental note to mention the gap to Lynda.

"Oscar's troops found the back door unlocked. Walter said it must have been that way when he got home. He came in through the garage, however."

"Unlocked? That's hard to believe, especially in that that neighborhood and with their money. And what about the burglar alarm? They must have a burglar alarm." That didn't just come to me. I'd thought of it when I'd read Johanna's story.

"They do indeed. Every house on their street does, according to Oscar. Unfortunately, a burglar alarm is only effective when it is activated. Oscar reports that Walter cried when he explained that he frequently chided his wife for not turning on the alarm."

I could relate to that, but still . . .

"If one were cynical," I said, cynically, "one could point out that Walter's explanation is convenient for him if anyone suspected that he was the one who shot his wife."

"Well, she was in the house at the time, old boy. Do you always activate the burglar alarm when you are in residence?"

"Yes." *But then, I'm Jeff Cody.* "Lynda doesn't always," I admitted. "But she does lock the door."

"Most admirable! I, for one, am not so diligent. As you know, I enter this house through the back door. I have to acknowledge that on occasion I have forgotten to relock it upon entrance. One morning about two months ago, as I was leaving for St. Benignus, I realized that the keys were still in the lock from the evening before!"

"But you have an excuse. You're an absent-minded professor."

Mac chuckled. "What really puzzles me is why the purse was rifled, almost as if the intruder were looking for something."

"But wasn't that just camouflage, part of the attempt to make it look like a robbery?"

"That is entirely possible. And yet, why merely rummage through Cassandra's purse? Why not ransack her husband's home office? That would have greater verisimilitude for the robbery scenario."

I decided it was time to confront the pachyderm in the room. "Let's look at the bottom line, Mac. It looks like Cassandra Ellicott was killed by somebody she knew. People are going to suspect Walter. Lynda already suspects Walter! The husband is always the first suspect. Never mind that he looks too boring to be a cold-blooded killer. I've never been able to figure out that whole love, marriage, homicide thing, but it happens."

Mac sighed deeply. "Yes, it happens. Well, Oscar appears to have the case well in hand and neither you, nor I, nor anyone close to us is imperiled by his investigation. Surely this is one murder that we can stay well out of."

Even geniuses are wrong sometimes.

Chapter Seven
Funeral Rites

The Sunday edition of the *Erin Observer & News-Ledger* offered a more in-depth look at the late Cassandra Todd Ellicott, along with a few boilerplate sentences about the continuing investigation. Oscar told Johanna Rawls there were not yet any suspects but that "we are following some leads." He expressed his confidence that one of them would lead to the killer. Apparently he didn't correct Johanna's assumption that he was still looking for a burglar.

On Monday, the last day of February, I half expected Mac to wander into my office or call me on my phone with some excuse for getting us involved in the case, but that didn't happen. He was teaching an undergraduate class (a rarity for a full professor) and deep into writing his latest Damon Devlin mystery novel, so maybe that kept his restless mind busy enough.

Ralph Pendergast, in my office to discuss a news release about a new dean, took the time to wax sympathetic about his friend Todd. "The directors of the Convention & Visitors Bureau want him to take a leave of absence," Ralph reported, "but he refused to take more than a couple of days off. He wouldn't even accept the loan of our condo in Destin."

You own a condo in Florida? Hey, I could use some time off!
"Everybody handles grief in their own way."

A lean specimen with a sharp nose and wire-rimmed glasses, Ralph nodded gloomily. "There but for the grace of God . . ."

I make no apologies for this exchange of bromides. Everybody is reduced to platitudes in the face of death.

Trying to shove Lynda's suspicions to the back of my mind so they wouldn't affect my interactions with Walter Ellicott, I went to Cassandra's visitation on Tuesday afternoon. Maybe my job as St. Benignus communications director didn't oblige me to attend the funeral rites of a trustee's spouse, but it seemed right to me.

The Hawes & Holder Funeral Home was packed. At first I was surprised to see my sister Kate among the milling crowd. Mac wasn't with her. I didn't think she knew any of the Ellicotts all that well. But then I remembered Mac telling me that she felt ashamed of herself for making a catty comment about Cassandra ("She has expensive taste, but not good taste") the last time she'd seen her. My sister is hard as nails and soft as butter.

"Hello, Jeff."

Startled out of my reverie, I turned around to see the smiling face of seventy-something Fred Gaffe. Fred looks like somebody's white-haired, benevolent grandfather —or maybe everybody's—though I'm not even sure he has any offspring.

"Oh, hi, Fred. Friend of the family?"

"No, I go to almost all the funerals in town. Gathering material, you know."

Fred writes a column called "The Old Gaffer" in the *Observer & News-Ledger*. Lynda used to edit it, which was not an easy task but worth it. No great writer, Fred is a top-notch storyteller, with a way of connecting topical events to interesting but little known slices of local history.

"I thought you already knew everything about Erin and everybody in it," I said.

"Trying to, anyway."

"Care to share some of your wealth of knowledge for a faithful reader?" I looked around. Lincoln Todd and Walter Ellicott, united in loss, both stood somberly next to the closed casket as they greeted mourners. "For instance, how do Walter and Linc get along?"

"They're close," Fred responded without hesitation. "They speak the same language, both being business types. Somebody—never mind who—once told me that Walter is like the son that Linc never had."

Nobody would ever say that about my father-in-law and me. But maybe that was my fault. I made a mental note to get to know Col. Teal better.

"Poor Walter!" I emoted. "To lose a spouse has to be horrible, but when it's murder . . ."

The Old Gaffer caught my subtext. "I've known a few widowers whose tears were borrowed from a crocodile, Jeff, but I hear Walter's really torn up." Already speaking *sotto voce*, he made his voice even lower. "He told Betty that if Cassie were alive he'd never take her for granted again."

"Who's Betty?"

"His secretary—who happens to be my niece. I'm surprised that Jamie Ellicott had the nerve to show up." He nodded toward the third Ellicott brother, who was studying a display of photos at the back of the room. He wore a blue blazer over a pair of jeans, his dark hair touching the jacket collar.

"You mean Ivanhoe," I stated.

Fred snorted. "He can call himself Thoreau if he wants to, living out there by himself in that cabin in the woods. But he's still Jamie Ellicott who was one of June's students at Malcolm C. Cotton." June was Fred's late wife. Cotton is Erin's public high school.

I thought I knew the reason Fred was surprised to see the Prodigal Son at the funeral. "I understand he doesn't get along with his brothers and that Cassandra couldn't stand him."

"That's an understatement. But it wasn't always like that. Jamie dated Cassandra throughout his college years—she followed him up the road to Miami of Ohio—until she broke it off. That may have been why he went to Wisconsin for graduate school and never came back to Erin."

"I thought he left town to get away from his family."

Fred nodded. "He did. But my guess is that he wouldn't have if he hadn't broken up with Cassandra. Getting her to go away with him would have been tough. Cassandra was such a daddy's girl she wouldn't even date a guy that Lincoln Todd didn't like."

I filed that away for future reference. "Where's the other brother—Samson III? I assume he's here."

"Trey is standing near the wall to your left, right beneath that painting of flowers."

Shorter than either of his brothers, Trey chatted unsmilingly with a chestnut-haired woman about his height. He wore a gray pinstriped suit, with all three buttons of the coat buttoned. Not only is this the wrong way to do it, it emphasized the thirty pounds or so he would have been better off without. Not that I would have told him that. Something told me that, graying hair notwithstanding, he could have decked me—and would have.

But it was his conversation mate who interested me. She was the woman who'd been sitting with Ivanhoe at the City Council meeting, the one with the build of a runner or volleyball player. I'd assumed she was his girlfriend. And now she was with his oldest brother.

The Old Gaffer followed the direction of my eyes. "That's the sister, Karen Ellicott. She's the only one in the family that Jamie talked to even when he was out of town."

"And that didn't put her on the outs with the rest of the clan?"

"Family relationships can be complicated." *I know. I've met Lynda's parents.* "She works in the Ellicott business. I don't know what she does, and if I did I wouldn't understand it anyway. It's something very technical. She was a high school classmate of Cassandra."

Hold your fire for a minute, Fred, while I draw a relationship chart. I can add to it later.

"Walter's the top legal talent at Samson Microcircuits and Trey, being the oldest, sits in the corner office, right?" I said.

Fred nodded. "Trey is definitely Big Brother."

Just then, Ralph Pendergast entered the room. He crossed in front of me, acknowledging my existence with a brief nod, and walked over to the father and the husband of the deceased. After exchanging a few perfunctory words with Walter, he focused his attention on Lincoln Todd. I don't think he said a whole lot but, in the way of friends, he didn't need to. His face, never an especially cheerful visage, reflected his old friend's pain. I always knew deep down that Ralph was human—his fondness for jazz and for his wife showed that. But it wasn't often that I saw it demonstrated. Most people wouldn't have even noticed, but I felt like a voyeur.

"Sad," Fred said.

There wasn't much I could add to that. The whole death thing fills me with so many emotions I can't even sort them out, but sadness is near the top.

"Well, let me know if you hear any good gossip about the Ellicotts, Fred. They fascinate me."

"I prefer to think of my stock in trade as living history, not gossip."

Whatever helps you sleep at night.

The Old Gaffer drifted away to gather more living history. I bided my time. As soon as there was a clear path to Walter, I girded my loins and approached him. What can you say to a grieving husband that hasn't been said already? But I guess the bereaved aren't looking for originality.

Walter didn't smile, but something in his eyes said he was glad to see me.

"I'm sorry about your loss, Walter. You have my deepest sympathy."

"Thanks for coming, Jeff. I'm glad you're here because I was planning to reach out to you anyway."

I cringed—inwardly, I hope. Who started all this reaching out, anyway? Every day half a dozen people, most of whom I don't know and don't want to, tell me they're "reaching out" to me. That creeps me out. Sometimes I want to say, "Let's just not go there," but that's a cliché, too. Instead, I responded with:

"Is there something I can do for you?"

"I hope so." Walter put a hand on my shoulder and guided me into an empty side room apparently reserved for the family of the deceased. "I'm not happy with the way Chief Hummel is conducting the investigation of Cassie's murder. Why is he asking *me* so many questions? He should be trying to find the killer."

That's what he's doing, Walter. As the husband, you're the chief suspect. Oh, and as for that business about an intruder killing your wife? That's baloney.

"I'm sure it's frustrating, but you have to understand that police routine takes a long time. It involves a lot of data-gathering that may not make sense to laymen like us. Oscar's doing his best, I can assure you."

"That's cold comfort, Jeff. I'm afraid his best may not be good enough. I have no confidence in the man."

I should have defended Oscar as a solid officer with decades of experience, first in Dayton and then in Erin since his retirement from the bigger city force. But all that came out was, "Well, he's the only police chief we have."

Walter shook his head impatiently. "Not good enough. This is my wife we're talking about. I want Sebastian McCabe on the case. Him I have confidence in. Maybe he can get a lead on the killer from his contacts in the underworld." *There is no underworld in Erin, Walter. And if there were, Mac wouldn't have any contacts there. He writes fiction.* "Can you get him to do it? I'd be very grateful to you and to St. Benignus."

He didn't say that his gratitude would be demonstrated in the form of a large check for the university's capital fund drive, but I got the drift. I was only mildly offended. Actually, even without the bribe it was in our best interest for Walter to be an innocent victim. Even though no headline would ever say "St. Benignus Director Arrested in Wife's Murder," Walter Ellicott's connection to the university would be noted.

"I might be able to twist Mac's arm," I allowed. "He told me he didn't plan to get involved, but that doesn't mean he—"

My sentence was drowned out by an angry bellow.

"Who the hell are you to say?"

Have you ever noticed how much murmured conversation, even some laughter, there is at a funeral visitation? All of that died a quick death at the shouted words. I spun around to see who had yelled.

James Ivanhoe was right in his oldest brother's face, which required him to look down. "What business is it of yours?"

I didn't think they were talking about the St. Patrick's Day Parade.

Trey Ellicott, five or six inches shorter than his brother and built along the lines of a fireplug, didn't back up an inch. "If you had any class, Jamie, you wouldn't have to ask."

Walter Ellicott stepped between his two siblings. "Maybe you'd better go, Jamie." He sounded nowhere near as self-assured as his older brother.

"Why, Walter? Because Trey says so and you always do what he says?"

Walter colored. "*I* say so. Please leave."

Ivanhoe clenched his fists, but didn't raise them. His eyes darted between his two brothers. "You're going to be sorry I ever came back to Erin."

"We already are," Trey said.

"Stop it!" Karen crossed the room to stare down her three brothers with a pair of bright green eyes. If looks could kill, she would have quickly been the last Ellicott standing.

Ivanhoe opened his mouth, closed it, and stalked out without saying another word.

Chapter Eight
Ancient History

"Tell me everything that happened at the funeral home," Mac said, mug of beer in hand. "Skip nothing."

He'd already agreed, with an unconvincing show of reluctance, to play amateur sleuth. Sitting by the man cave fire just a few minutes after leaving the visitation, I gave him the play-by-play of what I'd witnessed, quoting dialogue as precisely as I have in this report. I took my time. Lynda was at a post-partum exercise class and my two nieces, Rebecca and Amanda, were spoiling Donata.

Mac raised an eyebrow twice—once at the intel that James Ivanhoe, née Ellicott, had dated Cassandra years ago, and once at Ivanhoe's blow-up at his big brother.

"How did their sister react to that?" Mac asked about the latter.

I shrugged. "I couldn't say. I was too riveted by the main actors to notice the supporting cast."

"Next time, old boy, notice."

Next time, you go.

"The only Ellicott I know is Walter," I said, "and I now realize that I don't really know him. Ivanhoe implied that he's dominated by Trey, but he seemed to stand on his own two feet when he told Ivanhoe to take a hike."

"Not quite. Granted, you have described him as being assertive. However, remember that he was echoing Trey in front of Trey. That is hardly standing on his own." He quaffed his Christian Moerlein Barbarossa Double Dark lager. "The family dynamics of the Ellicott clan certainly intrigues me."

"They aren't exactly the Waltons. But I'm sure their internecine warfare has nothing to do with Cassandra's murder. Walter seemed really bent out of shape that Oscar asked him so many questions, but you and I know that's pure routine. If the killer wasn't a burglar, the chief's got to be figuring the odds are on the victim's husband. It's hard to believe Walter's too naïve to get that. Do you think he could be playing cute—asking you to look into his wife's murder to deflect suspicion from him because he did it?" *What was I saying? Of course he didn't—he's a St. Benignus board member!*

"That is certainly not beyond the bounds of possibility. The client who turns out to be the guilty party is something of a mystery fiction staple. It even happened in a very late Sherlock Holmes story. Of course, the ploy did not succeed in that case. And if Walter Ellicott is responsible for his wife's death, I can assure you that he will regret that he ever sought the assistance of Sebastian McCabe."

The following day, Wednesday, was the funeral, so we met with Walter in Mac's office at St. Benignus on Thursday, March 3. Mac wore one of his favorite bow ties for the occasion, dark blue with yellow polka dots.

The widower watched in disbelief as Mac struck a match off of the "Thank You for Not Breathing While I Smoke" sign on his desk and lit a cigar. The ashtray overflowed with soggy butts. Neither the university nor Kate allows Mac to smoke indoors, but he only listens to Kate. I live in fear that he will someday ignite one of the towers of books and papers that cover every available surface of his office.

"Whom do you suspect of your wife's murder?" Mac asked Walter after expressing sympathy for his loss.

"Suspect?" From the look on his face, Walter hadn't expected that. "How should I know? I don't know any burglars."

"I am sorry to inform you that no larcenous intruder killed Cassandra. Chief Hummel is convinced, as am I, that her murderer was someone whom she knew, and likely someone whom you know as well."

Mac had warned me that he was going to drop that bomb on his non-paying "client." He knew that Oscar would be hopping mad at him for it, but he wanted to see how Walter reacted.

Walter stared. "You mean—you can't—"

He stalled out.

Was that the startled reaction of an innocent man? Damned if I could tell!

He tried again. "But if that's true, why did Hummel tell me, and the *Observer*, that it was a burglar?"

"The *Observer* story said the crime was being *investigated as* a break-in gone awry. That was Oscar's very natural initial theory, refuted by a closer examination of the scene. Your wife's murder was not an unintended by-product of a home invasion robbery. For the time being, the chief would rather the killer not know that he knows that."

If Walter caught the implication that he was on the chief's suspect list, but apparently not on Mac's, he didn't show it.

"But who would want to hurt Cassie?" That's what Mac had asked, but I didn't interrupt. "It just doesn't make sense, McCabe. She was sweet and kind and generous to a fault. I miss her already."

"So you had a perfect marriage?" The tone in my voice might have been skeptical. Call me a cynic, but it did seem that he was working overtime to make it clear that he was no happy widower.

But Walter shook his head. "I couldn't claim that. I should have paid more attention to her. I know that now."

Light dawned in his eyes. "That's why Hummel and his man Gibbons asked me all those questions, isn't it? I'm their number one suspect—the husband. Oh, God. What a nightmare!" He put his head in his hands. I didn't blame him.

Mac stroked his beard. I don't know why he does that; he can't be stimulating his brain cells. "Who else is there to suspect? How about a business rival?"

That angle hadn't occurred to me—a motive connected to her resale shop, Cassandra Couture.

Walter snorted. "I don't think the St. Vincent de Paul Store or the Salvation Army took out a contract on her, if that's what you mean."

I certainly hope not; that's where I buy most of my clothes.

"The classic question of motive is *cui bono*—who benefits," Mac lectured.

Walter interrupted before he could rattle on. "Cassie came from a respectable family—she's Lincoln Todd's daughter—but she didn't bring a lot of money to the marriage. Her will isn't going to make anybody richer, least of all me." He threw up his hands. "This isn't getting us anywhere, McCabe."

"I was about to say, the benefit to the killer need not be financial. Perhaps Cassandra stood in the killer's way or possessed some knowledge that threatened the killer's security. Does that strike you as likely?"

Walter stood up. "No. Is this the best you can do?"

Hey, jerk, you came to us! I might have actually said that if Mac hadn't responded with a patient, "At the moment, yes. What was your brother James so upset about at the funeral home the other day?"

He sighed as if reconciling himself to what he considered an irrelevant question. "Trey told him he wasn't welcome. And he wasn't!" Walter's phone boinked, as if for emphasis. He took it out of his pocket, typed into it rapidly with both thumbs, and put it away. "Jamie resigned from the family thirteen years ago when he left Erin. He didn't even come back for Mom's funeral. But when he got word that Dad wasn't going to live much longer, he danced back like nothing had ever happened. That didn't sit well with Trey or with me."

This was déjà vu all over again for me because I'd overheard Walter telling Saylor-Mackie about it at that reception months before. But Walter didn't need to know that.

"Your father, however, reacted differently," Mac commented. "As I understand it, he welcomed the wayward offspring back like the father of the Prodigal Son in the Bible. And the will reflects that, does it not?"

Walter smiled grimly. "That's right—Jamie inherits a share of the business along with us who helped to build it, Trey and Karen and me, plus an equal part of everything else he had. But Dad wasn't competent when he executed that will because he was under the influence of powerful painkillers. Trey and I aren't going to roll over for that. We're in the process of hiring the best estate attorney we can find to challenge the will. But what does Jamie have to do with Cassie?"

"She dated him before he left town, did she not?"

He nodded. "That's how I first met Cassie, although I didn't really know her very well then. We reconnected a few years later. She dated a lot of people in between. This is a small town, McCabe. Everybody's either related or having relations. I consider my wife's old boyfriends, including my brother, to be ancient history."

"Perhaps so. And yet, history has a way of leaving its mark. Were that not true, Walter, you would not have felt the desire to eject your younger brother from the funeral home."

Walter let that sink in. "Still," he said finally, "I don't see what happened years ago or what's in my father's will could have to do with Cassie's murder."

"Nor do I," Mac said. "I am simply trying to understand what is known in Biblical criticism as the *Sitz im Leben*, the 'setting in life' or context in which your wife operated."

"In other words," I said, "he's getting the big picture, collecting information, some of which may actually be helpful."

"Precisely. Well said, Jefferson! Let us move on. If there is no obvious reason why someone would want to kill your wife, Walter, then there must be an unobvious one. And since no one is an island, someone other than the killer must know what that reason is. Is there anyone to whom Cassandra might have confided her joys and sorrows—a friend, or perhaps a business associate?"

"She had a lot of friends. Cassie was a very friendly person, highly emotional. And she was very close to Linc, her father."

"How about—I'm sorry, Walter—but how about, well, a male friend?" I hated to ask the grieving husband, but I figured that Oscar or his men had already done so if they weren't asleep at the switch.

Walter squirmed in his chair.

"Well?" Mac pressed.

"The cops asked about that." *See.*

"What did you tell them?"

"The truth: I don't know. But just between us, it's possible."

Chapter Nine
Empty Nets

"Why didn't he tell us that in the first place?" I asked after Walter had gone.

"Would you, in his position? His reluctance to speak about a matter both personal and embarrassing is quite understandable. Besides, he has no more than a suspicion based on a perceived furtiveness by his wife."

"You know that wouldn't even be a speed bump for Oscar. Just admitting that he had a suspicion of infidelity gives Walter a gold-plated motive for murder. Why didn't you press him on his alibi?"

"I have every confidence that Oscar will have done that already. It seems solid if the airline confirms it."

The coroner's report indicated that Cassandra's death, a day shy of a week before this discussion in Mac's office, had taken place in the morning. This was supported by the fact the she had consumed breakfast and not lunch. Walter claimed to have been at LaGuardia Airport or in the air all morning on his way back from a business trip. Or was it monkey business? I made a mental note to take that up with Oscar.

"Do not lose sight of the fact that this hypothetical boyfriend also has a number of potential motives," Mac said. "For example, perhaps he wanted out of the relationship and she threatened him with exposure. Or perhaps she wanted out and he was obsessed with her."

"So the boyfriend who *may* have existed *might* have reasons to want Cassandra out of the picture. That helps a lot."

"I concede that we are operating at a high level of conjecture, Jefferson. We need a solid base of facts lest we begin to build a structure of theories on a base of sand. Let us see what friend Oscar and his troops have been able to ferret out."

After a quick sandwich at Beans & Books, we dropped in on the chief in his new digs. After more than a century in the basement of City Hall, the police department and Erin's small jail had been moved to a new location just a few weeks earlier. They now occupied an old Art Deco building on Court Street that had once been home to the long-defunct Fifth National Bank of Erin.

The political maneuvering that it had taken to accomplish this would fill another book. Some members of City Council had wanted the city to get out of the jail business altogether and let the county Sheriff's Department handle the minor offenders as well as the major ones, but they got outvoted by the mayor's allies. County prosecutor Marvin Slade, a political rival of Her Honor, wound up on the short end of that brouhaha, along with the sheriff.

"What took you guys so long?" Oscar said when we walked in. "I thought you'd be on my case over the Ellicott murder before we had her body in the morgue freezer."

Nice image there, Oscar.

"I like the curtains," I said. Unlike the old office, this one had a picture window facing the street. The glass was bulletproof.

"Popcorn picked 'em," Oscar said.

I wouldn't doubt that she had also picked the semi-circular wood desk and the baseball memorabilia hung on the wall. Oscar had been keeping company with my irreplaceable assistant, a widowed grandmother of three, for two or three years. Sometimes his mother tags along. I'm never sure which of those crazy kids she's trying to protect. Both in their mid-fifties, I doubt that they will move near a school if their romance ever leads to wedding bells, which I also doubt.

"Are we here to admire Ms. Pokorny's decorating skills, not discuss the Ellicott case?" Mac asked.

Oscar grunted at this lame sarcasm as he stuck a huge mug, an artifact from the old office, into his new Keurig coffee maker. **I SEE NO REASON TO ACT MY AGE**, the mug proclaimed. So, naturally, Oscar handed it to Mac when it was filled with high-test java. Then he stuck in a decaf cartridge for me while he said:

"Walter Ellicott, who is not an official suspect, has made no secret that he thinks Inspector Clouseau— remember him from those old Pink Panther movies?— could solve his wife's murder faster than yours truly. He's been yapping about it all over town. That's just what I would expect Mr. Ellicott to do if he'd killed his wife, by the way. Happens all the time. But he's not an official suspect. Did I mention that? He is a trustee of St. Benignus University, though. So I thought maybe you guys would be interested in the case."

Oscar looked like a man who needed a cigarette to go with his own coffee. Not that he smokes them anymore —he vapes instead. I credit Popcorn for that, though I'm not sure the e-habit is any more healthful than the traditional kind. Her makeover had not yet extended to Oscar's donut-shaped body or his bald pate, but give her time.

"Yeah, we're interested," I confirmed as Oscar passed me my decaf. "So how's it going? Off the record." Even with Lynda on maternity leave from journalism our conversations with Oscar were always off the record. But I was trying to be reassuring.

"Off the record, we're almost finished interviewing all the Ellicott neighbors and anybody else who might have seen something. That wasn't as easy as you might think. Hardly any of the homeowners in that ritzy neighborhood are home during the day, except the ones who are retired and don't look out their windows much. But we had to track down all the people who come in to clean houses, some of which were afraid we were from the Immigration and Naturalization Service. Also, it was both trash collection and recycling day on Skylark Lane, so we had to track down those guys."

"And all that for nothing, I suppose?" I said.

"You could say that. Nobody saw any strangers or anything unusual."

"I presume you checked Walter Ellicott's alibi—as a matter of routine, of course," Mac said.

Oscar frowned. "It checks. He was on that plane, which was late. It didn't get into the airport until two-o'clock, about an hour and a half before Ellicott called us. That's about how long it would take to get home, with waiting for luggage. Have I ever told you how much I hate the hassle of flying?"

I filed that question under "rhetorical."

"And I suppose you checked that he was really in New York on business?" I said.

"Yeah. It was some kind of lawyerly thing involving a contract with a big supplier. Gibbons said the supplier verifies that there was a meeting and Ellicott was there."

It was nice to know that Walter's alibi was solid, but if you Google "murder for hire"—as I just did—you'll get 10.9 million hits.

"We might as well tell you that we are here because Walter Ellicott requested our involvement," Mac said. "As you indicated earlier, he is not pleased with the pace of your investigation."

Oscar didn't actually say "What the hell?" but that was the expression on his face. "Did he also tell you that he admitted owning a 9mm Glock—that being the size bullet that killed his wife—but says he doesn't know where it is?"

"No, that did not come up."

"It doesn't matter that he didn't tell *us*," I chipped in. "The important thing is that he told *you*. Why would he do that if he had something to hide?"

Mac answered that one before Oscar could. "In theory, that could have been a pre-emptive strike, knowing that there would be a record of it."

Thanks, Mac. Remind me again: whose side are you on?

But Oscar shook his head. "No, he already told us there's no record of his ownership. He bought it at a gun show years ago when he decided to take up the manly art of target shooting. He said he's been too busy lately to put holes in defenseless targets, so he hasn't used the gun in such a long time that he doesn't even remember where he put it."

Just then I had a happy thought: Walter's gun being used was actually a good thing, given his alibi. Because if Walter hired a hit man, wouldn't the assassin bring his own weapon? When I have work done on my house, I just pay for it; I don't supply the tools. But just in case Oscar hadn't Googled "murder for hire," I didn't say that (although I did make the point later to Mac, who was suitably impressed).

"Well, a lot of people have guns," I said instead. "The 9mm thing could be just a coincidence."

Oscar nodded, causing the light to shine off his dome. "Could be, sure." He took a swig of coffee. "Stranger things have happened."

"Have you any thoughts on motive?" Mac asked. My brother-in-law is very big on motive, in his fiction and in real life.

The chief sat back comfortably in his wide, leather, taxpayer-purchased new chair. "Mrs. Ellicott was an attractive lady quite a bit younger than her husband. No disrespect to the dead intended, but I can connect the dots as well as anybody."

"You suspect a dalliance?"

"No, I think she could have had a boyfriend. And you know what that means. You guys are mystery writers. I don't need to draw you a map from there to a motive."

Why was Oscar suddenly connecting dots and drawing maps? Enough with the artwork analogies! And that crack about us being mystery writers, plural—was that a snide reference to my seven unpublished Max Cutter private eye novels? At least I finished them. Oscar's attempt at a locked room mystery involving a tree house had stalled out around chapter ten, thank heavens. He hadn't even mentioned it in months.

"Do you have anything more tangible than a suspicion pointing to the existence of this Romeo?" I asked. Never mind that the widower himself had shared "just between us" his suspicions that Cassandra might have had a beau.

"Not yet. I had Gibbons check the deceased's smartphone for calls, e-mails, and texts to a person of the male persuasion other than her husband, but he didn't find any."

If he didn't find any, that means there weren't any. Lt. Col. L. Jack Gibbons, Oscar's assistant chief, doesn't make mistakes.

"Good idea, though," I said.

I had a flashback to Ivanhoe talking negatively about just such threats to privacy in his *Bookmarks* TV interview. I also remembered a triple murder in Cincinnati a few years back where the killer's texting habit, and the indiscrete nature of those texts, resulted in his change of address to death row. Lynda and I kept in touch all day long through text messages, although so many of them were in the private code of lovers that I'm not sure anyone else would even find the suggestive parts suggestive. Their loss!

"Of course, the killer could have wiped the texts, if he had the presence of mind to do that," Oscar added. "Anyway, this is not exactly a cold case. The murder happened a week ago tomorrow. We'll catch the perp. Tell Mr. Ellicott he doesn't have to worry about that."

Mac raised an eyebrow. "Why, Oscar—you've just committed irony!"

Sounded like sarcasm to me, and I'm an expert.

Oscar ignored the badinage. "Meanwhile, I think it's time for a change-up on this case. I'm going to let Johanna Rawls know that Cassandra's murder was, if not necessarily premeditated, at least not a side action to a burglary. That should be a page-one story, and it might stir the pot a bit. Maybe somebody will remember something when they know we're not looking for a guy in a mask and black sneakers. If there's anything to remember, that is. I have my doubts."

"Are you going to tell the victim's husband that before you tell the news media?" I said.

"I'll give him a courtesy call, but I bet he already knows."

"Of course Walter knows," I muttered to Mac as we walked toward his car, a whale-sized 1959 Chevy the color of a fire engine. "We told him."

Mac nodded, but his mind was elsewhere. "Oscar has set all the appropriate nets and landed not even a minnow."

"Try not to look so happy about that. Maybe his new tactic of going public with the info that the killer wasn't Raffles will pay off. What now for us?"

"We should talk to Cassandra's father."

"I'm not looking forward to that."

"It must be done, old boy."

I sighed. "I know Lincoln Todd better than you do. I'll give him a call tomorrow and see if he'll meet with us."

When I got home, Lynda was watching PNN with Donata on her lap. She muted some story about a crackdown on illegal sales of technology to China and asked me how my day went.

"You already know the storyline from my texts," I said. "Walter Ellicott says Oscar's not doing enough to find his wife's killer. Oscar, on the other hand, says they're on it like black on licorice and that Walter is not a suspect—which means he's the prime suspect but also part of a well respected family with more than a few dollars."

"Sometimes licorice comes in red, you know."

I reached into my left pocket for my smartphone but it wasn't there.

"I wish I could help find the killer." Lynda looked up from our blissfully sleeping baby. *Why can't she do that at night—Donata, I mean?* "Cassandra seemed nice."

"That's right—you knew her. I keep forgetting that." I checked my other pocket, even though I knew I couldn't feel it there. I felt a rising tide of panic.

"What are you looking for?"

"My iPhone."

"Try your briefcase."

"I never put it in my briefcase."

But I looked anyway. It was in my briefcase. I must have swept it off my desk with my other junk at the end of the workday. A feeling of relaxed relief flooded through me as I sat down on the other end of the love seat after a quick glance at Facebook. I noted with satisfaction that my reposting of the meme **YOU CAN HAVE MY OXFORD COMMA WHEN YOU PRY IT FROM MY COLD, DEAD, AND LIFELESS HANDS** had attracted 47 Likes.

"Did you ever get the idea that Cassandra had a boyfriend?" I asked.

Lynda's gold-flecked brown eyes widened. "No! Did she? I didn't know her that well, just from our work together for Serenity House."

"I didn't say she did. Speak no ill of the dead and all that. I was just asking a question based on a notion that somebody had. You know how people speculate. And it's off the record!" There is no such thing as an ex-journalist, and this one was just on maternity leave. *Change the subject, fast!* "How did your day go?"

She smiled and snuggled with the baby. *Hey, do that with me!* "Playing with Donata is the best. But watching news when she's asleep is very frustrating."

"You miss the game, eh?" Lynda's corporate job at Grier Ohio NewsGroup technically disqualifies her from being called "working press." But she still had an office in the newsroom at the *Observer & News-Ledger* and she was still involved in story development across the NewsGroup's various media in the state.

"That's not the problem, Jeff." She sighed. "Now that I'm not in that rat race anymore, I realize that most of the stuff my colleagues dish out is crap. And not even good crap. I mean, it's trivial. This morning, one of the channels devoted about half a minute to showing the inside of an apartment trashed by a bad tenant in Calgary. Calgary! And it was about ten seconds of the same video shown three times! Then there was a report about all the gross germs found in men's beards."

I hope Mac saw that.

"Maybe you should just stick to the local news."

"That was *on* the local news, Jeff! Even though it wasn't local."

Not sure whether this insight was the result of post-partum depression or the scales falling from her eyes, I didn't hasten to pile on. Instead, I tried to reassure her.

"You've done a lot of great work with the TV stations as well as the newspapers and websites," I said stoutly.

"Thanks. A lot of us did. But things are changing very quickly. Every news organization is chopping jobs, especially the veteran reporters and editors who get paid more, and it shows. I even read that some newspaper publishers talk about 'managing decline.'" She looked down at our baby. "It would be hard to leave her. Maybe I shouldn't go back to work."

Donata wiggled and smiled in her sleep. Lincoln Todd must have seen his daughter do that when she was the same age. I repressed the thought.

I'm known to be a tight man with a dollar—or a dime, for that matter. But I've come to realize that you can't put a price tag on happiness.

"We can afford it," I said, "so don't rule it out."

"Thanks, *tesoro mio*, but I'd hate to let Megan down. I think she expects me to be around for a long time."

So that was the sticking point—loyalty! Megan Whitlock, president of Grier Ohio NewsGroup, had taken Lynda under her wing and promoted her from news editor of the *Observer* into a new corporate position created to take advantage of Lynda's talents as a newshawk and social media whiz.

"I'm sure she'd understand, if that's the road you choose," I said, making a grossly unjustified leap of faith. "But for now, just enjoy maternity leave."

Chapter Ten
The Right Ellicott

KILLER KNEW VICTIM, Johanna's story screamed across the top of page one on Saturday. It was substantially a one-source article, with liberal quotes from Oscar spiced up by a few expressions of shock from friends of Cassandra.

Lincoln Todd had declined to talk to Johanna, but he agreed to a sit-down with Mac and me. We visited him at his office late Monday morning, just after Popcorn and I finished reading the page proofs of the university-themed spring edition of *Ben*, our quarterly alumni mag.

Todd's grief-ravaged appearance hadn't improved much since Cassandra's funeral, his haggard features looking more Lincolnesque than ever. We sat around a small table in his large office. Even in shirtsleeves with a cup of coffee in his hand, Todd didn't look relaxed.

"I never thought anything could hurt so much," he said in response to Mac's expression of sympathy. "I have to remind myself that I'm not the first father who's ever lost a child."

"It must be hard to think of anything else," I said.

"I'm trying, though. That's why I'm here."

"'Work is the best antidote for sorrow,' as Sherlock Holmes told the grieving Watson," Mac said.

If Todd was put off by having his anguish compared to that of a fictional character—as I would have been—he kept it to himself.

"Somebody told me that when my wife died. Sometimes it works, at least for short stretches. That's why I got back to work as soon as I could. Besides, I'm still worried about the St. Patrick's Day Parade on Sunday. The PNN crew is in town and they've already lined up Brett McGee for an interview. And they told him that some professional busybody named Nelson Abbott is coming to town to support Jamie Ellicott—or Ivanhoe, as he now calls himself. Apparently Abbott has some minor reputation in obscure circles as an opponent of Artificial Intelligence."

The name was new to me. But then, what I know about AI is confined to a handful of machines-take-over movies, which I've never taken seriously.

"I have found his work to be thought-provoking, although his articles are not themselves deeply thoughtful," Mac opined. "G.K. Chesterton did better fictionally with the robot servants of 'Smythe's Silent Service' in his classic detective story, 'The Invisible Man.' However, I am inclined to think the danger to our humanity is not so much machines acting like humans as humans acting like machines."

Time out! This is over my head already.

"So is this Abbott dude a member of the Ned Ludd Society, or an ally, or what?" I asked.

"My reading of it is that he's an opportunist," Todd said. "He's undoubtedly hoping to get attention for his cause by hopping on Jamie's bandwagon. He's launched a petition drive on Change.org in favor of letting the Ned Ludd Society's banner be unfurled in the parade."

"Wait a minute." Somebody had to be the adult here, and I nominated me. "Isn't it a bit hypocritical to use the Internet to repeal the twenty-first century? That's like the Ludd group tweeting."

"Which they are," Todd asserted, in case I was kidding.

"How Chesterton would have loved the paradox!" Mac boomed with unseemly enthusiasm. "Emerson, on the other hand, already had that covered with his famous observation that a foolish consistency is the hobgoblin of little minds."

That doesn't help. "What a circus! We have everything but the clown."

"Oh, Mr. Abbott will fill that role admirably," Todd said bitterly.

I grasped at straws. "At least they're talking to Brett for some balance. You know they'll be all over Ivanhoe. The cabin in the woods will be perfect for the visuals."

"What cabin?"

"The one Ivanhoe lives in."

How could Todd not know about that? The word was all over town, as well as in Ivanhoe's every media appearance lately.

Mac cleared his throat, a sound roughly equivalent to the rumble of my Volkswagen's engine starting on a cold morning. "We understand that Cassandra dated Ivanhoe, then still James Ellicott, before he left Erin for graduate school."

The expression on Todd's haggard face told me that this was a mixed memory. "Jamie was a likeable rascal in those days, always protesting something with such ignorant sincerity that I got a kick out of debating him. Immature for his age, but I thought he would grow up. It looks to me like he hasn't yet. I'm not just talking about his latest cause. I was shocked by the embarrassing scene he caused at the funeral home." He shook his head. "At one time, when she was very young, Cassie thought Jamie was her windmill-tilting knight. But she married the right Ellicott. I couldn't have been happier for her. Walter is solid." *So is a block of wood.*

"She wasn't exactly a part of Ivanhoe's Ned Ludd cheering section, was she?" I remembered Cassandra staring at her ex-boyfriend during the City Council meeting.

"No."

"I presume you saw Johanna Rawls's story in the *Observer & News-Ledger* about Chief Hummel's new theory—that someone she knew killed Cassandra?" Mac said.

"How could I have missed it? But that story raised more questions than it answered."

"The primary one, of course, is who had a reason to kill your daughter," Mac said. "The police, guided by long experience, will cast the cold eye of suspicion upon her husband."

"That's ridiculous." Todd jumped up, agitated. "Walter loved Cassie."

"Perhaps so," Mac allowed. "And perhaps she loved him. However—and forgive me for saying so at this painful time—lovers have been known to stray. I am sure that Chief Hummel and his men will be on the hunt for indications of a paramour as he seeks to establish a motive for Cassandra's murder."

"My Cassie?"

"Or Walter, for that matter." *Why did I say that?*

"No, no. I won't believe it." He might as well have said "I don't want to believe it."

"Then who do you think killed your daughter?" Mac pressed.

Todd was shaking his head before Mac even finished the question. "I just can't imagine that anyone would."

"But somebody did," I said gently. "She didn't kill herself."

"No, of course not. She didn't kill herself. And neither did Walter. That's all I know."

Chapter Eleven
Nobody Home

Within half an hour we were riding out to Ivanhoe's cabin east of town in Mac's car. I checked my office e-mail while Mac piloted his moving ashtray and pontificated.

"The motive for Cassandra's murder is not evident. Therefore, it may well involve a secret. Many secrets are family secrets. Who better to betray a family secret than a disaffected member of the family?"

I looked up from my smartphone. "If his sister-in-law had a lover, I hardly think she'd tell Ivanhoe. She loathed him. The feeling was probably mutual, given that whole relationship-gone-bad history between them."

"That is the very reason that someone might share negative information about her, or related to her, with Ivanhoe. It is certainly worth asking him."

In other words, it was the only line worth casting right now.

"After you've softened him up," I said, "I'll try to goad him into telling me what kind of protest he's planning for the parade." That would be highly useful intel in advising Brett about a response.

Mac raised an eyebrow. "Goad?"

"If he tries to play coy about his plans, I'll hit his ego. From what I've seen of him, that's a big target."

Turning back to my phone, I saw that the e-mail traffic flow was light. Father Joe sent me a thumbs-up symbol in reaction to a speech draft I had sent him, and

Ralph wanted assurance that our float for the parade would be on time and on budget. By the time I edited the snark out of my response to Ralph, we had almost arrived at Ivanhoe's cabin in the woods barely inside Erin city limits. I'd obtained the directions from Johanna Rawls, who had talked to Ivanhoe there for her story about the parade brouhaha the previous fall.

"At least he doesn't have to worry about noisy neighbors," I observed.

The log structure, with solar panels on the south-facing side of the roof and no DirecTV antenna, sat about a quarter-mile off the main road. We drove down a gravel driveway to reach it. If there were any houses within a mile or so, they were hidden by trees.

"One certainly does not get the sense that visitors are encouraged," Mac commented as we got out of the car. "However, the traditional NO TRESPASSING sign is notable by its absence."

"Maybe he'll just shoot us."

We hadn't called ahead because Ivanhoe didn't have a phone, as he'd told the hyphenated PBS interviewer. That alone was enough to make me turn in my membership card in the Ned Ludd Society, if I'd had one.

From the outside, the house reminded me of a shrunk-down version of a place Kate and I had once stayed with our parents and three other families in the Smokey Mountains when we were kids. It had a stone chimney and wrap-around porch. But it was small, probably under eight hundred square feet, with no second floor. The curtains were closed. Landscaping was minimal—a few water-hungry bushes beneath the front windows.

"No sign of life," I said. "Not even a cat."

Seeing no doorbell, Mac rapped forcefully (the only way he knows how) on the front door. No answer. I looked around me at a whole lot of nothing. There wasn't a car on the road. Mac knocked again, with the same result.

Undaunted, he lifted his hand a third time when my cell phone burst out with the Indiana Jones theme song. The phone number on the screen didn't have a name attached.

"Hi, Jeff. This is Walter Ellicott. I was just wondering what you've been able to find out."

This didn't seem the time to fully debrief him on our morning.

"We've been very active," I reported. "We talked to Chief Hummel and to Lincoln Todd. We're at your prodigal brother's house right now."

"Jamie? What the hell do you want to talk to him for? Cassie wouldn't give him the time of day."

Actually, that could be a good motive for murder. Is that what Mac really had in mind? A lover scorned more than a decade ago, a rejection that he never got over? Stranger things . . .

"I don't want you talking to him," Walter stormed on. "He's dead to me."

Walter yelled that so loudly that you probably heard it. Mac certainly did. He ripped the phone out of my hand.

"Sebastian McCabe here, Mr. Ellicott. Please refresh my memory on a point about which there seems to be some confusion. Did you or did you not approach Jefferson with the request that we make some inquiries regarding the death of your wife?"

"What? You know that I did."

"That was certainly my understanding of the situation. I also was given to believe that you said something to Jefferson about having confidence in me. Perhaps I am in error, however, for if that were the case you surely would not be questioning the lines of inquiry I have decided to pursue."

Mac held the phone out to me so that I could hear Walter's stammered apology. It ended with: "It's just that I get a little emotional about Jamie, that shithead." He managed not to actually cry, but I judged it a near-miss.

I took the phone back, told Walter that his brother wasn't answering the door anyway, and promised to bring him up to speed in more detail later.

"Seems a little edgy," I told Mac after I hung up.

"Perhaps 'prickly' would be closer to the mark."

I opened my mouth to suggest "jittery" as a compromise when I noticed that we weren't alone in the unpaved driveway anymore. A horse and buggy kicked up the gravel as they approached us. The buggy stopped and the sparsely bearded, stocky figure of my Amish friend Amos Yoder got out.

I remembered that Amos had built Ivanhoe's cabin.

"Stopped by to admire your work?" I joked, knowing that would be a very un-Amish thing to do.

Amos smiled. "I recognized Professor McCabe's car. Just drove back to say hi."

"It looks like a very fine cabin," Mac said.

This is one subject on which I, being the son of a successful real estate broker, have it all over Mac. I actually know something about home construction and design. But I wasn't thinking of hammer and nails at the moment.

"I'd get lonely out here all by myself," I said. That's why I'd lived in Mac's carriage house all those years.

"Oh, he's not really by himself."

Tell me more!

Mac raised an eyebrow.

"His sister comes out here a lot," Amos explained. "She picked the kitchen cabinets and countertops."

Oh.

"You must come out frequently as well in order to know that," Mac said.

Amos nodded. "I'm still finishing up some detail work."

"The next time you see Mr. Ivanhoe, please do us the favor of telling him that we'd like to speak with him."

Mac handed him a business card.

Chapter Twelve
Big Brother

Back at my office, I spent what seemed like a long afternoon fielding pesky questions from Maggie Barton at the *Observer*. She'd heard complaints from some alumni and others that the university's online courses and aggressive outreach to international students were making St. Benignus into a diploma mill. (Will that woman never retire?)

"Who said that?" I demanded. Normally I would never ask a reporter such a thing, but Maggie and I go way back. I knew her when her hair was white instead of pink.

"James Ivanhoe, for one."

"Oh, *him!* A man who uses an alias! And he's not even an alum. Scratch that, Maggie. I never said it. But he's wrong."

Maggie had me a bit discombobulated because I thought I'd tamped down that kind of talk last spring, around the time we'd announced our change to university status. I wasn't happy that Ivanhoe's obsession with going retro had invaded my workspace. But I managed to retrieve my old talking points from the Cody memory banks within a few seconds.

"Our online courses fill a real need." *We need more money.* "Distance learning has been around since correspondence courses became popular in the nineteenth century. The difference today is that the Internet enables students to participate in classes in real time, interacting with other students and with the world's greatest teachers from the comfort of their home. Even such educational powerhouses as Harvard and Johns Hopkins have seen the advantages of this."

"But Mr. Ivanhoe says . . ."

Etc., etc.

The phone call at four o'clock from a briskly efficient yet friendly female voice came as a welcome break from such work-a-day drudgery.

"Mr. Cody? This is Tamara Najinski, executive administrative assistant to Mr. Samson Ellicott. Mr. Ellicott wondered if you and Mr. McCabe would be available to meet with him at his office in half an hour."

My Spidey sense tingled. Sometimes when you shake a tree, the fruit that falls on your head isn't the one you expected – and an outreach from the oldest of the Ellicott siblings was definitely unexpected. But welcome.

"We'd be delighted. What's the address?"

The offices of Samson Microcircuits, composed of glass, curves, and metal, look like something designed by Frank Lloyd Wright—for the Jetsons.

Ms. Najinski, whose appearance matched her voice except that she didn't wear glasses, ushered us into a huge corner office with large paintings on the walls. The artwork looked like the kind of thing people paid a lot of money for so they could tell people they paid a lot of money for it. The nameplate on the door said **SAMSON I. ELLICOTT, III.**

But he looked more a "Trey" as he stood up behind his chrome and glass desk when we entered. He thrust out his hand. "Thanks for coming, gentleman."

Below medium height, wearing another suit not tailored well enough to cover his extra pounds, he strongly resembled the portrait of his father that hung in the entranceway. In his late forties, his hair wasn't as gray as the clan patriarch's had been but it was getting there. He pumped our hands as if he were milking a cow. The art of the firm but friendly handshake must not have been covered in his M.B.A. courses.

"Have a seat over there. Make yourselves comfortable. Coffee?"

I'm reasonably sure that if we had said yes, Ms. Najinski would have made a return appearance with a two-hundred-dollar chrome carafe. Trey had divorced years ago and never remarried, I'd heard, but clearly he had a highly efficient office wife. Mac and I declined the offer of java. We planted ourselves, as invited, on the brown leather couch at the other end of the room from his desk and waited for Trey to show his cards. He took over a chair facing us.

"First, I want to thank you for agreeing to look into Cassie's death for Walter. This tragedy has devastated him, as you might imagine. I'm sure that seeking your assistance made him feel better, even though I have great confidence in Chief Hummel." Was I just imagining that Trey thought making Walter feel better—not a solution to the murder—was the only likely outcome of Mac's investigation?

"However, Walter is very upset that you chose to drag our former brother, Mr. Ivanhoe, into the matter." Nice touch, that Ivanhoe business—ironic, condescending, and yet James Ivanhoe himself could hardly object to being referred to by the name he chose to adopt. "Walter doesn't think you should talk to the man."

"So he told us." Mac stopped there. Considering his propensity for verbosity (as he might put it), I figured that was a strategic choice.

Trey was quiet for a while, too.

"Well," he said finally, "I just wanted to make sure you got the message."

Loud and clear—especially clear.

"May I ask whether Walter asked you to speak to us?"

Trey put up his manicured hands in a "heavens no" gesture. "Not at all. I happened to go into his office a little while ago and he looked very upset. I could see there was a problem, and when I see problems I solve them. That's what I do. So I asked him what was wrong."

Mac raised an eyebrow. *You had to ask that, Trey?*
"His wife was murdered a little more than a week ago."

Samson I. Ellicott, III, problem-solver, looked chagrined. "No, no, not Cassie's tragic death. Walter was disconnecting a phone call as I walked in. I knew from the look on his face that something upsetting had just happened." He took a breath. "Walter is my little brother by three years, gentlemen. I've always taken care of him."

Big Brother knows best. I know how that works, only in my case it's Big Sister who likes to call the shots. But I love her!

"James Ivanhoe is also your brother."

Trey shook his head. "Not anymore. He has repeatedly made that clear by his words and deeds and non-deeds over the past thirteen years."

The wheels must have been spinning in Mac's head, but I had no idea what they were spinning toward. The expression on his face was unreadable as he said: "Internecine warfare is always most unpleasant. I gather from the observation of others that Cassandra shared your strong negative attitude toward the man we will call Mr. Ivanhoe."

"Everybody in the family did, except for Karen." The expression on his face softened as he mentioned his little sister's name. "Sometimes that girl is just too sweet for her own good. She's the closest of us kids in age to Jamie, just two years younger, and she's always had a special relationship with him. That's somewhat understandable, I suppose. She also adopts stray cats and volunteers at an animal shelter."

I made a mental note of that in case a cat ever tried to move in on me. But Mac didn't linger over the niceness of Karen Ellicott.

"Presumably, then, she is not joining the lawsuit contesting your father's will?" Mac waved his hand as if he had a cigar in it. "I admit that I ask out of vulgar curiosity."

Trey frowned. "No, of course she wouldn't. You know, it's not about the money, our suit. It's a matter of principle. Jamie went his own way all those years ago when he left town. He even changed his name. Fine, if that's the way he wanted it. But then he danced back right before Dad died and managed to con his way into a share of the estate. Well, Walter and I don't want any of that money to fund Jamie's lunatic causes."

"Nor, I daresay, would you countenance the thought of him becoming an owner of Samson Microcircuits."

"The prospect is appalling, even though he'd only be a minority owner."

That's not how I saw the math. "There are four of you. If Karen joined forces with Ivanhoe on some disputed management issue, that's half the owners, right? There could be a stalemate."

Trey shook his head. "The will gives Jamie an equal share in the rest of the estate, but not Samson Microcircuits. He gets ten percent of the company and the rest of us get thirty percent each, presumably because we helped to build Samson while he was punching away on his typewriter. But ten percent to him is still too much to suit me."

"I suppose an attorney might say your father's discernment among his children in the will, giving the prodigal son less than the others, indicated that he very much knew what he was doing and was therefore of sound mind," Mac pointed out.

"An attorney might say anything he's paid to say. That's why I don't respect them."

Does that include Brother Walter, your corporate mouthpiece?

"One would think that the family firm would be anathema to your youngest brother. Perhaps he would be happy to sell you his inherited shares."

"We hope to save him the trouble." Trey leaned forward. "If you start asking Jamie questions about Cassie, and he found out that Walter asked you to look into the murder, he might think Walter has some cockamamie notion that Jamie was involved. And that might send him even further over the edge. We'd rather avoid that."

"Is that really such a cockamamie notion?" I asked. "After all, your sister-in-law and your youngest brother had a history before Walter, and it didn't end well. Time doesn't heal all wounds, despite the cliché."

An uncomfortable ten seconds of silence followed. If I were a betting man, I would bet that Trey was trying to convince himself to give in gracefully and admit that I had a point. But he just couldn't do it.

"That was a long time ago," he said finally.

Mac didn't repeat his meme about ancient history leaving its mark. Instead, he said, "Chief Hummel has concluded that Cassandra's killer was not a burglar, meaning that he or she was someone Cassandra knew and perhaps you did as well, acting for some personal motive. Who do you think that might be?"

Trey shrugged. "Do I look like Sherlock Holmes?"

No, but neither does Mac.

"I am not asking for deductive reasoning. What is your intuitive sense?"

"If I had to guess, I'd say it was somebody she met at that place where she volunteered—some homeless person who developed a crush on her and got rebuffed."

"What a crock!" Lynda said. She said a few saltier things, too, in reaction to Trey Ellicott's toss-off theory about his sister-in-law's killer.

"Serenity House serves women and children." *So what?* That didn't rule out the crush theory. A woman or an adolescent could have developed an obsession for Cassandra. But I kept my mouth shut while my dearest stormed on. "And if you're going to go in that direction, why assume the fatal attraction involved one of our clients? It could just as easily have been one of her customers at the resale shop—if it wasn't Walter."

This is what passes for witty cocktail hour banter at Chez Cody. I'd just finished giving Lynda a rundown of my day, mostly focusing on the various members of the Ellicott family. Donata slept serenely through it.

"Yes, it could have been," I agreed, ever the affirming husband. Privately, I wondered how many of Cassandra Couture's customers packed guns. *Probably a lot*, I answered myself after a moment's thought. Gun owners come from all social and economic classes. Exhibit A: Walter Ellicott. "Either way, Lyn, that doesn't limit the field a lot unless we can establish more than a nodding acquaintanceship between Cassandra Ellicott and somebody at the House or at her shop. Isn't tomorrow your regular day to volunteer at Serenity House now?"

She set down her Manhattan, a look of suspicion darkening her oval face. "You know it is."

"Just checking. Mac and I may stop by tomorrow and talk to a few folks."

She started to protest, but I put a finger on her delectable lips.

"You know how Mac is," I said soothingly. "No stone unturned and all that. It's not that he's buying what Trey's selling. We're going to Cassandra's shop right afterward to ask a few questions there, too. The shop's still in business until Walter can figure out what to do with it. What's for dinner?"

Chapter Thirteen
Serenity and Couture

Ralph stomped past Popcorn and into my office on Tuesday morning before I even had a chance to decide what to worry about first. He held up a copy of the *Spectator*, the St. Benignus student newspaper which I had once edited as a student myself. The headline blared **HEAVY BURDEN**, elucidated by the lengthy subtitle *Working-Class Students Pay Hidden Fees to Subsidize Money-Losing Athletic Program.*

"This is terrible, Cody!"

It certainly is, Ralph! Student fees weren't nearly that high in my day.

"It's not what I call positive press," I admitted. "The new editor is feeling her oats, flexing her muscles, and strutting her stuff." I hate it when I babble in trite phrases, but Ralph didn't seem to notice.

"This reporter, this Hadley Reams person, doesn't understand the economics of student athletics." *That makes two of us.* "Why didn't you block the story?"

I counted to ten. "I've explained this before, but let me try one more time. Censorship doesn't work. If I tried to muzzle the student press, that would more than likely become a big story in the real-world press. Then thousands of people who would never see the story in the *Spectator* would find out about it from other media in the region, or possibly even far beyond Erin. Call it the boomerang effect, achieving the exact opposite of what you wanted."

"But can't you do *something*?"

"We could write a letter to the editor under your name setting the record straight if there were any errors of fact. Were there any?"

He just stood there, his nose seemingly getting sharper by the minute. Finally, he said, "You knew this was coming. You're quoted in the story. You should have alerted me." *So you could circle the wagons?*

He was right, though. That was basic CYA 101: Never let your boss be surprised. Sometimes I had to deal with Ralph on a story because he was the source of the information and the person to approve the talking points. This time I'd worked with the athletic director and chief financial officer, leaving Ralph out of the loop. That was a mistake.

I'd taken my eye off the ball because of the Cassandra Ellicott business. I could tell myself that I'd been trying to help a St. Benignus board member, but that wouldn't cut any ice with Ralph. True, the provost himself takes great pains to cultivate and even protect board members, but right now he had visions of students marching on his office.

So I girded my metaphorical loins and looked Ralph in the eye, thinking how much he looked like a myopic hedgehog. "You're right. I muffed that. I'm sorry, and it won't happen again."

He regarded me, as if searching for sarcasm. Finding none, for a change, he finally snapped, "See that it doesn't, Cody."

"Yes, sir. That reminds me. Maggie Barton is working on a story for Sunday's *Observer* about the criticism of our push to get new student populations, especially with distance learning."

This was a particularly sore spot with a man who was one big sore spot. Ralph had championed the expansion of St. Benignus beyond the physical limits of our campus as a way to boost both the brand and the bottom line. He regarded its success as one of his triumphs.

"What criticism?" he asked sharply.

"Oh, you know, the usual. We're becoming a diploma mill and all that."

"That's ridiculous! Our online courses are as academically rigorous as those that are classroom-bound. They have to be in order to meet the standards of our accreditation authority."

"I told Maggie that. That's why I think the story she's working on could actually be a good thing for us. Think of it as publicity, reminding everybody of the university's dynamic and forward-thinking approach. And then we can reinforce our talking points by having Father Joe write an op-ed piece for the *Observer*."

Ralph nodded thoughtfully. "Which you will write, of course."

"Of course."

"All right. I like that." *Whew!* "Write a memo to Fr. Pirelli outlining the plan, copied to me. Now, what's this I hear about some kind of dance party in the halls on Fridays?" *Uh-oh.* "A friend of mine saw it on that YouTube. It sounds thoroughly undignified and unprofessional for the administration of an institution of higher learning." Although I happen to know that Ralph likes jazz after five o'clock, he builds a Chinese wall between work and leisure. He thinks everybody else should as well. "I assume you had something to do with it, and probably McCabe as well."

Round up the usual suspects.

"We've been doing it for weeks now." I tossed this off, no big deal. "Popcorn and I make the videos; Mac's not involved. It's a stress-reliever for faculty and staff and shows prospective students and their parents what a fun place St. Benignus is. We have to give them something for their student fees." *Why did I have to bring up student fees?*

Change the subject fast! "Our St. Patrick's Day float is ready, by the way. It's going to be a stand-out."

In addition to giving Mac a chance to play his bagpipes to a captive audience along the parade route, the float was an opportunity to highlight our still relatively new status as a university. A model of the landmark Gamble Building, the impressive Georgian structure with columns that dominates the older part of campus, was decorated with our new logo and festooned with shamrocks. It would be flanked by Mac on one side and smiling Father Joe on the other. The tall women of the NAIA champion Lady Dragons basketball team (subsidized by student fees) would be marching alongside a green dragon.

Ralph knew all this, so I didn't elaborate. He gave me a sour look. "I'm sure it will be lovely. However, I am greatly concerned about the controversy surrounding the parade this year."

The whole Ned Ludd thing, with Ivanhoe's veiled threats of protests, AI skeptic Nelson Abbott coming to town, and PNN here to record the circus, had fallen off my radar. I hadn't forgotten about it exactly; I just hadn't been giving it any of my precious worry time with Cassandra's murder on my mind.

"That won't hurt St. Benignus," I assured Ralph, assuming that was his anxiety. "We aren't a party to the debate."

"Perhaps not, but this kind of publicity will do Erin no good. Don't be so parochial, Cody."

Civic-minded me? I'm the one who's on the parade committee!

"You should be the head of the Convention & Visitors Bureau," I said.

He appeared to take that as a career suggestion, not snark. After a moment of seeming to consider the idea, he shook his head. "The job isn't open. I suspect that Linc can have it as long as he wants it." *Maybe we can work a trade.*

"Now, about this dancing in the hallways during working hours . . ."

"Are we in trouble, Boss?" Popcorn asked when he'd finally left.

"No more than usual." I summarized Ralph's whines *du jour*.

My efficient assistant's face fell at Ralph's critique of our Dance Party Friday.

"Don't worry," I hastened to reassure her. "That's my job."

"And you're very good at it."

We spent the next couple of hours parallel playing. I worked on that memo to Father Joe while Popcorn tapped out press releases about a spring arts show and a new dean of students. About eleven o'clock I left the office to go with Mac to Serenity House. Well, I didn't really leave the office. As long as I have my smartphone, my office goes with me. And I *always* have my smartphone. Take that, James Ivanhoe!

"How goes the battle, old boy?" That was Mac's idea of a good-morning greeting.

"Ralph stopped by."

"Oh? What have I done now?"

I filled him in as we walked.

The signature building associated with Serenity House, which is actually a network of social services housed in a number of different locations, is a former mansion on Front Street. Like Mac's house and many others, it had once been a stop on the Underground Railroad. A few decades later it had been owned by a Prohibition-era attorney, pharmacist, and bootlegger named Franklin W. Galton. He had put the secret room in the basement to good use.

"I am always impressed by the high level of activity here," Mac observed as we walked through the unlocked front door of the building. The place hummed, all right, as I knew from my own previous visits. In one room, young women prepped for job interviews and learned how to dress for success. In another, their children played. Upstairs, classes in sewing and jewelry-making were underway.

We told the receptionist, who was about eighteen and pregnant, that we were looking for Ms. Teal or Ms. Cody, whichever name she knew her by. Lynda tries to be Cody while not earning her paycheck, but sometimes slips.

She appeared about a minute later with Donata in her arms and Serena Mason at her side. The nice thing about babies that age is that they are easily portable. And when you put them someplace, they stay put.

My wife gave me a friendly kiss. I knew that she could do better, but I didn't press it. When I'd left her at the house she was still in pajamas. Now she wore a bright yellow dress that until now she hadn't been able to fit into since she'd started to show the previous summer.

"I thought you'd like to talk to Serena," she said.

The widow Mason had a tall paper cup of Books & Beans coffee in each hand and a smile on her face. Without a word, she handed me the one labeled *Decaf* and Mac the other.

"Excellent," Mac said. "I thank you seven times seventy times."

"My pleasure."

Serena Mason is probably the richest woman in Erin, and certainly one of the nicest. A long-time widow now closer to seventy than sixty, she spends a lot of time giving away her late husband's inherited railroad wealth as chair of the Mason Foundation. Serenity House benefits from her personal involvement as well as check-writing prowess, although whether the institution was actually named after her nobody will say.

"I'm very eager to see that justice is done for Cassandra," Serena said, favoring Mac with her wide hazel eyes. She ran a hand through her short, salt-and-pepper hair (mostly salt). There was some steel in that magnolia, as I'd observed before.

"No more eager than Jefferson and I, I assure you," Mac said.

"But I don't think it's very likely that one of our clients killed her. We help desperate women and children."

"I place no special credence in Trey Ellicott's suggestion. However, you must admit that it is not unknown for a disturbed or addicted individual to kill the very person who helped him or her."

"Hardly ever *her*," Lynda retorted. That seemed a rather broad statement, but I didn't say so. She could be right.

"Cassandra came in a few hours a week and read to the kids," Serena said. "The parents of the kids, if they paid attention to Cassandra at all, wouldn't have any reason to know that she had anything worth stealing. She didn't dress like it." I remembered what Kate had said about Cassandra and later regretted—that she had expensive taste, but not good taste. Serena herself wore a simple white blouse with charcoal slacks. I happened to know that the strand of pearls around her neck was costume jewelry that she'd bought at a Serenity House fund-raiser.

"You forget: Cassandra's murder does not appear to have been the byproduct of an attempted robbery," Mac said. "She let the killer into her home. The disarray in the house that suggested a search for things to steal was only a smokescreen. That is Chief Hummel's conclusion and it appears credible." Mac stroked his overgrown beard. "Of course, that does not preclude the possibility that something was taken, something the killer knew was there and worth killing for."

Serena shook her head. "I'd be willing to swear that she didn't have more than a nodding acquaintance with any of our adult clients."

"Perhaps the executive director would know . . . ?"

"You can talk to Vicki, if you want, but she didn't know Cassandra nearly as well as I did. This building is only part of Serenity House, and it's not Vicki's job to be here every day."

We took a pass on Vicki.

"I have an idea," Lynda said to me. "Meet me for lunch at Daniel's after you finish at Cassandra's store." Then she clammed up, as uncommunicative as Mac when he thinks he knows whodunit but won't say who.

Cassandra's Couture had taken over a former gift shop in a brick building on Broadway, just across from the Lyceum Theater.

"It would make things a lot simpler," I mused, "if we could prove that Terri was dipping into the till and killed Cassandra to cover it up."

That would be Terri Beddoes, Cassandra's only full-time employee in the resale shop. Neither Mac nor I had ever met her. Walter had supplied us with her name.

"What would you think the odds of that are?" Mac asked.

"About the same as the odds of me winning the Ohio lottery, unfortunately."

Mac raised an eyebrow. "You play the lottery?"

"No."

"Then I do not think the possibility is quite that remote. It might be worthwhile for Walter to have a forensic audit done if we sense some financial shenanigans."

We walked in the door assuming the pose of two cheap husbands out to buy their wives a gift that looked more expensive than it cost. Or rather, Mac was posing. I was dead serious.

Terri Beddoes turned out to be an attractive, vivacious woman, maybe just a little younger than me, with dyed black hair gathered in a bun. She wore a yellow and orange dress that I thought Lynda would have liked, but it would have been big on Lynda.

"Can I help you gentlemen today?"

"We'd like to buy something for our wives." I thought I might as well make it clear up front that we weren't shopping for ourselves.

"Well, you've come to the right place. Were you thinking of a blouse, slacks, dress . . .?"

"My wife likes dresses." And I like my wife in dresses.

So she took me over to a rack and I started looking, concentrating on Lynda's favorite colors of red and yellow. *What dress size is 38-26-38?*

"This is a well merchandised and well organized store," Mac said, looking around. "Do you own it?"

Terri's face darkened. "No, I just started here part-time in the fall when my youngest daughter started all-day kindergarten. I just moved up to full-time. The owner, Mrs. Ellicott, got herself *murdered.*" She lowered her voice at the last word. I don't know why; we were the only people in the store.

"Murdered!" Mac repeated. "How ghastly!"

"You must have heard about it. Somebody shot her in her own home. Can you imagine something like that happening out there on Skylark Lane? I can't. Anyway, I'm just holding down the fort until her husband decides what to do with this place."

"Is business always this slow?" I asked.

She nodded. "Mostly. I think it was really kind of a hobby for Mrs. Ellicott. Her husband has money out the wazoo, which is why she lived on Skylark Lane. There's lots of good stuff here, though. High-end goods that the carriage trade only wore a few times. This is a Donna Karan New York." She held up a backless black dress with a low neckline. It looked like it would fit Lynda very nicely. Very nicely indeed! She would complain that it offered too much cleavage, but maybe if I bought it . . .

Mac dragged the conversation back on topic.

"How disconcerting to think that the murderer could be anyone your late employer knew—perhaps even a customer! You may have met the villain."

Terri Beddoes shuddered, probably not even realizing that she was enjoying herself immensely. "I don't believe it. I have no idea who could have killed her, but not one of our customers—clientele, Mrs. Ellicott always called them."

"Why not? It certainly seems possible."

She shook her head. "Mrs. Ellicott was a nice lady, but she didn't socialize with the help and she didn't socialize with the customers, if you know what I mean. She was on a first-name basis with a lot of the clientele, but her real friends didn't shop here. At least that's my take. I just work here. And I don't know how long that's going to last."

Mac waxed sympathetic. "Ah, yes. Her husband owns the business now, but surely that is little comfort to him. The poor man must be devastated."

"You would think so, but Mrs. Ellicott let it slip more than once that he paid more attention to his smartphone and his tablet than he did to her."

I noticed that Terri, wrapped up in telling everything she knew and then some, still held the black dress. I could just imagine the dark honey curls of my beloved spouse's hair contrasting against the dark of the Donna Karan New York creation. Lynda likes bright colors, but they say every woman needs a little black dress. I tried to remember whether she owned one.

"No wonder she was stepping out on him," Terri added.

Chapter Fourteen
Little Sister

"I wouldn't take it to the bank," I told Mac as we walked toward Daniel's Apothecary. I carried Lynda's black dress in a bag. "She admitted she was just guessing based on behavioral clues."

"That is precisely what Sherlock Holmes did, old boy. He called it deduction. Besides, women know these things about other women. Therefore, I give weight to Ms. Beddoes's conclusion."

"How do you account for the fact that Oscar couldn't find a digital trail—no text messages or phone calls to the hypothetical boyfriend?"

"As Oscar noted, such things can be deleted. And that is not the only possible answer. There were no text messages of a romantic nature, as we understand it. There were also no phone calls to likely paramours. However, suppose the paramour was not a likely one. Suppose the person was a business associate, male or female, with whom Cassandra might logically be expected to be in communication?"

"That's a lot of supposing. You might as well suppose we're all fictional characters in a mystery novel while you're at it."

"Well, I do not insist on it. I merely offer it as a possible answer to your question."

Not being known as a spontaneous spender, I was expecting to surprise Lynda with the dress. But Mac and I got the surprise when we arrived at Daniel's, downtown

Erin's throwback-to-the-fifties eatery right next to the *Observer* offices. Sitting across the table from Lynda and Donata, reaching across to play with the baby, was Karen Ellicott.

"I didn't know you two were acquainted," I said after the introductions. And that's not the kind of thing Lynda would forget to tell me.

"We just met," Lynda said. "I gave her a call and asked her to join us because I thought she might want to help your investigation into Cassandra's murder."

What a woman!

"I would hardly call it an investigation," Mac protested mildly. Was this an attempt at modesty? If so, that was a rare trick from him. "We are simply making a few inquiries at Walter's request."

"Cassie and I were close," Karen Ellicott said. "We went to high school together. I was the first Ellicott she knew." She shook her head sadly. "Poor Walter. This has hit him so hard. He really loved Cassie."

"Their personalities seemed much different," Mac observed. "By all accounts, Cassandra was giving and outgoing." Maybe that was just an idle observation. Or maybe Mac was drawing a contrast to Walter's bland deportment.

Karen sipped a 1,200-calorie chocolate milkshake from a straw. Either she didn't do that very often or she had a gym membership and the metabolism of a hummingbird, judging by her Serena Williams physique.

"Walter has no personality, God love him. We get along fine—I get along with all of my brothers, more or less—but Walter's only interests are the company and whatever Trey tells him to be interested in. He doesn't even have any hobbies. My father, who was a gun nut, once tried to get him interested in target shooting. I think he went to the range all of one time." *But the gun got used again.*

"Well, no wonder Cassandra married him," Lynda said. "He swept her off her feet." The woman has absorbed a flare for Codyesque sarcasm. I approve.

If I read the expression on Karen's face and eyes correctly, Lynda's comment and the question it implied activated her mental Way-Back Machine. "I suppose Walter's biggest attraction for Cassie at first was that he wasn't Jamie."

When Karen paused, seemingly lost in her thoughts, Mac said, "Would you care to elucidate?"

"Jamie was, and is, a romantic and a rebel and handsome to boot. What teenage girl wouldn't fall for a guy like that? But by the time Cassie was a sophomore at Miami and Jamie was a senior, she had a practical side that came from being Lincoln Todd's daughter. She didn't want to hook her wagon to a falling star.

"When she pressed Jamie to get serious about making a plan for his life with more future than a master's degree in history was likely to get him, he pushed back. They were both a little stubborn. I'd say the parting was mutual, but Cassie's the one who actually pulled the plug. Basically, she thought Jamie was a dreamer who would never be more than a teacher and she couldn't handle that."

Mac raised an eyebrow. Or rather, Professor McCabe did. *What's wrong with being a teacher?*

I wondered whether Cassandra had ever realized that her ex-beau's dreams were what had put his name on the *New York Times* best-seller list. He had made plenty of himself, never mind that he was a royal pain in the ass and, IMHO, a bit of a fruitcake. It would be interesting to get his side of this first hand if he ever responded to our request, via my Amish friend, that he talk to us.

Karen sighed. "I lived through all this, too, you know. They both cried on my shoulder. That whole relationship was always awkward for me because I kept secrets for both of them. And when it exploded, well, I was afraid I was going to be collateral damage. But I managed to stay on good terms with both parties. In fact, I invited Cassie to a family vacation on Fripp Island about ten years ago. Jamie wasn't there, of course, and that's where she met up with Walter again. She'd known him only slightly when she was dating Jamie."

Lynda listened intently. Donata, cradled in my arms, seemed less interested.

"Walter was older, almost fifteen years older than Cassie and me, but that just meant that he was a settled commodity and not a work in progress. They hit it off and got married within the year. By that time Jamie was already working on his first divorce, which I suppose proves his lack of stability." She finished the last of her drink, sucking it loudly in accordance with milkshake protocol. "We've gotten way off topic, haven't we?"

"Perhaps not," Mac rumbled.

"What do you mean?"

I figured she deserved to have it straight. "Cops are trained to play percentages. By that measure, Walter is the leading suspect. Husbands kill their wives with dismal predictability in real life, and occasionally even in fiction. And we heard a whisper that maybe Cassandra had a boyfriend."

She avoided my eyes. "My father would hate this. So do I."

"A paramour would be a solid suspect," Mac pointed out.

"Or it could give Walter a motive." No flies on Karen! She stood up. "Look, I have to get back to work." *You own part of the company.* "I have no idea who killed Cassie, but I hope you catch the bastard."

She threw a few dollars on the table and hurried out.

"She knows who the boyfriend is," Lynda said. "What's in the bag, Jeff?"

Chapter Fifteen
Dead Bolt

The dress was a big hit. Lynda's just waiting for the right occasion to wear it. It's not what you'd call a housedress.

On Wednesday morning, at twelve minutes after three, I woke up with a start. Lynda, lying next to me, was nursing Donata. Her curls were in disarray and she had bags under her eyes. Call it New Mom Syndrome.

"Ivanhoe," I said groggily.

"What about him?" Lynda yawned.

"He was Cassandra's boyfriend."

"Yeah, so? I had boyfriends in high school and college, too."

Let's not talk about that.

"I don't mean years ago. I mean since he came back to town—or maybe that's even why he came back." My subconscious mind must have been working hard on this all night because it had everything all worked out. "It all fits. Casandra's smartphone didn't show any texts or phone calls to a likely lover because Ivanhoe scorns post-*Mayflower* technology."

"But Cassandra gave him his walking papers before he went to graduate school."

"Call it seller's remorse. Thirteen years ago Jamie Ellicott didn't have a book on the *New York Times* bestseller list and probably nobody, Jamie included, imagined that he someday would. Cassandra's fears for his wasted future didn't come true, unlike the predictions of the Trojan

Cassandra in mythology." Confession: I'd remembered almost nothing about the Cassandra of Greek and Roman literature until Mac had bent my ear about the subject a few days earlier.

"So you're saying she was attracted to him now because he became successful? That sounds pretty shallow, and not like the Cassandra I knew."

"No, I'm not saying that. I'm saying that what she once saw in him as a defect, the lack of worldly ambition and practicality, may not have seemed like a defect after nearly a decade of being married to his brother. She complained to Terri Beddoes about Walter paying more attention to his smartphone and his tablet than to her. I can believe that because I've seen him in action. And that certainly wouldn't be a problem with Walter's Luddite younger brother. See what I mean? Does that make sense?"

Lynda yawned. "Right now it does. You might want to ask me again in the morning."

"And Cassandra's well-known loathing for her brother-in-law was camouflage. But I bet Karen knows the real score. That's why she dodged the boyfriend question. If I'm right, that makes Jamie a suspect and Walter an even better suspect than he was before. So two of her brothers are on the hook."

"Even worse, one of them may be guilty. And Cassandra was Karen's friend. That's awful, Jeff. How am I supposed to get back to sleep now?"

Later that morning, at breakfast, my conviction that Cassandra's dalliance (Mac's word) was a family affair still looked like a winner. That is, it worked for me. Lynda was still asleep. I tried to share my brainstorm with Mac but he didn't answer his smartphone. I would have bearded him in his office when I got to campus, but I got swamped with a media relations issue in my own workplace.

Maggie Barton had been tipped by someone that our scheduled commencement speaker had tweeted over-the-top harsh comments about a certain political figure two years previously. Popcorn saved the day by discovering that she, the speaker, had already apologized and blamed the instant nature of the Twitterverse for making it too easy to be mean in 140 characters. The politico had accepted the apology, which made it easy for Father Joe to embrace the virtue of mercy and not replace the speaker. I got back to Maggie with a quotable quote and the issue turned out to be a one-day wonder. There were a few nasty comments posted when the story ran online, but two days later nobody remembered the teapot-worthy tempest.

Also on the commencement theme, I drafted Father Joe's commencement address for a Catholic high school in Cincinnati. I was just crafting a memorable line when Ralph came in to complain bitterly about an escort service ad running next to our Dance Party Friday videos on YouTube. I tried to explain to him that goes with the territory and that YouTube is perfectly respectable—even the Vatican has its own channel.

"Will this day never end?" I asked Popcorn gloomily in Ralph's wake after an agonizing ten-minute verbal wrangle.

"Cheer up, Boss. It's almost lunch time."

About ten o'clock the next morning, as I was polishing off a press release announcing next fall's visiting artist, my phone burst out with "You're So Vain," my ringtone for Mac. A photo of his bearded face took over the phone's screen.

"You have reached the voice mail of Jeff Cody, croquet master and *bon vivant*," I announced in the stiff cadence characteristic of most VM messages. "I'm sorry that I can't clear up your mess right now, but I'm busy getting a pedicure. Please leave your name and credit card number at the tone." I beeped.

"Very droll, Jefferson!" Mac boomed. "You are developing a distinct touch of a certain pawky humor, to paraphrase the Master."

"Where have you been? I left you a message more than twenty-four hours ago."

"I apologize, old boy. I accidently dropped my phone in the toilet, rendering it useless. My only exculpation is that I had never done that before."

"The first time is the hardest." *Believe me, I know.* "The reason I called is that I think I figured out who Cassandra's playmate was."

I laid it on him. The silence that followed made me think he wasn't buying it. But no, he was just looking at it from all angles and five moves ahead, like the great chess player that he was. (I bet he could beat Amy Quong, who once beat me in six moves, without a chessboard.)

"By thunder, Jefferson, I believe that you could well be right!" he finally bellowed. "I really must congratulate you. I wonder if Oscar has tumbled on to that possibility?"

I didn't actually puff out my chest (does anybody really do that?) but I was so startled by Mac's quasi-endorsement of my theory that I spilled decaf on my Frank Lloyd Wright design tie.

"Let's find out," I said as I patted the tie with my handkerchief.

A couple of hours later, after Mac finished teaching a class, I told Popcorn that Mac and I were going to see her beau at the police station.

"Should I give him a kiss for you?" I teased.

"No, thanks," she replied with dignity. "I can handle that myself."

"Coffee?" Oscar asked.

Mac accepted, but I said, "No, thanks. My tie's had enough for the day. The reason we dropped by is that we think Cassandra Ellicott did have a boyfriend"—dramatic pause—"and it was her brother-in-law, James Ivanhoe."

Oscar stopped in mid-pour and set down the coffee pot. "Now that's a helluva coincidence."

"How so?" Mac asked.

"Karen Ellicott called me not ten minutes before you walked in the door. She's worried about Jamie, as she calls him. She hasn't heard from him in days. She went out to his cabin and the mail is piled up. He has diabetes, so she's afraid he might be lying there alone in a diabetic coma. I agreed to meet her at the cabin with Phil Oakland, the locksmith over on Spring Street. When I called Phil, he said to tell her to look for a spare key under a doormat or a rock or something because people almost always tuck one there, thinking that nobody will look."

"Makes sense," I said.

Oscar nodded. "So I called her back, but she said she'd already done that. The upshot is that Phil and I are going to posse up with Ms. Ellicott at the cabin. He said I had time for a cup of coffee on account of he has to finish whatever I interrupted. Want to go along?"

"Surely," Mac said.

He and I both stood, with some apprehension in my case.

"Is this even legal?" I wondered. "I mean, there *is* the U.S. Constitution and that whole 'a man's cabin is his castle' thing."

Oscar waved away my concern. "With his sister making the request and the medical issue, I'm pretty sure a judge would say I had just cause for entering the domicile without a warrant."

"Is a locksmith really necessary?" Mac wondered. "I am a fair hand at picking locks."

"I didn't hear that," Oscar said.

Phil Oakland, a stocky guy with sandy gray hair and wire-rim glasses, beat us to the cabin. He was on the front porch with Karen Ellicott when we pulled up. As soon as he saw us, he started working on the lock. Karen raced over to Oscar's cruiser, moving like the runner she probably was.

"What took you so long?"

"I brought my unofficial deputies." *Is that what you call your unpaid help?*

Mac glowed.

I looked around. Nothing seemed to have changed since we'd been there on Monday, three days before, except that the mailbox was even more stuffed. That wasn't a good sign.

Phil turned from the door. "It's a good lock, a Schlage dead bolt. But I got it. It's all yours now." Phil's conversation tends to be terse, even though he holds a master's degree in philosophy. Or maybe because of that. I've never read his thesis on Kierkegaard. He stood aside.

Oscar nodded at Karen. "You first, Ms. Ellicott."

She pushed in the door.

I'll never forget the smell, and I'll never be able to adequately describe it.

The door opened into the main living area of the cabin. On our right as we entered was a fireplace with ashes in the grate and a love seat in front of it. Straight ahead lay a compact but modern kitchen, with an island, a refrigerator, a stove, etc. To our left were two rooms that undoubtedly would have been designated as bedrooms on a floor plan.

Inside one of those rooms, with an impressive array of knives, swords, crossbows, and battle axes on the walls, the decaying body of James Ivanhoe lay slumped over a manual typewriter with a hole in his right temple and a gun in his right hand.

Karen Ellicott screamed and screamed and screamed.

Chapter Sixteen
Too Many Reasons

James Ivanhoe's death, ironically, was first announced to the world at large in a tweet from Johanna Rawls: *Best-selling Erin author and techno-skeptic James Ivanhoe found dead in cabin of apparent self-inflicted gunshot wound. He left a note.*

The tall, Nordic reporter had arrived right behind Oscar's troops. If Oscar had used his cell phone to summon Lt. Col. Gibbons and his small corps of crime scene investigators instead of the police radio, he could have avoided that. When Johanna pulled up in her silver Prius behind the two police cruisers, I could see Oscar's day going from bad to worse. He went out to meet her, the rest of us tagging along.

"Suicide or murder, Chief?" Johanna asked.

"That's for the coroner to decide officially, Ms. Rawls. But judging by the weapon in his hand and the suicide note on his typewriter, I'd say suicide."

"What did the note say?"

"That's not a public document at this time."

"Why not?" She made it sound more like a point of idle curiosity than a challenge. Tall Rawls belongs to the "catch more flies with honey" school of journalism.

"I'd rather not say now. I hope I can tell you more tomorrow."

"But everybody will have it tomorrow, Chief!"

Oscar shook his head. "No, you asked first so I'll release it to you first. I promise."

I had to admire his poker face. He didn't give a clue that he, Oscar, was sitting on dynamite. The note still in the typewriter beneath Ivanhoe's body said:

```
Why live if I cannot write? My creative juices
have dried up. The guilt is too much. I killed
Cassie.
```

The typed missive was the second thing I had noticed after entering the main room of the small cabin. The first, of course, was the mortal remains of James Ivanhoe, née Ellicott. Judging by the condition of the corpse, he must have already been dead when Mac and I had come out to see him on Monday.

"Is this your brother?" Oscar had asked Karen in a surprisingly gentle voice.

The screaming all out of her, she was sobbing too much to respond in words. But she nodded.

"I'm sorry. I know this is very difficult for you. You have my sympathy. Please don't touch anything, miss. This is a potential crime scene."

"Perhaps you should sit down," Mac suggested.

Karen ignored him. She stood over the body and saw the letter in the ancient Remington. "Oh, Jamie, Jamie, why did you do it?" she wailed.

The answer seemed obvious then, although not so much later on.

Oscar pulled out his police radio and called Gibbons. I'm pretty sure it was his use of the words "Ivanhoe" and "dead" that had attracted Johanna's attention as she listened to the police chatter with half an ear in the *Observer* newsroom.

"Who else needs to be notified, Miss Ellicott?" Oscar asked when he had finished his thirty-second call.

She shrugged. "He still had a business relationship with his second ex-wife."

"I don't think that qualifies as next of kin." He ran a hand over his balding noggin. "This is just bizarre. I never figured him for a suspect in Mrs. Ellicott's murder. I just knew the two of them had a history."

"More than that," Karen said. "It can't hurt to tell you now." And she did, confirming my deduction about the Cassandra-Ivanhoe fling—and also my suspicion that Karen had known about it. "It wasn't right. I don't always see eye to eye with Walter, but he's a good man. He deserved better from Cassandra. I told her that, but it was like she was a teenager again smitten with the bad boy. Oh, I don't mean that Jamie was bad, really. I loved him so much. But he never grew up. He was irresponsible, like Peter Pan."

That image isn't quite working for me, what with the gun and all.

"Walter Ellicott needs to know about the contents of the suicide note before I make it public," Oscar had said, thinking aloud. "I'll be the one to tell him, got it? I think I owe him that for putting him in the hot seat."

So that's how we got to Oscar promising Tall Rawls that she would get the contents of the suicide note before anybody else, but not yet.

"That's all I can tell you now," he said. "You can all go. In fact, you should have never been here." His weary look did not exclude Mac and me. "This is a crime scene. We professionals have work to do here." Sure enough, Gibbons and another officer were stringing the yellow crime scene tape while a third took photos.

Karen walked quickly toward a red Fiat parked right in front of the cabin, Johanna on her heels.

"Ms. Ellicott, may I—" Johanna began.

"No. I have nothing to say to the media."

She got in the car and tore off.

Johanna shrugged. "To be honest, I don't blame her. If I weren't in the business, I wouldn't talk to somebody like me at a time like this. What about you guys? What are you doing here?"

"Just lucky, I guess," I said.

"Chief Hummel asked us," Mac said at the same time.

"Okay, then how did the Chief know that Ivanhoe was dead? Walk me through this step by step, and don't forget the details. I need some color."

Johanna didn't have to ask Mac twice. He gave her everything, just as if it were a scene in one of his overwritten but popular Damon Devlin mystery novels. He even caught the pause after Phil Oakland unlocked the door and before we all piled in.

"So what did the suicide note say?"

"Nice try," I said before Mac could blurt it out word-for-word. "Next question?"

"What does the inside of the murder room look like?"

"What one notices first," Mac said, "is that all four walls are decorated with antique weapons, as perhaps befit one who so often explored earlier time periods in his novels."

"Like what kind of weapons?"

"Battle axes, swords, knives, spears, maces, a crossbow."

"Is that what he killed himself with—some Braveheart kind of deal?"

"Far from it," Mac said. "It was a 9mm Glock to the side of the head." He knows enough about guns from shooting them and from research to have made the identification without Oscar's help.

If Johanna's hands hadn't been busy with pen and notebook, she probably would have scratched her head. That was the expression on her face. "Doesn't that seem kind of odd? I mean, here's this guy with all these past-century weapons and he offs himself with a modern handgun?"

My mind was going in a different direction that had nothing to do with this seeming paradox: Apparently Walter Ellicott's missing Glock was no longer missing.

"It is hardly unknown for a suicide to act in peculiar ways," Mac said. Actually, Ivanhoe's method of dispatching himself wasn't even peculiar, given the confession in the suicide note, but Mac couldn't say that.

"Why did Ivanhoe kill himself?" Johanna asked. "And what does this have to do with the death of his sister-in-law two weeks ago tomorrow? I can't believe that's a coincidence."

"You ask excellent questions, Johanna!"

Her blue eyes narrowed. "You know more than you're saying, Mac."

"Do I? How do you reach that conclusion?"

"Because if you didn't know anything, you'd be talking non-stop—dishing out a whole menu of possible theories."

She sure had his number, right down to the food metaphor.

But Mac chuckled as if this were the silliest thing he'd ever heard. Some people wouldn't recognize themselves in a mirror with all the lights on.

"Why was the sister here? Can you at least tell me that?"

"She got worried when she hadn't heard from him," I said. "She drove out here and saw the mail piled up. That's when she called the Chief to report her concern. Karen and Ivanhoe were always very close."

"The Ellicotts are an interesting family, aren't they?"

You don't know the half of it.

"Ivanhoe had to be more than just a hair off-center," I said to Mac as we drove back to town in his boat. "As I read his suicide note, the bottom line is that he killed himself because killing Cassandra gave him writer's block." I shook my head. "I wouldn't use that in fiction."

"Nor would I, albeit possibly for a different reason." Mac's eyes were on the road, but his head was somewhere else. "You seem to imply that the stated motivation is insufficient. On the contrary, I find it excessive. Look at the wording of the note. Ivanhoe actually gives two separate reasons for killing himself—related reasons, admittedly, but still separate. Would not the fact that he felt guilt over killing his paramour be motive enough? And yet the note tells us first that he cannot write, that his 'creative juices have dried up.'

"And something else bothers me about that note, Jefferson: The sentences are too short. The average length of those four sentences is just five words. That was not James Ivanhoe's style. The sentences in his novels are much more prolix."

"But those are novels," I protested. I learned in Writing 101 to use different styles for different kinds of writing, although I have to admit I've never studied the genre of suicide notes.

Mac rubbed his facial forest, ignoring my protest. "In fact, the very existence of the note is rather dubious. Seventy percent of all suicides do not leave notes. One's natural suspicion of such a missive is then amplified by the fact that the note was composed on a typewriter, not in the victim's handwriting."

Stevie Wonder could see where this was going, and I didn't like it.

"This is a gift horse, Mac, and you should stay away from its mouth. Ivanhoe always used a typewriter. Look, Walter wanted us to find Cassandra's killer. We did that. His body is in that cabin back there. Obviously, the family affair between the in-laws somehow went wrong. My guess is that Cassandra wanted out a second time for some reason—guilt, disappointment, whatever—and he couldn't take it so he did her in. And then later he felt so much remorse that he couldn't even write. He killed again, this time himself. Case closed."

Mac sighed. "I am sure that Oscar will readily agree. Murder-suicide is such a satisfactory solution, so neat and tidy and no loose ends."

Too bad it wasn't the true solution.

Chapter Seventeen
Not Buying It

"Jamie didn't kill himself," Karen Ellicott insisted, sitting in Mac's office the next morning.

"You didn't say that yesterday," I pointed out. I had a vivid memory of her moaning over the body, "Oh, Jamie, Jamie, why did you do it?"

"Yesterday I was in shock."

Johanna Rawls's front-page story in that morning's *Observer* stuck with the standard "apparent self-inflicted gunshot wound" phrase. She quoted Oscar; noted the presence of Mac, Karen Ellicott, and yours truly on the scene; and even squeezed a few words out of Phil Oakland, not about Kierkegaard. Somewhere around the middle of the fifteen-paragraph story Johanna recapped the St. Patrick's Day controversy and snagged an expression of sorrow about Ivanhoe's death from Brett McGee.

"Now that you are unshocked, to adopt a neologism, on what do you base the conviction that your brother did not take his own life, if anything?" Mac asked. "It is not unusual for survivors to deny that a loved one killed himself or herself. Suicide used to be considered rather disrespectable."

Karen looked small sitting in one of Mac's big chairs. "I loved Jamie, but he thought too much of himself to deprive the world of him. And if he did kill himself, he wouldn't have used a gun. He hated guns and he had plenty of other weapons—you saw them on his wall. He'd been collecting antique arms for years."

That had bothered Tall Rawls, I remembered.

"I don't think he could kill himself with a battle axe or a crossbow," I said.

"He had knives and swords. On top of all that, his 'creative juices'"—she made air quotes—"hadn't dried up. The last time I talked to him, a week ago yesterday, he was excited about the new book he was working on."

"Not mourning his murdered lover?" I said in faux surprise. "That was the day after her funeral."

"When the real world let him down, Jamie retreated to his own. He was like that even as a kid. But you saw him at Hawes & Holder. He was very upset about Cassie's death, and even more upset that he wasn't welcome at the visitation. He didn't kill her."

The fervor in Karen's voice was almost enough to convince me.

"You make a good case," Mac told her.

My phone rang. Well, actually it played the Indiana Jones theme song. I looked down and saw that Walter Ellicott was calling. I turned off the ringtone. "Sorry." I made a mental note to call him back, even if he didn't leave a message.

"Was your brother left-handed or right-handed?" Mac asked Karen.

"Right-handed."

And Ivanhoe was shot in his right temple, with the gun in his right hand. Thank heavens! The old it-couldn't-be-suicide-because-the-victim-was-left-handed trope is so old its beard is white.

Mac cleared his throat with a rumble. "Perhaps your brother's talk of his next book was only a brave front for his favorite sibling. Chief Hummel has suspected all along that Cassandra was killed with a gun that belonged to her husband. It is conceivable that the two illicit lovers argued, the argument turned into a real fight, Cassandra brought out the gun, there was a struggle over it, and the gun went off. Devastated by what he had done, Ivanhoe took the gun from the scene and used it to end his own life as a form of poetic justice. Surely that is a plausible sequence of events."

"Did the police find any evidence of a struggle anywhere in the cabin?"

"Not to my knowledge."

I made a mental note to ask Oscar about that. My mental notebook was getting filled up.

Karen gave Mac the hairy eyeball. He responded with a slow half-smile. "I must admit that I have been playing Devil's Advocate, Ms. Ellicott. The scenario I have outlined is likely to be Chief Hummel's, but it is not mine. I have my own grounds for suspecting that the convenient tableau presented to us at the cabin in the woods was staged to conceal a homicide."

"Whoa!" If I'd had a whistle, I would have blown it. "Have you forgotten Phil Oakland opening the cabin door? That door was locked and dead-bolted. You can't secure a dead bolt without a key. And even you didn't have a key, Karen. And the windows were locked."

"There must have been a back door."

"Sure—also dead-bolted." I'd checked that with Oscar shortly before Karen arrived, knowing what she wanted to talk about.

"I don't care. Jamie didn't kill himself."

Well, that's a solid line of reasoning.

Mac's wasn't much better. "Locked room murders are far from unknown, Jefferson."

"In *fiction!*" I came perilously close to shouting.

"Let us not discount the possibility of life imitating art. After all, there is something Gatsbyesque about a man who changes his name and then woos and re-wins his lost love, is there not?"

F. Scott Fitzgerald's *The Great Gatsby* is one of the best hard-boiled crime novels ever written, according to me and a few other discerning critics. Mac, however, regards it as merely The Great American Novel. I didn't see the parallel with James Ellicott alias Ivanhoe, though. He didn't have a swimming pool, for one thing. Besides, Gatsby believed in the green light. What did Ivanhoe believe in—Greenpeace, maybe? Or just himself?

I took a breath. "Do you know anybody who did have a key to the cabin, Karen?"

"No."

"Okay, we'll put 'means' on hold. How about 'motive'? You have reasons why you think your brother didn't kill himself. Do you know of any reason why somebody else would want to kill him?"

She gave that a think, and came up dry. "I just don't know. He made a bit of a stir over marching in the St. Patrick's Day Parade under the Ned Ludd name, of course, but I can't believe that somebody . . ." She shook her head.

Mac rubbed his beard. "The killer—"

"If there is one," I inserted.

"—chose to blame James for Cassandra's murder. Perhaps that was no more than what it appears to be on the surface, an attempt to provide a motivation for suicide. However, it suggests to me that the killer knew of the past relationship between your brother and your sister-in-law, and perhaps the current one as well. Who knew about their *affaire de coeur*?"

She shrugged. "People talk. But maybe fewer people than you might think in a small town. Folks have a way of not knowing things they don't want to know."

"Including Walter?"

"Especially Walter. He wouldn't have noticed. And yet he would be devastated to find out. I hope that doesn't have to happen."

Fat chance. "It's probably only a matter of time before it's in the *Observer* and little old ladies talk about it at the bridge club," I opined.

Maybe I could have put that more diplomatically.

Karen got up and left a short while later, taking with her Mac's cell phone number and his assurance that he would share his doubts about the murder-suicide scenario with Oscar Hummel. We walked her out.

Her face flushed when she saw who sat in the small reception area outside Mac's office.

"Walter!"

He looked like he'd been hit by a Mack truck. His suit was wrinkled and he'd cut his mustache slightly more on the left side than on the right. The bags under his eyes looked like they were packed for a trip to Europe.

"What brings you here, Karen?"

"Haven't you been listening at the door?"

"Of course not!"

The door is too thick.

"Jamie didn't kill himself."

"What? Sure he did." Walter's voice was just this side of hysterical. "But if he wasn't already dead, I'd kill him myself. He murdered Cassie! And he was having an affair with her! It's like a bad joke. I thought she hated the jerk."

"How did you find out otherwise?" I asked.

"Chief Hummel called me last night and asked me to meet him at his office. I asked if I should bring a lawyer, but he said it wasn't that kind of meeting. When I got there he laid it all on me. He said he wanted me to know first, before he told the media, the reason for Jamie's suicide. Why didn't you tell me?"

"The Chief felt that was his responsibility," Mac said.

"Nice of him. He even sort of apologized for suspecting me about Cassie. And then he asked about the gun that Jamie used on himself. I told him I couldn't be sure—there weren't any identifying marks or anything—but I thought it was mine. He said he's sure the ballistics tests will prove that it killed Cassie, too."

"Where did you keep the Glock?" Mac asked.

Trick question? We already knew what Walter had told Oscar earlier.

Walter shrugged. "Unlike my father, I never cared very much for guns. I lost track of it when I quit target shooting. I know that doesn't sound very responsible, but it's not like we had kids in the house. How was I supposed to know that my brother was going to use it to kill my wife and himself?"

"He didn't do it, Walter," Karen snapped. "Not Cassie, not himself. How do you think Jamie happened to find your gun when even you didn't know where it was?"

Somebody found it!

"Your favorite Ellicott," Walter said bitterly. "You always defended Jamie, no matter what crazy bad thing he did."

"And you and Trey always treated him like a stray dog with a bad case of fleas. That's why he changed his name."

Walter pouted. "He didn't even come home—"

"For Mom's funeral. I'm sick of hearing that! He didn't come back because I told him not to. I knew the kind of reception he'd get. I suppose I should be glad you didn't give him the same treatment at Dad's services that you gave him at Cassie's visitation." She slung her purse over a well-formed shoulder. "But I'm not going to stand here and argue with you. I'm going back to work."

She stalked out.

"Karen!" Walter called after her. But his sister kept walking.

I suspected that no air conditioning would be needed this summer in the management suite of Samson Microcircuits if things didn't change between those two.

"She's kind of stubborn," Walter murmured, as if to apologize for his sister.

"That is one perspective," Mac acknowledged. "Now, presumably you came here today for a reason. How can I help you?"

"You already did—when you agreed to look into Cassie's murder, even though you didn't come up with anything. Thanks for trying. I really just came to tie a ribbon on it, to tell you what happened yesterday with Chief Hummel." He shook his head. "I still can't believe it. Not any of it. I never suspected that Cassie was cheating on me. And with Jamie!"

Isn't cheating something you do in a game? It always seemed to me that using the term as a euphemism for marital infidelity trivialized the act.

And yet, I couldn't help thinking that, for a tragic figure, Walter had really lucked out. His wife, who was fooling around with his brother, had been killed with his gun. But the killer had confessed and then killed himself.

Mac had ironically referred to the murder-suicide scene as a "convenient tableau." The person for whom it was most convenient was Walter Ellicott. I pushed that thought to the back of my mind because I didn't like what it implied. I do that a lot. By now the back of my mind must be about ready to ooze out of my ears.

"I fear you have affixed that ribbon prematurely," said Mac, never one to resist the temptation to wordplay. "I do not believe that your brother killed himself, and I am far from certain that he killed your wife."

"I don't blame Walter for being skeptical," I told Mac after our former "client" had left in a huff that gave his sister's a run for the money. "You just want it to be double murder because murder-suicide leaves you nothing to solve."

"Really, Jefferson, you wound me. Did I in any way indicate an interest in making further inquiries into this matter?"

As if you had to draw me a map! I ignored the question. "Forgetting the dead bolt lock on his cabin door for a minute, who do you think killed James Ivanhoe? You didn't give Walter or Karen a hint." Not that Walter would have listened. His parting shot was something about Mac sticking to fiction writing. Since I was inclined to agree, I didn't point out that to Walter that this was a complete one-eighty from his attitude during his first appearance in Mac's office a week and a day earlier.

"Mr. Ellicott is happy believing that he already knows what happened," Mac pointed out. "Ms. Ellicott, being an intelligent woman, could doubtless enumerate the possibilities herself—as could you."

"Well, sure I could. But I like to hear you talk, so give."

He sighed. "Very well, then. Let us imagine some credible scenarios:

"Perhaps a technophile who had reached the limits of his endurance with Mr. Ivanhoe's comments challenging certain aspects of the digital age decided to make him permanently unavailable for interviews.

"Or perhaps the killer was in Ivanhoe's own camp—either a rival technophobe who disagreed with his tactics or an associate in the modern-day Luddite movement who hoped to take over his position of leadership."

I threw up my hands. "You're joking!"

"Not at all, old boy! None of those motives is without precedent—and I do not mean within the pages of fiction. However, if you would prefer a more personal motive, possibilities are not lacking. Lincoln Todd, for example, might have killed Ivanhoe in retribution for the murder of his daughter."

Mac was spinning cotton candy, but I pushed back as if he really believed it. I can play the game as well as he can.

"Linc is so straight I bet he pays the sales tax on Amazon purchases. His best friend is Ralph, for heaven's sake. A guy like that would leave it to the forces of law and order to deal with his daughter's killer, not go vigilante. Besides, how would he know who the killer was? You didn't figure it out." *Sorry; low blow.*

"Perhaps he threatened Cassandra at some time before the deed and she told Todd. By all accounts, father and daughter were quite close."

"Then that would be evidence that Todd could have taken to Oscar. Bereaved parents testify in court all the time about domestic violence against an adult child that eventually led to murder. I've seen it on TV. Yet Linc never hinted at that after Cassandra died. I'm sure if he had, Oscar would have told us."

Without acknowledging the sagacity of that observation, Mac dropped the subject of Lincoln Todd to spin other theories. "Also in the personal vein, someone might have killed James Ivanhoe to inherit his money or something else of value. In that case, Cassandra's death was completely unrelated. The killer evoked that crime in the note merely to give Ivanhoe a reason for the staged suicide.

"Or perhaps one of Ivanhoe's brothers reacted with extreme negativity to his threat at the funeral home. What were his exact words?"

"The last thing he said to his brothers that day was, 'You're going to be sorry I ever came back to Erin.' I wouldn't call that exactly a threat. It was more like a safe prediction."

"One man's prediction or promise is another man's threat, old boy. The question of what Ivanhoe meant by the comment is relevant, but not so important as how the brothers perceived it."

My head felt like a pool table full of ricocheting billiard balls, not an uncommon occurrence when I was in the presence of Sebastian McCabe road-testing potential murder solutions out loud.

"So what's your next step?" I asked.

From the top of a filing cabinet he picked up his bagpipe, surely the most hideous instrument of cruel and inhuman punishment known to humankind. I can't listen to the thing without earplugs. "I must practice for the parade on Sunday."

"You actually practice with that monster? I thought you just let it attack you."

He sucked in a bushel of air and started to play "Danny Boy." I beat it.

Chapter Eighteen

The Circus Comes to Town

When I got back to Carey Hall, Oscar Hummel's sizeable rump was firmly planted in the chair in front of Popcorn's desk. He had covered his nearly-hairless head with an Erin Eagles baseball cap, the Eagles being our new minor league team.

"Please don't arrest my assistant, Chief," I jested. "No work would ever get done around here." *Besides, she's already your prisoner of love, ya big galoot.*

Not being particularly skilled at witty repartee, Oscar just glared at me while Popcorn smiled at the veiled compliment. "We were just going to lunch. Care to join us?"

The message in Oscar's look couldn't have been clearer if he'd written on a large whiteboard: *Three's a crowd.*

"I'll take a rain check. Say, Oscar, I just saw Walter Ellicott. He said you hauled him in for a chat."

He snorted. "There was no hauling about it. I invited him to come to my office because I didn't want to break the news over the phone that his wife was diddling his brother."

"Oscar!" Popcorn's prim rebuke rang rather hollow in my ears. For research purposes, I once read one of those Rosamund DeLacey romance novels she devours. I had to wash my eyes out with soap afterwards.

"He's very upset, as anybody would be," I said. "But when he says he doesn't believe it, he means just the opposite. He believes it; he just doesn't want to. His sister and Mac, on the other hand, are convinced that Ivanhoe's self-execution was staged by a murderer."

Oscar's broad face assumed a look of wariness. "And just how does Mac figure that?"

"The suicide note."

I explained.

Oscar sat back and folded his arms. "Let me get this straight. Your genius brother-in-law doesn't believe that Ivanhoe killed himself because he left a suicide note? And also because he thinks the sentences in said note are too short? And also because Ivanhoe wrote this note on a typewriter—he being known for writing his novels on a typewriter? Do I get all of that right?"

I nodded. "Not that I agree with him."

"When has Mac ever been wrong about a thing like that?" Popcorn asked. Like the other women in my life (Lynda, Kate, my mother, and probably Donata), Popcorn has the totally inexplicable conviction that Mac is not only a charming teddy bear but also walks on water.

While I was still trying to think of a time Mac had been wrong—there must have been at least once, early in some case—Oscar said, "He's overdue."

"When do you think the coroner will rule on the cause of death?" I asked.

Oscar shrugged. "She says she's got so many heroin overdose cases that she's backed up." Not a county in America is immune from that. Something similar happened the year before in suburban Cincinnati in the case of a woman shot by her husband. It took the overloaded coroner months to rule the death an accident during a tussle over the gun.

"It shouldn't be a hard call," I asserted. "If Ivanhoe killed himself, he should have gunshot residue"—GSR, to *CSI* fans—"on his hands and maybe his clothing."

But Oscar shook his head. "Not necessarily. Even suicide victims can test negative for GSR. I've seen it happen. The stuff is kind of delicate—it wipes off pretty easily." Oscar leaned back, rubbing the nape of his neck with a big paw. "Besides, a positive GSR just means he was in the vicinity of a gunshot. Even if it was all over his hands, that doesn't mean he was the one who pulled the trigger." He got a stricken look on his face. "What am I saying? There's nothing solid that says Ivanhoe's death wasn't just what it looks like. Mac's murmurings don't count.

"Meanwhile, in the interests of transparency"— apparently a word recently added to Oscar's vocabulary—"I already called Johanna Rawls and gave her the gist of the suicide note. Not the exact wording, but close enough. She's probably put it on the *Observer* website by now. I also gave Lincoln Todd a heads-up so he wouldn't be surprised."

"That poor man!" Popcorn said.

"At least he has the satisfaction of knowing that his daughter's killer is six feet under. No waiting around for the state to get the right drug combo for a lethal injection. All's well that ends well. I can go back to worrying about security for the St. Patrick's Day Parade. But I'm not really worried about it. With Ivanhoe out of the picture, all the protesting nut-balls will go away."

Oscar and Popcorn weren't gone five minutes, merrily on their way to lunch, before I found out how wrong he was about that.

I settled into my chair to draft Father Joe's op-ed piece for the *Observer*, his response to Maggie Barton's upcoming story about criticism of the university's expanding into online courses and wooing international students. Father Joe didn't know about it yet, by the way.

Just as I finally had the first paragraph nailed, my phone started playing *Bolero,* my special ring tone for the love of my life.

After a few affectionate sallies back and forth, the nature of which prompted me to suggest that I go home for lunch, I quickly found out that Lynda had other things on her mind.

"Nelson Abbott is holding a news conference today in front of City Hall."

My mind being focused on other things just then, it took me longer than it should have to remember Abbott as the crusader against Artificial Intelligence. He had announced before Ivanhoe's death that he was coming to Erin to support the Ned Ludd Society. He'd even launched a petition drive on Change.org for Ivanhoe's "right" to march under that name in the St. Patrick's Day Parade.

"So the leader is dead but the cause goes on," I said.

"Looks that way. I'm intrigued. I'd like to go the news conference."

"Great idea! Getting out of the house would be good for you."

"I'm glad you think so, Jeff. The news conference starts in twenty minutes. I'll drop Donata off in about ten."

"Eh? What?" *I think I missed something.* "Why are you dropping her off?"

"I might want to ask questions and take notes, of course. I can't do that while I'm holding her, can I? Besides, who would take me seriously with a baby in my arms?"

"But I—"

"So thank you, darling. You are a wonderful father and an exemplary spouse. Did you see Johanna's story on the *Online Observer?*" The separate branding, i.e., its own name, for what Grier News Ohio liked to call "the online product" had been one of Lynda's innovations just before she'd gone on maternity leave.

"No." Oscar had mentioned that he expected Johanna to post the story soon, but I'd been too busy wrestling with the first paragraph of that op-ed piece to look for it.

"Check it out. I'm proud of that girl. Love you. Bye."

I immediately pulled up the newspaper website on my desktop. **IVANHOE CONFESSED MURDER** yelled at me from the screen. That said it all, really. The story just filled in the details.

> The suicide note left behind by Erin native James Ellicott, who wrote best-selling novels under the pen name of James Ivanhoe, included a confession to the Feb. 26 murder of his sister-in-law, Cassandra Ellicott.
>
> In an exclusive interview with the *Erin Observer & News-Ledger*, Erin Police Chief Oscar Hummel declined to reveal the exact wording. He said, however, that Ivanhoe ...

How many citizens of Erin would be saying "I told you so" to their spouses? When a suicide closely follows a murder in a small town, tongues will wag. Johanna's story danced lightly around the relationship between the deceased in-laws, noting only that they had dated many years ago in high school (for her) and college. The fifteenth paragraph recycled the parade controversy.

By the time Lynda and the baby showed up at my office, I had a plan.

"I'm going with you," I said. "I can hold Donata." The aforementioned smiled in her sleep.

"Okay. You can start now." Lynda handed the baby over. The beautiful burden seemed very light to me. The diaper bag with all the paraphernalia was another matter. "Is this your lunch hour?"

"No, I'm on the clock. I think it's my duty as communications director for SBU to find out what this Abbott character is up to. If he's going to raise a ruckus at the parade, I want to be prepared."

"Maybe Mac would want to go along."

Four's a crowd.

"He's practicing his bagpipes, not that that will help any. If there is music in hell, it must be played on bagpipes.

"Aw, I love the sound of bagpipes, especially on 'Amazing Grace.'"

"Nobody's perfect."

A block away from City Hall, we could see a small crowd of media. As we got closer I recognized Tony Lampwicke from WIJC-FM, the campus station; Morris Kindle, AP; and Tall Rawls. TV cameras were there, too. Bruce Gordon, Ivanhoe's champion on City Council, stood at the periphery, hands on his suspenders.

As we joined them, Tony Lampwicke was asking a question in his pompous attempt at Oxford English. (He was born in Hamilton, Ohio.)

". . . but aren't electronic devices actually more green than paper?"

The man on the other side of the microphone, Nelson Abbott, strongly resembled a Scottie dog. He had thick salt-and-pepper hair combed straight back, a neatly trimmed beard, and black horn-rimmed glasses, also thick. I estimated his age at early fifties.

"That's debatable," he fired back at Tony. "A lot of minerals go into hand-held devices, which are to all intents and purposes assembled by slave labor. And then they consume a lot of electricity in use. You have to recharge yours every day, don't you?"

He didn't wait for an answer to his question.

"But I'm not here to make an environmental point, important though that is." Abbott stuck out his chin, as if he were posing for a heroic statue. "It's time to rage against the machine. If we human beings don't stop letting machines do everything for us, including our thinking, evolution will leave us behind."

"Isn't that going a little far?" Johanna asked.

"Ask a Neanderthal."

I'm not sure that made any sense.

"But surely you don't want to turn back the clock on all the advancements that computers have made possible," Morris Kindle stated. When Morrie got his first newspaper job, pecking out copy on a manual typewriter was state-of-the-art rather than an eccentric affectation.

"That phrase 'turn back the clock' is a cliché that implies going in the wrong direction. But are we really going in the right direction as a society and as individual human beings when we can't find Main Street without a GPS device to which we have given a personal name and refer to by a female pronoun?"

Lynda calls hers Gretchen. She has an English accent.

"That's just one mild example of how we have come to be completely dependent on computer technology. We haven't yet begun to see the real dangers of Artificial Intelligence. Robots will soon replace people if we don't stop AI now. Don't take my word for it. Johann Rupert, the South African billionaire who owns Cartier, last year predicted massive social unrest as a result of unemployment caused by robots and AI taking away jobs from humans."

"Mr. Rupert's glum prognostications aside, do you sometimes feel like a lonely voice crying in the wilderness?" asked a tall black man with a shaved head and small mustache and goatee. He stood next to a female videographer whose camera said PNN. *Uh-oh.*

"Not at all, Mr. Lee." So Abbott knew the cable network reporter, at least by sight. "Many scientists and engineers are concerned about where AI is taking us. They have seen the future and it is scary. And, as you know, the late James Ivanhoe and the Ned Ludd Society are on record as sharing my belief that we must either master technology or be mastered by it." Abbott held up a thick sheaf of papers. "I have here a printout of 30,000 names on a petition demanding that the Erin St. Patrick's Day Parade Committee allow the Ned Ludd Society to march in

Sunday's parade. And speaking of marching, I am going to march these petitions to the chairman of the parade committee right now."

With the same detached professionalism that causes me to watch the Sunday morning interview shows to see how the politicians avoid answering questions, I admired Nelson Abbott's showmanship. He had a parade of his own as the reporters followed him two blocks down Main Street and three blocks down Market Street to Bobbie McGee's Sports Bar. As he walked, he talked. The visuals later on PNN were great.

"Mr. Ivanhoe's death is a great tragedy . . . Yes, we met a few times and admired each others' work . . . No leader is more important than the cause he leads." And so forth.

The lunch crowd had packed Bobbie's, much of the trade coming from City Hall and the nearby Sussex County Courthouse. Bobbie McGee, who works all the high-traffic times, met Abbott just inside the door. She's a big gal with more brains than hair under her Stetson—and she has a lot of hair, wavy and brown. So I'm sure she knew that something was up, and maybe even what. But she played it cool.

"Welcome to Bobbie McGee's. How many do we have this afternoon?"

Lynda squeezed in close so she wouldn't miss a word, which also cleared the way for Donata and me. Being six-one, I could see as well as hear.

"I'm not here to eat, thank you," Abbott said with a stiffness that my dry cleaner could only dream of. "I have a petition to deliver to Mr. McGee."

"He doesn't work here." The local reporters laughed, knowing that was true. At this time of the day Brett was probably shaking hands at his car dealership. "But he might stop by for lunch. I'd be happy to give that to him."

Nonplussed for the moment at the mammoth intel fail that had put him in the wrong place, Abbott stumbled around a bit before he finally mumbled, "Yes. Thank you. Please do."

Bobbie took the papers. "Sure you don't want lunch?" She must have majored in hard-sell at the Wharton School of Business. But Nelson Abbott was a man on a mission, that being to stage part two of his press conference. Just outside the door he addressed the assembled cameras and notebooks.

"I am hopeful that Mr. McGee and his committee will realize that thirty thousand signers of this petition can't be wrong"—*why not?*—"and will stop stifling the First Amendment rights of the Ned Ludd Society."

Actually, Nelson, the First Amendment only refers to government action: "Congress shall make no law . . ."

The slumbering Donata was starting to get a little heavy in my arms—still terminally cute, but heavy. How long was this going to drag on?

"With James Ivanhoe dead," said a husky female voice, "who is there to march under that banner?"

He looked gratefully at the questioner, Lynda Teal (Cody). He had set a trap, and my beloved had sprung it by asking the question that any good journalist would.

"Yes, James is dead but his cause lives on. I plan to pick up my good friend's fallen banner and carry it myself." He looked around, making eye contact with each of the journalists in turn. Scotties do that. "Whether the parade committee relents or not, I will march in the parade in honor of James Ivanhoe. If I have to go to jail for the privilege, so be it. I am willing to engage in an act of civil disobedience to assert our constitutional rights."

"Martyr complex," I told Lynda later over my fruit salad and her meat loaf sandwich. Lunch at Bobbie's suited us just fine, and the crowd had thinned by the time the news conference had petered out. "Whether he realizes it or not, Abbott actually hopes he gets arrested—with PNN getting it all on video for a national audience. And I'm sure Oscar would be happy to accommodate. He enjoys having guests in the new jail."

My wife's forehead wrinkled. "Abbott almost talked about Ivanhoe as if *he* were a martyr, even though his death had nothing to do with a cause."

"Yeah, he did." I fiddled with my fork. "He could make a lot of hay with that, couldn't he?"

"What do you mean?"

"Every movement needs a martyr, either figurative or literal. Ivanhoe will bring more attention to his cause in death than he did in life. What a stroke of luck for Abbott—if that's what it is."

Chapter Nineteen
A Joyful Noise

A priest, a rabbi, and a minister walked into a bar.

Yes, I know I've used that line before in these chronicles, but this time it was no joke. The bar was Bobbie McGee's later that Friday, and the clergymen were three tenors who performed under the Biblically-inspired name of Joyful Noise.

And noisy it was. Bobbie's is not exactly a Christian Science Reading Room on any Friday night, but the Friday before St. Patrick's Day tipped the place into sensory overload. Joyful Noise, booked to perform on a bandstand for the parade, sang "Molly Malone" over the sound of boisterous laughter as Mac, Kate, Lynda, and I entered. Mac's mom, broken in by six kids of her own, was watching Donata at home and spending the weekend.

Familiar faces were all around the room. Lincoln Todd hoisted a dark brew, and I wondered whether he'd seen Johanna's story about Ivanhoe's suicide note. Karen Ellicott sat at a table talking to Neil Carboy, the Samson Microcircuits veep who had spoken at the City Council meeting. A pitcher of reddish beer separated them. If they were talking business strategy, their body language said it was monkey business. I made a mental note of that. In the opposite corner of the ring was Ivanhoe's champion, Bruce Gordon. Was that a glass of whiskey neat I spotted in his hand? The glass was too small for it to be tea. A few people were actually eating—there was a special on corned beef.

"Ah, the news media have preceded us," Mac said.

"That's not the news media," Lynda sniffed. "That's PNN."

They referred to Bennington Lee, he of the shaved head and goatee from Nelson Abbott's news conference. I knew his full name because I'd looked him up on the PNN website. I'm not a regular viewer of the cable network, although I land on it from time to time while channel surfing. Lee had his cuff links off and his shirtsleeves rolled up—just one of the guys. The camera was rolling as he held a microphone up to the face of a twenty-something woman with green hair and beer to match. Her sleeveless blouse, likewise of an emerald hue, showed off body-builder muscles and a Hello Kitty tattoo.

"He's getting some local color," Bobbie McGee said, startling me. I hadn't heard Bobbie's cowboy boots come up behind us.

"I'll say," Kate quipped. I think Hello Kitty offends her sensibilities, although I don't understand why. Heck, she's an artist herself.

"Is it true there's no such thing as bad publicity, Jeff?" Bobbie asked.

"No."

"I didn't think so."

Nothing good for Erin could come of this. PNN, presumably in the person of Lee's producer, had had a story about the parade controversy in the works since before Cassandra had died. I remembered Lincoln Todd fretting about that before he had bigger concerns. All hope that something more newsworthy would come up to distract the network from the story had surely been eliminated by the spectacular death of James Ivanhoe.

An Irish sports bar was a natural place for Lee to chat up the locals for their opinions on murder, suicide, and the threat to humankind posed by GPS. And chief among them would be Brett McGee, chairman of the parade committee. He had agreed in a telephone conversation with Lee to submit to an on-camera interview at the bar.

But Brett would not be unprepared. I had met with him for an hour in the late afternoon to prep him.

"Get yourselves drinks," Bobbie invited. "First one's on me." She moved on, wending her way through the crowd to keep the customers satisfied.

Joyful Noise, having just finished a rousing rendition of "When Irish Eyes Are Smiling," took a break. Finally! Now I could think. And what I thought was that everybody was trying too hard to have fun. This was a town that had really taken it on the chin from the Grim Reaper of late, and some of the people most affected were drinking and laughing as if trying to anesthetize themselves.

"I should have brought my bagpipes," Mac said.

No, really, that's all right.

"That was lovely, Father O'Boyle," Lynda told the short, white-haired leprechaun in a Roman collar who led the tenors. "You guys are really a holy trinity."

"Isn't that sacrilegious?" asked Rabbi David Goldman, the tallest and baldest of the trio.

Reverend Fred Sutterlee of the Apostolic Holiness Church of the Holy Spirit (and Erin City Council) looked like he was thinking that over. Maybe he was having second thoughts about his bar outreach ministry.

"The singing was great, but I think Erin could use your ecumenical prayers," Kate said. "There's a lot of tension in the air this weekend."

"The community is hurting," Rabbi Goldman agreed. "Maybe we should step forward as religious leaders and provide a space for healing."

"Free will is a wonderful and terrible thing," observed Father Francis Xavier O'Boyle who is retired but not retiring. "Suicide is a great sin, but God's mercy is greater than any sin." *I'm counting on that, Father O.* "The pain we're all feeling, even if we didn't know the deceased, is a reflection of the communal nature of sin."

"Our great God has not abandoned us," intoned the Reverend Sutterlee, whose heart is as big as the rest of him. "But sometimes I do suspect that he is sleeping. Maybe that is why so many of the Psalms tell us to 'make joyful noise' unto the Lord."

Mac caressed his whiskers. "Theologically speaking, Reverend—"

"Weren't we just on our way to the bar?" I interrupted. "Bobbie offered us drinks on the house. You know, as in beer."

"Eh? Oh, yes. Lead on, old boy!"

Patrons stood about three deep at the bar, but we finally got in our orders for Caffeine-Free Diet Coke (for me), beer (Mac), a Manhattan (Lynda), and Bailey's Irish Cream (Kate). We brought them back to our spouses. With more hope than confidence, we looked around for a table where we could sit together.

"Ms. Teal! Lynda!" came a familiar voice out of the crowd.

"Oh, hi, Johanna!"

"How's maternity leave? That baby of yours is so cute. We sure miss you around the office."

And so forth. I worked on my drink while they caught up.

Tall Rawls, who looks to Lynda as her role model, wasn't so tall this evening. At six feet even, she usually looks down on me by a couple of inches in her three-inch heels. But tonight she wore flat sandals, appropriately enough with her Fighting Irish T-shirt and blue jean shorts.

"This is my friend, Seth Miller."

Johanna's date could have reached maybe five-six if he stood up straight, not that it matters. Hey, I'm not a sizeist! But the contrast between the lanky blond, with her long legs and straight blond hair, and her dark-haired, bespectacled date seemed to prove the adage about opposites attracting.

Young Seth—approximately mid-twenties, like Johanna—shook hands all around. "Good to meet you." I doubted it. He probably felt like he was meeting a double helping of surrogate parents just before the prom.

"Do you happen to have the time?" Mac asked the poor guy.

Seth looked at his left wrist. His eyes popped like a cartoon rabbit. "My watch—it's gone!"

"Not far, I assure you." Mac held out both hands, showed that they were empty, made a fist, then opened it to show Seth's watch.

"Awesome!"

Childish! Any other former professional magician could have done the same trick. This Seth fellow was too easily impressed.

"So, what's news?" I asked Johanna. Lynda rolled her eyes.

"Lots. I've been hopping today. Did you see my exclusive story about James Ivanhoe's suicide note?"

We all admitted it.

"Good work," Lynda said.

Johanna blushed prettily. "Thanks. And then there was the news conference. I couldn't believe that Bennington Lee showed up for it!"

Apparently he was a big deal in the 24-hour-news-cycle world.

"Can you believe that he's here now?" Kate said dryly.

"You're kidding!"

"Not in the least." Mac pointed across the room. Lee, looking earnest, was listening intently to Bruce Gordon. That could go on all night, if Lee didn't fall asleep.

"What's he doing here?" Johanna asked.

"Being bored by the world's most contrary florist," I said. "But to answer your real question, PNN has been planning a story on the Erin St. Patrick's Day Parade since before Cassandra died." I thought back to my advice to Lincoln Todd: Show up for the interview in an Amish buggy as a joke. A lot had changed since that afternoon. "The carnage was just icing on the cable news cake. Anybody want another drink?"

Seth Miller walked with me to the bar.

"So, how did you meet Johanna?"

"On the job."

"She interviewed you?"

"No, I cleaned her teeth. I don't know anything about journalism."

Neither do most reporters these days.

"Let me tell you, being married to a journalist can be a challenge," I said.

"Married?" Seth didn't actually turn pale, but he did sort of gulp. "This is only our first date and it's already a challenge. I haven't had a chance to talk to her all night. She seems to know everybody here."

"You'll get used to that." *If you stay an item long enough.*

After we ordered drinks, I glanced back toward the little group we had left behind. Bennington Lee and his camerawoman seemed to be navigating right toward them. I gave Seth a clump of greenbacks. "Do me a favor and pay for the drinks, including your Jameson's and Johanna's wine. I don't want to miss this. And tip twenty percent."

By moving aggressively, I managed to worm my way back to Lynda and the others at just about the time Lee got there.

He addressed Johanna. "I recognize you. You were one of the reporters at the news conference today."

"That's right. Johanna Rawls, of the *Erin Observer & News Ledger*." She stuck out her hand for a shake, very coolly and professionally. Gone was the star-struck, small-town reporter of a few minutes ago. Lynda watched with an appreciative half-smile.

"Perfect," Lee said. "I'm doing a story about James Ivanhoe and the controversy surrounding the St. Patrick's Day Parade here in town. Could you talk to me on-camera for a few minutes, give me your perspective as a journalist?"

She looked at Lynda as if to get permission from Grier Ohio NewsGroup. Lynda nodded slightly. Scribes and bloggers appear on TV all the time; it's great publicity. Besides, I'd heard Lynda say that every reporter should be the subject of a news story at least once to experience what it's like being on the other side.

"Sure."

"Great. Great."

After getting Johanna to say her name and spell it for the record, Lee threw her a softball. "In a little more than a week, a prominent family in this small town has suffered a murder and a suicide. What have these tragedies meant to the residents of Erin, Ohio?"

Johanna gave that some thought before responding. Good girl. No need to rush it. "This isn't the first murder we've ever had in Erin." *Not by a long shot.* "But the deaths of two one-time sweethearts in less than a week shocked a lot of us. It didn't seem like it could be a coincidence. And as I reported exclusively on the *Observer*'s website today, it wasn't." Johanna was clearly playing to the camera, as if she were auditioning for PNN. *Maybe she was!* And she was doing a bang-up job of it. "Erin Police Chief Oscar Hummel told me today that James Ivanhoe confessed to the murder of his sister-in-law, Cassandra Ellicott, in his suicide note."

Sensation! Lee's jaw dropped, almost comically. Apparently he hadn't read the *Online Observer* today, as a really good reporter parachuted in to cover a local community would have. He scrambled to regain control of the interview.

"And how is Erin reacting to this latest surprising news?"

"It's too soon to say, Bennington. But I think a lot of people who read my story in the print edition of the paper tomorrow will be stunned." *Just like you were, Benny.*

"I've talked to a few folks in town who don't believe that James Ivanhoe—or Jamie Ellicott, as some people here still remember him—really killed himself. What do you say to them?"

She shrugged. "That would mean his suicide was an elaborately staged fake. Maybe it was. But that's not what law enforcement thinks at this point. When the coroner makes an official ruling"—Johanna smiled winningly—"I hope to be the first to report it."

Lee ignored the younger journalist's hopes. "Even before the two deaths, Erin was a town torn apart by the controversy over whether to allow Mr. Ivanhoe's so-called Ned Ludd Society to march in the St. Patrick's Day Parade. Will that rift ever be mended?"

"I don't know about torn apart, Bennington. People have different opinions about the issue, but I haven't seen anybody throwing fruit at each other in Kroger's."

Way to go, Johanna! She had intuited one of my professional rules: Never let a reporter's incorrect premise go unchallenged.

"But Nelson Abbott delivered thirty thousand names on a petition today calling for the Ludd group to be admitted to the parade."

"I've seen it. In fact, I wrote about it. Very few of the names were local. It's not hard to get thousands of names on a digital petition once it goes viral."

Was that sweat I detected on Bennington Lee's forehead? I wondered how much of this interview was going to wind up on the digital cutting room floor.

"Thank you, Ms. Rawls. I appreciate your time."

Not only had he had enough of her, Lee had spotted bigger game: Brett McGee had just come in the door of his wife's establishment. Lee made a beeline toward him, the camera following close behind.

"You were awesome!" Seth Miller told his date.

"Thanks," she beamed. "That was kind of fun, but I feel a little wobbly now." Johanna grabbed the Chablis out of Seth's hand and downed it in two gulps. I always have the same urge after a TV interview, despite my customary abstemiousness. I attribute it to nervousness in retrospect.

By this time, I would have expected the tenors to be remounting the little stage, if not already belting out "The Irish Rover" or "Black Velvet Band." Instead, a relative quiet had settled over the room. Patrons nudged each other in the ribs as Bennington Lee and his videographer closed in on Brett.

Surprisingly, our baseball legend pounced first. "Welcome to Erin, Mr. Lee," he said with his easy smile. He shook the reporter's hand while most of room applauded, including the very corporate-looking Neil Carboy. Karen Ellicott, sitting next to him, occupied her hands pouring another beer.

After a few perfunctory words of thanks for agreeing to the interview, followed by some fussing by the woman with the video camera, Bennington Lee got down to it.

"Brett McGee, you're as famous in the sports world as James Ivanhoe was to readers of fiction. Two national celebrities, one small Ohio town." The comparison was a bit of a stretch, but close enough for TV work. "And yet you two have been engaged for some months in a dispute over his desire to march in your town's St. Patrick's Day Parade under the name of the Ned Ludd Society. How did you react to his death?"

Gosh, that pitch had a long windup!

"Like everyone else in town, Bennington, I was stunned. My heart goes out to Jamie's family. He was a great writer, and Erin is proud to call him a native son. His death was a real tragedy. We'll miss him." *Like I miss my last kidney stone.*

Considering that the deceased loved his brothers like Cain loved Abel, anybody in the know would snicker at that. But Brett's audience wasn't those in the know; it was those who would watch on PNN or, later, see the clip via social media. That's why I had coached him to begin with an expression of sympathy. Not surprisingly, that wasn't what Bennington Lee had been looking for. He tried again to elicit a piece of YouTube-worthy video.

"As you probably know, Mr. Ivanhoe reportedly left a suicide note in which he confessed to the murder of his sister-in-law. Would you care to comment on that?" I have to give Lee credit for making it sound like this was old news to him, not something he had learned less than five minutes previously.

Brett shook his head solemnly. "No, Bennington, I wouldn't." I gave him full points for delivery because he didn't sound like he wanted to punch his interrogator in the face, which I felt fairly sure he did.

"Given the contents of that note, do you still think his death was a great tragedy?"

"That's what I just said, and my opinion hasn't changed in the last thirty seconds." I probably wouldn't have said that to a reporter, not even if I had Brett's smile, but I loved it.

Lee moved on. "Have you thought of letting the Ned Ludd Society march in the parade in honor of their fallen champion, who was prohibited from doing so before his death?"

"It's not entirely up to me, you know. The whole parade committee has discussed this several times. We even had a conference call this afternoon. But look, the Ned

Ludd Society, if there still is one, is perfectly welcome to march in the parade and always has been. They just can't carry a sign or a banner with that name because it's tantamount to making a statement. The rule is that nobody gets to use the parade to promote political or social causes."

"Even though thirty thousand people signed a petition calling for you to let the Ned Ludd Society march in the parade?"

Brett's interior struggle to keep his temper must have been mammoth, but it didn't show. As I had advised, he kept his temper in the face of invincible ignorance. "I don't think most of the people who signed that petition really understand the issue. Besides, how many signatures on a petition would it get you to violate *your* principles?"

If you like that line, thank you.

Lee, recognizing the question as a rhetorical one, didn't answer. "When Nelson Abbott presented the petition at a news conference this morning, he indicated that he's going to march in the parade under the Ned Ludd flag, if you will, even if he gets arrested for doing so. He calls it an act of civil disobedience to stand up for his constitutional rights. How do you feel about that?"

"I'm offended by the implicit comparison to the civil rights movement. The implication is that participation in our parade is on a discriminatory basis. That's untrue. All individuals are welcome, and no causes are. I hope that Mr. Abbot doesn't attempt to disrupt the St. Patrick's Day Parade, but if he does I don't think he'll be successful. He'll be one lone voice out there among hundreds of other people having a good time."

Karen Ellicott, clearly under the influence of the former contents of the pitcher at her table, stood up on unsteady legs. Neil Carboy, looking horrified, tried to pull her back down. She swatted him away.

"He won't be alone," she slurred. "I'll be with him. And Carol Landis will be with me."

Chapter Twenty
Alibi for the Dead

In the confusion that followed, I didn't find out who Carol Landis was until the next day.

Predictably, Johanna's scoop about Ivanhoe's confession in his suicide note was splashed across the front page of the *Erin Observer & News-Ledger* on Saturday. But my breakfast-table conversation with Lynda was more about the author of the story than the by-now-familiar contents.

"She looked so at ease in front of the camera," Lynda said, buttering her toast. Donata, having a clear conscience, slept soundly upstairs. We could hear her on the baby monitor. "I wonder if she'd be interested in moving over to TV news at one of our stations?"

"I thought you were down on TV. Besides, she'd be great in a job like mine." I mixed low-fat yogurt and blueberries into my granola for a parfait. Who says I can't cook?

"Well, if she wants to go over to the *dark* side—"

Lynda's jocose rejoinder was cut off by the sound of the doorbell. Wondering who would be interrupting our domestic harmony at eight-forty on a Saturday morning, I jumped up to answer it.

When I opened our front door, Karen Ellicott, hair in disarray, looked at me blearily from half-open lids. Diagnosis: major hangover. At her side stood a woman I'd never seen before, well dressed in earth tones to match her long ash-blond hair. I found out later that she was thirty-eight, but right now she looked younger than Karen.

I greeted them cheerily.

"Is McCabe here?" Karen asked, in lieu of an equally cheery response.

I've heard stranger questions, but not many.

"Uh, no. He usually isn't on a Saturday morning. Can I help you?"

"I thought you lived together."

Light dawned. She was operating on a misunderstanding of outdated information. "I used to live in an apartment over his garage, but I moved out after Lynda and I got married." *Too long after, actually.*

Lynda joined me in the hallway. Sizing up our visitors and arriving at a quick diagnosis, she asked Karen, "Can I get you some coffee?"

Karen nodded like a bobble-head. "Strong. Black. Please."

"The same for me, please," the other woman added.

In the kitchen, while Lynda poured cups of freshly brewed high-test for Karen and her companion, Karen introduced the latter. "This is Carol Landis. She was Jamie's literary agent—and his ex-wife."

And I think *my* life is complicated! And it got even more complex a moment later.

"I'm also Jamie's alibi." Carol Landis wrapped long fingers around a coffee mug, showing off nails painted Cherokee red. "He couldn't have killed his sister-in-law because he was with me that day in New York."

"That's what we need to tell McCabe," Karen said.

"You should talk to Chief Hummel."

"Take me to McCabe. Please."

I checked the time on my smartphone. I haven't worn a watch since Mac made mine disappear, even though he gave it back. Johanna's boyfriend (what was his name?) should learn from me. "It's almost nine o'clock. We might as well wait a few minutes and go over to the Quadrangle. He'll be there practicing his bagpipes."

Karen's face contorted.

"Do you need something for your head?" I asked.

She shook said head slowly, misery personified. "I want to keep this pain so that I remember never to drink that much again. I was arguing with my boyfriend last night and the madder I got the more I drank. Then I really blew it and told that reporter I was going to march in the stupid parade carrying a stupid Ned Ludd banner."

Lynda and Carol Landis both put comforting hands on her shoulders.

"So you said something you didn't mean when you'd had a bit too much to drink," my practical wife said. "That's easy enough to fix. Just don't do what you said you'd do."

"You don't understand. It's not that simple. I *have* to do it because Neil told me *not* to. He was furious when I got on camera. Ours has never been an easy relationship, and maybe this will finish it. But I can't back down now."

Ah, the old "I'll show him" routine.

So Neil Carboy, the buttoned-down-collar Samson Microcircuits exec, was Karen's boyfriend and not just a guy from work that she'd joined for a few after-hour brewskis. That was an interesting Ellicott factoid, but probably irrelevant.

"You realize," I said, "that while you're sticking your thumb in Neil's eye, you aren't going to make your surviving brothers very happy either."

"I'm used to that."

I tried again. "Look at it this way: The media have a short attention span and so do consumers of it. A week from now, neither Bennington Lee nor any of his viewers from outside of Erin will even remember the St. Patrick's Day Parade. But I bet your brothers will."

Was I trying to downplay the parade controversy or give Karen Ellicott some friendly family-relationship advice? Maybe I intended a little of both. But it didn't take.

"I will do what I said I was going to do—whether I like it or not." She gulped coffee.

"And she won't be alone," Carol Landis said.

"Let's talk to Mac."

We heard the hideous sound of "The Wearing of the Green" oozing out of bagpipes before we got within sight of the Quadrangle, a grassy area between the oldest buildings on campus. At least on Saturday morning the noise disturbed nobody but the birds. Poor birds.

"Is McCabe Irish or Scottish?" Carol asked.

"Yes," I said.

As we approached, I waved my arms to attract Mac's attention. He stopped playing. Was there ever a sound so sweet as that of no bagpipe music?

The introductions were quickly dispensed with and James Ivanhoe's ex-wife told her story.

"My understanding is that Cassandra Ellicott's body was found on Friday, February 26, and that she died that same day. Is that right? Okay, well, James was in New York with me that day, and the day before, and the morning after."

Mac arched an eyebrow. "I take it that your divorce did not affect your business relationship, Ms. Landis?"

"Or our personal one, for that matter." She flipped her hair out of her eyes with a wave of her hand. "In fact, we got along better than when we were married."

No details, please. That sounded too much like my in-laws. I try not to think about them.

"Did you have a key to his cabin?" I asked.

"No. Why do you ask?"

"Because door locks on new houses always come with a second key. Ivanhoe's wasn't in any of the usual hiding places, so somebody must have it and it's not Karen." I didn't even know that had been bothering me until I said it. "It probably doesn't mean anything."

Mac must have agreed—or so I assumed at the time—because he went back to Ivanhoe's alibi:

"His presence with you at the time of the murder does not rule out the possibility, however unlikely it might seem on the surface, that your ex-husband engaged someone else to kill Mrs. Ellicott and then shot himself with the same weapon."

"But it was probably her husband's gun!" I blurted out. What a waste of breath. Mac was just playing mind games again. He didn't believe what he'd said any more than I did.

He continued the game: "The assassin could have found the Glock in the house."

"James didn't kill himself," Carol said flatly.

"He died in a house dead-bolted from the outside," I pointed out.

Carol turned to Mac. "Karen tells me you solve mysteries, so you figure it out. But he didn't kill himself."

"What makes you so certain?"

"I told her what was in the so-called suicide note," Karen said.

"And it's total B.S.! James wouldn't use a corny term like 'creative juices.' And his creativity wasn't waning in the least. He was well into a great new novel called *Sunbelt* about an alternative timeline where oil is worthless and solar energy was developed early in the nineteenth century."

"That sounds like his idea of Utopia," I said.

She shook her head. "Hardly. Where there's no conflict, there's no story. Besides, he didn't believe in Utopia. So there's a snake in the garden, as there always is: The minerals the world needs for solar batteries are being rapidly depleted. And the greatest remaining source of them is under the control of a rogue nation—the Confederate States of America."

That's what's known in the trade as a high-concept plot, one that can be pitched in a few words and doesn't depend on subtle characters.

"James was at the top of his game with this book and we were hoping for a big movie sale. The last thing he ever wrote was probably a page of *Sunbelt*. He didn't write that suicide note."

"How regrettable that novel was never finished," Mac said. "No doubt it would have been a fine addition to the reading list for my course on dystopian fiction, along with the classics such as *Brave New World* and *1984*. I also strongly recommend James Hugh Benson's *Lord of the World*, but do not read it near an open window. I wonder if I might read the manuscript of *Sunbelt*?"

Carol turned to Karen. "I assume it's in his office at the cabin."

"I can't say for sure. The police chief didn't mention it to me, but there's no reason that he would."

"Is it true that your former husband wrote everything on a manual typewriter, or was that flimflam devised by a publicist?" Mac asked Carol.

"Absolutely true."

"Do you have anything with you that he typed?"

She thought a second. "I have a business letter from him in my briefcase back at the hotel. In fact, it's a letter discussing the storyline of *Sunbelt* and where he is with the writing of it. Why?"

If I were unkind I might characterize Mac's smile as "fiendish," but "triumphant" is good enough. "The right person could compare the typing technique on the two documents and determine with a high degree of probability whether James Ivanhoe wrote the suicide letter. That should get Oscar's attention."

Chapter Twenty-One
The Key

"Where would I find somebody who could do that?" Oscar demanded. "I haven't even seen a typewriter in—what?—twenty years maybe. That was back in the previous millennium."

"As it happens, I know just the person," Mac announced. The chief did not look surprised. "Professor Alexandra Powers at Bowling Green State University has a passion for typewriters. She has made a study of the typing techniques of Hemmingway and Fitzgerald, among other great authors. She once advised me when I wrote a Damon Devlin novel in which the plot turned on an old typewritten manuscript."

Mac and I were alone with Oscar in his not-yet-messy new digs, having left Carol Landis and Karen Ellicott with promises to shake Oscar's tree. But the chief didn't look too shaken, I must admit.

"I'm not sure that's a recommendation, but if she comes up with something, let me know. If it's credible, I'll take it to Slade." Marvin Slade was the long-time, highly political prosecutor of Sussex County.

"One other thing," Mac added. "In searching the crime scene, did your men find a partially finished manuscript of a new novel?"

Oscar's broad face was one big question mark. "That's not exactly something they'd look for."

"Please ask them to look for it."

"Why? What's so special about it?"

"It could contain James Ivanhoe's real last words."

"That sounds thinner than one of your plots, but I'll have Gibbons check." The trivial matter of potential homicide apparently dismissed from his mind, Oscar looked at a spreadsheet in front of him. "Gibbons thinks I should shell out overtime for extra parade security tomorrow, but I'm not so sure. I don't see that Abbott guy starting a riot."

"No, but Karen might," I quipped.

Oscar looked at his watch. "Oh, Jeez. I gotta get to the dry cleaner. I had my other uniform pressed for the parade and they close at one o'clock on Saturdays."

"So what if you have gravy on your shirt. Who would notice?"

"I would."

But I think he was preening for Popcorn.

"Just one more thing, Oscar," Mac said. "Do you have a list of the contents of Ivanhoe's pockets?"

"Sure."

He printed it out from his computer and handed it to Mac. The list read:

Swiss army knife
Three quarters
One nickel
Six pennies
Four dimes
House key
Small notebook

"What was in the notebook?" I asked.

"A shopping list," Oscar said. "It looked like he was planning to cook chili for one. Now get out of here."

Mac surprised me on the way out of the police station. "Do you know where your friend Amos Yoder lives, Jefferson?"

"Yeah. I dropped a check off at his house once. Why?"

"One key to the cabin has now been accounted for on Oscar's list. It was in Ivanhoe's pocket. However, your observation that new locks usually come with more than one key was a trenchant one. I would like to ask the man who built the cabin, and therefore provided the door, about that."

The Yoder house, only a few miles from Ivanhoe's cabin but outside the city, isn't a log cabin and it isn't small. It's a simple, solid, wood farmhouse with enough bedrooms to accommodate a young couple with three boys, three girls, and the gender tie about to be broken. The big house, with a modern windmill behind it, sits on several acres.

Amy Yoder, wearing the white prayer cap typical of Amish women, greeted us at the door. She couldn't possibly have been as many months pregnant as she looked. The traces of flour on her apron and the smell of apple pie wafting out from the kitchen made me feel like I'd stepped into a Norman Rockwell painting.

"Amos? He's out back fixing a wagon wheel. I'll get him."

She disappeared. The Yoder kids, wearing somber clothes and happy expressions, ran in and out of the house while we waited and looked around. As I'd noted on my previous visit, it looked a lot like your average *Englisher* house with a few tweaks. All the lights were gas lamps, for example, and there weren't any paintings or decorations on the walls.

"No television," Mac observed. "How refreshing."

"You could get rid of your five any time you want, you know."

Amos came in from the back of the house before Mac could respond.

"Hi, Jeff. Is this Professor McCabe?"

"Guilty!" That was me talking.

After the usual social necessities, Mac let me articulate the reason for our visit.

"This is kind of a professional call, Amos."

"You need something built?"

"Not right now. This has to do with James Ivanhoe."

"Oh, that was sad."

"Yes, it was. Mr. Ivanhoe had a key to his cabin in his pants when he died, but there doesn't seem to be another key. At least, it's not in any of the usual hiding places and the two women in his life—the two who are still alive, anyway—say they don't have it. You did give him a second key, didn't you?"

"Sure. But he gave it back."

Mac raised an eyebrow. "He returned it?"

"Yes, sir. I was still doing some work on the cabin and he was out of town a fair amount. He told me to just keep the key until I was finished. Who should I give it to now?"

I suggested Karen Ellicott, who had told us she was Ivanhoe's executor.

"Well, Jefferson, we have come a long way," Mac said when we'd climbed back into his car.

"Yeah—one big circle that brought us right back to where we started. Ivanhoe's cabin was locked from the outside and the only key other than the one in his pocket belonged to an Amish carpenter who wouldn't kill a vampire bat if it was making a main course out of his mother."

"Unless—"

Mac opened his car door.

"Now what?"

"Perhaps we asked Amos the wrong questions."

Amy Yoder called her husband to the door as soon as she saw us standing outside.

"Did you think of something else?" he asked.

Mac nodded. "Yes, Amos, I thought of a question that only you can answer. You built the cabin that James Ivanhoe died in. Was there any jiggery-pokery about it?"

Puzzled doesn't begin to describe the expression on Amos's simple face. "What do you mean?"

"Was it gimmicked in any way—windows that opened even though they were locked, a trap door, a concealed room, any sort of hidden exit?"

Amos shook his head with a smile. "That sounds like something out of a book. I would have told you if there was anything like that. The cabin was just a simple plan I've built about five times before."

"Ah, well," Mac said. "It was just a thought."

That evening, as I put on a clean pair of khakis for Luther Kressel's annual St. Patrick's Day party, Lynda called from the family room and told me to turn on the bedroom TV to PNN. On the screen, Bennington Lee stood in front of Bobbie McGee's. He was reporting for the network's nightly *American Scene* program, where the segments were longer than on standard news programs but more hot-news oriented than, say, *60 Minutes* or *20/20*.

". . . a big topic of conversation by everyone here at the Irish pub owned by the wife of Cincinnati Reds legend Brett McGee. And that includes talk by the slugger himself."

Switch to video of Brett inside the bar.

"Like everyone else in town, Bennington, I was stunned. My heart goes out to James Ivanhoe's family, the Ellicotts."

The girl with the Hello Kitty tattoo got her fifteen seconds of fame holding forth on the writer's demise. "Yeah, everybody's talking about it. I read every one of his books." *Really?* A quick sound bite of Tall Rawls followed: "The deaths of two one-time sweethearts in less than a week shocked a lot of us." She looked like a natural on the screen, as Lynda had commented at breakfast.

"The town's shock," Lee intoned, standing once again in front of the sports bar, "turned to utter amazement when Erin's police chief announced yesterday"—*in an exclusive interview with Johanna Rawls, you jerk!*—"that Ivanhoe had confessed in his suicide note to the murder of his sister-in-law."

We then got about ten seconds of Bennington Lee asking Brett his reaction to the dramatic news, and Brett refusing to give it. After the clip, the action shifted back to Lee, now walking down Main Street in downtown Erin toward City Hall.

"Brett McGee and James Ivanhoe, each nationally famous in his own sphere, were on opposite sides of a local controversy that the death of the best-selling author has failed to quell."

Lee (or his producer) made good use of file footage of Ivanhoe, bits and pieces from Nelson Abbott's news conference, and video of Abbott's march to Bobbie McGee's.

When the gaunt form of Linc Todd appeared on the screen, I felt satisfaction to see that he was driving an Amish buggy as I had suggested. He looked right at home in the vehicle, too, except that his beard wasn't long enough. Also, I'd never seen an Amish man as lean as Todd. They eat well.

Lee introduced the new character in the drama with a voiceover. "Lincoln Todd, president of Erin's Convention & Visitor's Bureau and a member of the parade committee, denies that his town is totally unsympathetic to the concerns of the so-called 'New Luddites.'" *So-called by whom? I bet you made up that term on the spot, Benny.*

The camera cut to a close-up of Todd's smiling face. He was playing it light. "We have a good-sized Amish community in Sussex County. The bankers love them because they always make their mortgage payments on time. So it's not like everything is high-tech in our little town. But we're not *all* Amish, either. Even James Ivanhoe, may he rest in peace, had a refrigerator in his cabin, not an ice box."

"What do you say to people who say that the Ned Ludd Society has a right to march in the St. Patrick's Day Parade?"

This wasn't the first time the PNN guy had resorted to the old "what would you say to people . . ." trope.

In answer, Todd looked like he was torn between "poppycock" and "balderdash"—or maybe even stronger words. But the fast-thinking civic leader settled on the more prudent course of dodging the question. "I say it's going to be a great parade. I wish I didn't have to be in it so I could watch it from Main Street."

Bennington Lee's report concluded—*finally!*—on the steps of City Hall. "Even though the unwelcome mat is out for the Ned Ludd Society at tomorrow's St. Patrick's Day Parade, Nelson Abbott vows to march for the group. And so does James Ivanhoe's sister, Karen Ellicott, who declined our request for an interview. There could be some real fireworks here on Main Street and we'll be on the scene for *American Scene*."

Oh, joy.

"Okay, let's go," Lynda said, walking into the bedroom with Donata in her arms shortly after the segment ended. "The party's already started."

The biggest difference between Luther Kressel's basement and Bobbie McGee's establishment is that Luther has a bigger bar. As president of the local Ancient Order of Hibernians—never mind that three of his four grandparents were German—he opens the taps to his St. Benignus colleagues every year in honor of the Emerald Isle's patron saint. He also dyes his white goatee green, that being the only hair he has. The greenery doesn't bother me, but I can never get used to the Bluetooth headset sticking out of his ear. He looks like Uhuru on the original *Star Trek*, except for the minor fact that he's not female or black.

"Don't just stand there looking sober," he roared as he opened his front door. "Come on in."

Was that any way for a professor of history and economics to talk? Luther has five master's degrees, at last count, but no Ph.D. "Life is too short to specialize," he once told me. "You wind up knowing more and more about less and less."

Descending to the basement, we found it already crowded with familiar faces from the groves of academe. Popcorn shamelessly held hands with Oscar, Sister Mary Margaret Malone drank Guinness out of a can, and Dante Peter O'Neill (black Irish?) softly played some Gaelic tune on a flute. I've been to worse parties, and with *much* worse company.

At the shank end of the evening, I sat at the bar and told Mac about the PNN report.

"The good part," I said, "is that when the parade is over tomorrow, it's over—at least until next year. No more media attention. I hate those stories that hang around and hang around. I want to get back to worrying about my press release for the summer term."

Mac raised an eyebrow. "What about the murders, Jefferson?"

Oh, them.

Carol Landis had shaken my confidence that all was as it appeared to be—a murder-suicide with no loose ends. "I have to admit that if your typewriting expert says Ivanhoe didn't write the suicide note, then it looks like we've got a double homicide. But what about the dead bolt lock on the cabin door? We can trust Amos that the cabin wasn't equipped with an escape hatch of some kind. And how could a killer just walk up to Ivanhoe and blow his brains out?"

I winced at my own word choice. The memory of what I'd seen in the cabin made me wish I hadn't referred to brains. But Mac just smiled and hoisted a beer.

"This is quite a three-cigar problem, old boy. The locked room mystery is one of the most hallowed conventions of the mystery-writer's craft. Surely you know that Edgar Allan Poe himself invented the concept in the first detective story, 'The Murders in the Rue Morgue.' And Sherlock Holmes tackled locked room murders in 'The Adventure of the Speckled Band' and 'The Adventure of the Empty House.' Such masters of the genre as Ellery Queen, Agatha Christie, G.K. Chesterton, Dashiell Hammett, Erle Stanley—"

"This would be very helpful if I were writing a history of detective fiction," I interrupted sourly.

"However, the unchallenged maestro of the locked room puzzle remains John Dickson Carr, who also wrote as Carter Dickson. I commend his often-complex novels to your attention. Do not miss in particular *The Three Coffins*, originally known as *The Hollow Man*—a title evocative of T.S. Eliot, is it not? You will find it quite instructional. The same goes for *The Peacock Feather Murders*, one of the Dickson books."

"Ooh, I'm crazy about Carr," said a voice at my elbow, about a foot shorter than me. Sister Mary Margaret Malone—Triple M—had snuck up on us.

"I thought you only read science fiction and horror," I said.

"Spooky mysteries, too! You can't beat Carr for atmosphere. My father put me on to him."

"If Carr had a defect," Mac pontificated, "it is that his plots were too brilliant. The explication at the end of the book often was the length of a short story. Occam's Razor does not apply in his world."

Occam's Razor is a principle, not a shaving tool. It says that the simplest explanation is usually the correct one.

"I hope it applies in our world," I said. "The simplest explanation would be that the killer used a key to lock the cabin after he had taken care of business."

"So who had a key?" Triple M asked.

"A man named Amos Yoder."

"I know Amos! He reads a lot."

"People without television often do. Anyway, he had about as much reason to kill Ivanhoe as you did. Plus, he told us he had the key, which he didn't have to do and the killer wouldn't have done. This case is a mess."

"Try not to lose any sleep over it, old boy," Mac said.

But I did. At three o'clock in the morning, Lynda woke up to nurse the baby and realized that I wasn't in bed. She wandered into the family room, where she found me with *The Three Coffins* in my hand and *The Peacock Feather Murders* on the side table next to me. They were both hardcovers with dust jackets intact. Mac had ducked home, plucked them from his massive library of detective fiction, and forced them on me before we left Luther's party.

"What are you doing?" she yawned sleepily.

"Going crazy."

She rolled her eyes. "Let's not go there, darling."

"I'm tearing through these locked room mysteries that Mac gave me, trying to beat him at his own game."

"Are they helping?"

"If I want to write one of those fantasies, maybe." I picked up the *Peacock Feather* book. "The amateur detective in this one is a profane old goat with terrible grammar named Sir Henry Merrivale. I like him, but I hate it that I like him. Never mind that, though. He gives four possible reasons for a murder to take place in a locked room. The first reason on that list is to make it look like suicide. Okay, that's the case here and we already know that. That doesn't help." I set the book aside.

"And the one you're reading now?"

I picked up *The Three Coffins* again. "Triple M must have loved this one. It's full of talk about Transylvania and vampires, very eerie in places. I just finished a chapter where a wheezy old gent named Dr. Gideon Fell delivers a lecture on locked room mysteries. The lecture takes up the whole chapter. He has seven explanations for murder in a hermetically sealed room, including suicide made to look like murder—just the opposite of what we have. Then he gives five ways for tampering with a door so it looks like it was locked from the inside."

"That sounds promising."

"If only," I sighed. "Removing the door wouldn't work on Ivanhoe's cabin because the hinges are on the inside. Tampering with a falling bar or latch won't work because there wasn't one. The others all involve having a key, the lack of which is our whole problem to begin with."

"I'm going back to bed."

"Okay," I said distractedly. "I was hoping that somewhere in these books I'd find the key to the—wait a minute, the key! That's it!"

Lynda yawned anew and stretched in a way that normally would have been most distracting. "It is?"

"I think what we need, my sweet, is a locksmith."

Chapter Twenty-Two
Here Comes the Parade

Sunday, March 13, which I had mentally tabbed "Parade Day," dawned sunny and pleasantly cool. Seriously sleep deprived, I arose bleary-eyed and cranky. My brilliant idea of the night before seemed like a long shot in the cold light of day—but a shot nonetheless, I told myself.

Lynda and I, baby in tow, went to early Mass at St. Edward the Confessor, followed by breakfast at home.

The parade was to start at one o'clock. By twelve-fifteen we three Codys had positioned ourselves in front of the *Erin Observer & News-Ledger* offices on Main Street, which had been renamed Dublin Boulevard for the day. The newspaper brandished an Irish flag, as did Daniel's Apothecary and the law offices of Farleigh & Farleigh on opposite sides of the street. The temperature had warmed considerably so that T-shirts were the order of the day. Lynda's, worn over yellow capris, was white with a green shamrock design. She'd painted her fingernails and toenails an iridescent shade of emerald and gathered her honey blond curls with a green ribbon. Donata looked quite fetching in an Oscar the Grouch diaper.

I looked around for the expected protestors. Sure enough, there stood Nelson Abbott across the street, holding a sign hand-painted on both sides. Every so often he would switch from **FACE TO FACE, NOT FACEBOOK** to show **ST. PATRICK NEVER SENT A TWEET**. As promised, he was accompanied by Karen

Ellicott and Carol Landis. Karen, fully recovered from yesterday's hangover, looked mortified to be there. Carol Landis hid behind large sunglasses.

"I think it's going to rain," Lynda said.

A few dark clouds were on the western horizon.

"Have faith, my sweet. I'm sure it won't rain on our parade."

She rolled her eyes.

"Wait here," I said. "I'll be right back."

I hoofed it over to Spring Street. As I'd expected, Phil Oakland stood out in front of his locksmith shop waiting for the parade to pass him by when it made the turn off of Main Street. His green sweater barely stretched over his stomach.

"You make keys," I said after a brief greeting. *What else would you do with a graduate degree in philosophy?*

He peered at me through his wire-rimmed glasses. "So does every big box hardware store these days. But, sure, I make keys. I view that as kind of a metaphor for unlocking the secrets of life. Why do you ask?"

"Because I think the metaphorical key to James Ivanhoe's death is a real key, a key to his cabin. He had one in his pocket when he died, and his builder has another. But I think there must be a third."

"There is."

It couldn't be this easy.

"You mean—"

"I made it."

Sometimes long shots pay off. That's why people bet on horse races.

"For whom?" I asked.

"For Mr. Ivanhoe, of course. That's how I know it was to his house."

"When was that?"

He shrugged. "A couple of months ago, I guess. Not too long after he moved in. He said he saw my sign on his way to the bookstore."

"Did he say why he needed another key?"

"Just that he gave his original spare to his builder. I figured he would have put the new one under his mat or some other foolish place, like most people do."

"Why didn't you tell Chief Hummel about this the day we found the body?"

Another shrug. "He didn't ask. Is it important?"

Important? It would open the door (so to speak) for Ivanhoe's death to be murder, not suicide. Dead bolts can be locked from the outside with a key.

"Maybe. If it is, you'll hear about it later."

I thanked Phil and headed back to Main Street, feeling like I'd done a good day's work in the sleuthing line. We now knew that there was a third key to the murder cabin. We just didn't know who had it. I texted Mac: *Phil Oakland made extra key to Ivanhoe cabin. Doesn't know for who.* Why didn't autocorrect fix that? I changed the last word to *whom* and sent it. Mac probably wouldn't see it right away, but it would be there for him after the parade.

On my way back to Lynda, I passed Lani Alvarez, the young socialist who'd had her say at the City Council meeting. Clad in a tight-fitting white T-shirt and faded jeans, she carried a homemade sign on white cardboard saying **FIGHT THE MACHINE!** It was illustrated with drawings of robots. The other side of the sign said **FREE SPEECH, NOT CAPITALISM!** I'm still scratching my head over that one.

I joined Lynda and told her what I'd learned.

"So there's another key," she said. "Who do you think has it?"

"That's the big question. Ivanhoe lived in that cabin alone. He might have given a key to Karen or Carol—either would have been logical—but both deny it. And we don't suspect them anyway."

"Maybe you should."

"But they're both adamant that Ivanhoe didn't kill himself. The killer wouldn't do that after going to all that trouble to make his death look like murder-suicide."

"Maybe that's just what she wants you to think, 'she' being either of them."

This stuff gives me a headache.

Just then the figures of Bennington Lee and his photographer caught my eye. They walked slowly down the street, and then stopped to talk with the Ned Ludd Trio, as I thought of them at that moment. I made a mental note to keep an eye on the man from PNN, who was wearing a green bowtie, but first I had to earn my salary.

Anticipation mounts! I tweeted at twelve-forty-five. Exactly fifteen minutes later, I wrote: *Sound of bagpipes! 63rd annual St. Patrick's Day Parade starting! St. Benignus University leads the way.*

Yes, thanks to no small effort on the part of yours truly, SBU had snagged the prestigious position of leading float in the parade. Only the 1960s-era green MG convertible carrying the grand marshal, Colleen Clancy (AKA Miss Ohio), preceded it. Silver-haired Father Joe, somehow looking both handsome and saintly, waved to the crowd from atop a replica of SBU's Herbert Hall while Sebastian McCabe squeezed alleged music out of his bagpipes.

Behind them were entries from all the major businesses in town and a lot of the minor ones—Mo's Mysteries & Marvels bookstore, Glad Tidings Church, Happy Homes Realty, Hawes & Holder Funeral Home, Artistic Ink Tattoo Studio, and The Speakeasy, our trendy new gastropub that had had such a difficult birth[4], plus

---

[4] See *Bookmarked for Murder*, MX Publishing, 2015.

Brett McGee's car dealership in Cincinnati. I tweeted all the names as they rolled by us.

Oscar Hummel, wearing his newly pressed police chief uniform, was not the only public servant on display. Mayor Lesley Saylor-Mackie and county prosecutor Marvin Slade, political rivals, were among politicos reminding the voters that they were Irish at heart, just like everybody else on St. Paddy's Day (which, of course, was actually four days away). Bruce Gordon waved to the crowd from his white Oldsmobile, but few of his City Council confreres joined him. Maybe they were afraid of being hit by flying shrapnel from this trumped-up media controversy. Voters only laud courage in politicians they agree with.

But no parade would be worthy of the name without marching bands. The university and both high schools had sent theirs. Lincoln Todd, wearing a stovepipe hat, rode right behind them in a vintage 1966 Lincoln convertible, black with white sidewall tires.

Looking around me, I couldn't help but notice that more than a few parade-goers had taken advantage of the "Kegs and Eggs" Irish breakfast offered at both Bobbie McGee's and The Speakeasy starting early that morning. The flexible term "kegs" included Irish whiskey as well as beer.

After a while, my eyes began to search for Bennington Lee. And there he was—talking to a short, elderly woman wearing turquoise glasses shaped like Catwoman's mask. She carried a sign that said **GO GREEN FOR ST. PATRICK'S DAY**. I sidled up behind the TV reporter and eavesdropped.

". . . the ecological damage just so people can be talking and texting on their damn mobile phones all the time. And do you ever think about those poor Chinese workers who make these electronic gadgets for less than two bucks an hour? If you don't know what I'm talking about, just Google the phrase 'Apple sweatshops.'"

Isn't there a Ned Ludd Society rule against using Google? If there was, it didn't apply to Catwoman anyway. I found out later that she wasn't a member of Ivanhoe's army, just a bystander with an opinion.

The interview finished, Lee positioned himself on the sidewalk between his camera operator and the parade in such a way that viewers would be able to see Nelson Abbott holding his sign above the rest of the crowd on that side of the street. Karen Ellicott and Carol Landis remained with Abbott, looking like kids forced to go to an opera and told to enjoy it. Lee began what sounded like the closing lines of his report.

"Clearly, here in tiny Erin, Ohio, the death of native son James Ivanhoe has done nothing to halt the budding movement that meant so—"

Abbott made his move. He put down his protest sign. The two women helped him unfurl a banner that said **THE NED LUDD SOCIETY** in big letters and *Remember the Past, Save the Future* in smaller ones. They walked toward the street, apparently to join the end of the parade.

"Hey, you people!" came a yell from a middle-aged guy with too much belly and not enough "Kiss Me I'm Irish" polo shirt. "You're not part of this rodeo! Get lost!"

With the sound of the Bernardin High School Band fading into the distance, he was quite audible. Lee stopped in mid-pontification and jerked around.

"We aren't going anywhere, sir," Abbott replied in a loud voice. "This is a public street, not the entrance to a gated community for the one percent."

"Maybe so, but this is a parade with a permit, not a picket line. And nobody invited you."

"We have a right—"

Lee's camerawoman zoomed in on Big Belly as he attempted the first punch. The guy had drunk too much breakfast, judging by the way he wobbled as he ploughed his fist in the direction of Nelson Abbott's chin. Abbott deftly avoided the blow with a quick move, while simultaneously hitting the man in his stomach.

"You can't do that to my friend!" someone yelled.

From there things moved quickly. In about a minute three men had piled on top of Abbott. Karen and Carol started pummeling them with the activist's abandoned protest sign. Lani Alvarez pitched in on their side with her own sign, throwing her socialist heart into it. The crowd, for the most part having no idea what was at issue, started to take sides anyway as the PNN and cell phone cameras captured the mayhem.

And then the clouds opened and it poured down rain.

Chapter Twenty-Three
Fahrenheit 451?

James Ivanhoe's funeral on Monday morning, cooked up by Karen Ellicott and Carol Landis, was one of the most unusual in my experience. I'm used to services in a church or funeral home with readings from Holy Writ. Ivanhoe's obsequies were at Mo's Mysteries & Marvels, and the readings were from his own books.

Funeral planning must have been a snap, though. The bookstore is majority-owned by my friend Mo Russell, who is affianced to Jonathan Hawes of Hawes & Holder, the funeral directors.

"He wasn't a religious man," Mo unnecessarily commented during the visitation period right before the service.

"A pity, that," Mac said.

"And he loved books," she added, "so his sister thought this was an appropriate place to say good-bye."

Fair enough, I suppose.

Mo's Mysteries & Marvels, in which Sebastian McCabe has a minor financial interest as Mo's supposedly silent partner, purveys mystery, fantasy, and science fiction books from the first floor of a former firehouse on Water Street. Ivanhoe, I recalled from that feature story last winter, had once signed copies of *The Whirligig of Time* there.

By design, the shop has more open space than the average bookstore. Jonathan had set out a couple of dozen or so wooden folding chairs in front of the plain wooden casket for the late-morning service. The deceased's sister and his ex-wife/agent both delivered better-than-average eulogies. They were interspersed with dramatic readings from Ivanhoe's novels by Jonathan Hawes, who acts in amateur dramas when he is not busy embalming and so forth.

"This world never quite met Jamie's expectations," Karen said, on the verge of tears at the end of her remarks. "We can only hope that the next one will."

Whether Karen actually believed in a next world or was just bowing to convention I had no idea, but I thought that closing line a good one. It would have been especially apt for a suicide, which she didn't believe her brother was.

Ivanhoe's ex was considerably less sentimental, for which I gave her high marks. "Jamie had a strong sense of priorities and humanity ranked at the top," she said with a bitter smile. "Individual people were a little lower down the list. Some of us found him easy to admire, but hard to live with." *Well, at least that's honest.*

Maybe Carol Landis was shoving metaphorical dirt on the casket, or maybe she was working through her failed relationship with the dead man. I'll leave the psychoanalysis to people who are paid for it.

The whole shebang only took thirty or forty minutes, so it was curiosity rather than boredom that caused me to glance around and see who my fellow mourners were. "A full house," Mac whispered. Actually, it was an SRO crowd. The surviving Ellicott brothers sat grimly at the back of the room, shouting "we'd rather be anywhere else" in body language. Terri Beddoes, Amos Yoder, and Fred Gaffe had all arrived in time to capture seats, along with a lot of folks I didn't know. But Bruce Gordon, Phil Oakland (looking uncomfortable in a tie), and Neil Carboy all had to stand. Carboy's presence hinted that he and Karen hadn't split over her performance the day before; but on the other hand, he wasn't sitting with her.

Tall Rawls hovered around the edges of the room, not taking notes but not missing anything either. Karen had told me that she'd pointedly disinvited Bennington Lee to the service. Word that he had stayed in town had ended my fantasy that last night's chaotic report would be his last one from Erin. Still, the parade was over and I could check that off my worry list.

The service ended with Jonathan Hawes leading a non-denominational prayer, sort of a "to whom it may concern" affair, and then giving instructions to those who were following the hearse out to the cemetery.

"Thanks for coming," Karen said when Mac and I emerged onto the sidewalk.

"Good crowd, considering," I said. "I noticed your friend Neil in the back of the room."

"We reached a cease-fire, but I still don't know where we're going."

Been there, done that, wouldn't recommend it.

"I was rather surprised that Nelson Abbott was not in attendance," Mac said, "given his relationship with your brother and with you."

"He's still in jail."

Mac raised his eyebrow. A respectable citizen charged with disorderly conduct in Erin normally would be released on his own recognizance unless he resisted arrest.

"He refused to be released. He claimed it was his right to go to jail."

"No lie, he really said that," Oscar affirmed. "Most of my guests are a lot more reluctant. The guy who threw the first punch bailed out."

If you have the idea that Abbott was behind bars a few feet away from Oscar's desk, you're thinking Mayberry. The lockup part of the police-jail complex was at the back of the building. Mac and I sat alone with Oscar in his office.

Oscar shoved Mac a mug of black coffee. "By the way, Gibbons said there was no book manuscript in the cabin. The only fiction he found was a letter Ivanhoe wrote asking the Prime Minister of England to re-establish the British Empire as soon as possible."

"And yet," Mac said, "I rather think Ivanhoe's next novel *was* there—in his fireplace. It has not been a cold spring, the windows of the cabin were closed and locked, and yet there were ashes in the hearth the day that we found Ivanhoe's body. I suspect that those were the remains of *Sunbelt.*"

I had visions of Ray Bradbury's *Fahrenheit 451*, another dystopian novel. That's the one in which firemen are people who set fire to books.

"We'll never know, but you're probably right," Oscar said. "Whoever started the fire apparently made sure it did the job. Gibbons sent the ashes, including a few large pieces he managed to preserve, to BCI." That would be the Bureau of Criminal Investigation, the state of Ohio's crime lab. Oscar picked up a report on his desk. "They were able to recover a few words here and a couple of phrases there, but not enough to add up to anything. They did establish that whatever it was, it was typed on a manual typewriter."

He handed the report to Mac, who returned it after a quick glance with a comment: "Sherlock Holmes was considerably more fortunate in 'The Adventure of the Three Gables.' When the villain's agents stole the manuscript of a novel, a thinly disguised *roman à clef*, they left behind a fragment that gives the plot away. The manuscript was later burned. Hum! Food for thought, that."

"If you say so. But here's the good news: BCI confirms that the Glock that Ivanhoe used to kill himself, Walter's gun—"

"Probably," Mac interjected.

"What's that supposed to mean?"

"I am merely being precise. Walter Ellicott believes the gun to be his, and it most likely is. However, he told us there are no identifying marks on the gun."

"Of all the hair-splitting—Never mind! BCI says the gun also killed Cassandra Ellicott. It's just what it looks like, Mac, murder-suicide. That's the ruling I expect from the coroner, if she ever gets around to it."

"The use of a single gun in both crimes proves no such thing. What about the possibility that a third party used that gun to kill both Cassandra and her brother-in-law, faking the latter's suicide? Or would you prefer the notion that James killed Cassandra and someone avenged her death, using the same gun as ironic justice?"

"No, I wouldn't. I mean, I wouldn't prefer either." Flustered, Oscar almost spilled his coffee. "James Ellicott-cum-Ivanhoe killed himself. And he did it behind a cabin door that was locked with a dead bolt!"

"If Ivanhoe's supposed confession was bogus, the convenient murder-suicide scenario falls like a house of cards and the locked room becomes a detail."

Even though he didn't bring it up to Oscar, Mac had been suitably impressed earlier by my sleuthing out the third key. ("Well done, old boy! I must congratulate you.")

"Is there really a chance the confession was fake?" asked an XX-chromosome voice. Tall Rawls, still wearing funereal black, had approached so quietly that I hadn't heard her. The twinkle in his brown eyes made me think that Mac had seen her coming and guided the conversation accordingly. Johanna and Oscar had a symbiotic relationship as reporter and source, so well established by now that his administrative assistant had probably thought it safe to wave her through without alerting the chief.

"There is every chance," Mac responded to her question.

"Maybe one in fifty," Oscar said with a scowl, "but even nags win once in a while." He was hedging his bets.

Johanna focused on Mac. "You seem convinced. Can you prove it?"

"I believe that I can. As you know, the note found in the murder cabin was typed on a manual typewriter and unsigned. However, an acquaintance of mine who has made a special study of typing patterns on such machines will be in town tomorrow. By comparing the typing on what we have been calling the suicide note and material that we know Ivanhoe typed, she can settle the issue."

"You mean she can tell whether the dead man actually typed the note on his typewriter?"

"That is my expectation. She has done something similar a number of times."

"Awesome!"

Johanna's pen flew across the pages of her reporter's notebook.

"You can't print that!" Oscar protested.

Doesn't that sound quaint? Print is such an old-fashioned concept.

"Nobody said this was off the record."

"She's got you there, Oscar," I noted helpfully.

"What makes you think Ivanhoe didn't kill himself, Mac?" Johanna asked.

"Not only I. His sister and his ex-wife are also convinced that he killed neither himself nor Cassandra Ellicott. We have several reasons."

He enumerated them: the surplus of suicide motives given in the note, the writing style of that note, the fact that Ivanhoe wasn't suffering writer's block, and the writer's narcissism (Mac's word, and a good one) as a counter-indication of suicide.

"There was no sign of a struggle, as far as I know," Johanna pointed out. "So how does somebody just walk up to a man and put a bullet in his temple? And then the man's body is found slumped over his typewriter?"

"That presents no great difficulties, Ms. Rawls. Any number of subterfuges would have worked. I would have presented Ivanhoe with an antique weapon for his examination. The walls of his study testified to his fascination for such items. While he was examining the item, and thus distracted, I would have removed the gun from its place of concealment on my person and quickly dispatched him."

I don't know whether he stayed up all night thinking up that scenario, but this was the first I'd heard of it.

"Awesome!" Johanna scribbled. *Curb your enthusiasm.* "But wait! Why would he do that while sitting down at his typewriter?"

"I, having never been to his cabin previously, would have asked to see . . ."

A familiar ping let me know I had a text. I pulled out my smartphone and found a string of three related messages from Lynda. Apparently she'd been thinking homicidal thoughts while Donata was asleep. Thoughts about homicide, I mean. She wrote:

Carol Landis!

I mean, what about her as killer?

The alibi she provided Ivanhoe for Cassandra's murder is also an alibi for her. How convenient!! Maybe she wacked both of them in a love triangle!

Chapter Twenty-Four
Love or Money?

"Ingenious!" Mac said when I'd told him about Lynda's brainstorm on our way back to campus.

"Yeah, but do you buy it?"

"I am afraid not, old boy. That theory contains a fatal flaw. Think about it."

I could have begged for a clue, since I didn't have one, but I don't like to grovel on an empty stomach.

Only an hour or so after I'd eaten lunch at my desk, Johanna posted a story on the *Online Observer*. It began with a bang: "The death of best-selling novelist James Ivanhoe may not have been a suicide, Sebastian McCabe believes."

The story also quoted Carol Landis, which set me to musing about Lynda's texts. There were a few problems with her nomination of the literary agent as a double killer, but not insurmountable ones. For example, how would Carol know where Walter kept his gun? Well, Cassandra could have known. Maybe she pulled the gun on Carol and Carol turned the tables on her after a struggle.

But wait! If Carol was the killer, and therefore staged the murder-suicide scenario, why would she so adamantly deny that Ivanhoe had killed himself? That must have been Mac's fatal flaw, the same one I'd raised with Lynda the day before. I made a mental note to point that out to her that evening, but not until cocktail hour was well underway.

"That's going to put Oscar in a bad mood," Popcorn said, reading the story on the computer screen over my shoulder.

"I'm sure you can mellow him out. Neck rubs always do it for me."

"You're not Oscar."

There was no way I could answer that one without digging myself into a hole so deep one of those big scooping machines couldn't get me out. But I didn't have to. My phone rang—the dumb one on my desk, not the smart one in my pocket. The phone number looked familiar, but I couldn't quite place it. So it must be a business call, I figured, not a personal one.

"Jeff Cody."

"Jeff! It's Todd."

The agitation in his voice told me to skip the small talk.

"What's up, Linc?"

"That reporter from PNN called me. He wants another interview."

Popcorn waved goodbye as she backed out of my office.

"Well, you did a great job last time, with the Amish buggy and all."

"That was different. I only agreed to do it if the reporter promised not to ask about Cassie, which he wasn't interested in at the time anyway. But now he wants to ask me about the report that McCabe doesn't believe Jamie's death was self-inflicted. He said he's going to try to talk to McCabe, too."

"Just say no." *If only Mac would do likewise.*

"I already did. That's not the issue. It's very painful to me to have my daughter's death become the subject of lurid cable TV coverage. Why can't they let her rest in peace? It was bad enough knowing that Jamie was responsible for Cassie's death. That was like a knife to my heart. But at least his demise brought closure—until McCabe opened his mouth to that *Observer* reporter. Can't you convince him that he's wrong this time?"

"That's what I thought at first, Linc, but now I'm not so sure. I guess we'll find out when Mac's expert gives us the verdict on the suicide letter." I gave him the back story on that.

"Aren't there so-called experts who practically make a living testifying to whatever you want them to say in court?"

I conceded as much.

"So much for experts, then. This negative media attention bothers me professionally as well. It's not good for Erin. Look, your business is PR. How can we put a positive spin this?"

It would be easier to convince Mac that he's wrong, which is impossible.

You know people are desperate when they use the phrase "positive spin." The very word "spin" has a negative connotation, and people can spot the phoniness of it a mile away. In other words, when you try to put lipstick on a pig, you just end up with a funny-looking pig.

I tried to think of something upbeat to say.

"PNN is just after a story, but I'm sure that you and Mac both want the truth. And the sooner that's established and justice is done, the sooner the story goes away." Okay, I was kind of sliding over the whole arrest, trial, and conviction part, but my intentions were good.

"That time can't come soon enough for me. If Jamie didn't kill himself, who does Mac think did?"

"On that point he remains coy. He hasn't named names. Do you have a candidate?"

"Jamie killed himself."

"But if he didn't, who would you think did?"

After a long pause, Todd said, "Maybe somebody in that Ned Ludd Society. You know, Malcolm X and George

Lincoln Rockwell were killed by members of their own movements."

My memory banks came up short on the three-part name. "Who was Rockwell?"

"The founder of the American Nazi Party."

Sorry I asked. And I sure wasn't going to ask whether he was related to Lincoln Todd.

"Why would some New Luddite kill Ivanhoe?" I said.

Mac, in the course of brainstorming possibilities, had suggested a rival within the movement who either disagreed with Ivanhoe's tactics or wanted to displace him as leader. But both of those seemed thin motivations to me. The movement wasn't big enough.

I could almost hear Todd shrug over the phone. "Who knows? Maybe they thought they needed a martyr."

That notion had flittered at the edges of the Cody brain a while back—not that the New Luddites needed a martyr, but many movements have been fueled by the blood of their leaders. "That's not crazy. I'll take it up with Mac."

After a few more minutes of holding Todd's metaphorical hand, I disconnected and called Mac.

"Did you do an interview with Bennington Lee?"

"No, Jefferson, I demurred. Ms. Rawls's story has already put our friend Oscar in an awkward position; I did not wish to exacerbate the situation."

"Well, Lee tried Linc Todd, who also declined the honor. Linc's pretty upset that his daughter is being posthumously dragged into all of this. He'd just as soon it be murder-suicide and be done with."

Mac sighed. "If only wishing would make it so."

"Linc wants to know who you think killed Cassandra if Ivanhoe didn't."

"That is a work in progress. As we have discussed, it may not have been the same person who killed Ivanhoe."

"Todd had an out-of-the-box idea." I explained the martyr scenario.

"Out-of-the-box indeed," Mac mused. "Implausible as it may seem, that motive certainly has the virtue of originality. I would have expected love or money to be the reason—or perhaps fear. Fear is a powerful motivator. I would like to speak to Nelson Abbott. Would you be available to accompany me on a visit to him later this afternoon at Oscar's bed and breakfast?"

We made a date to meet at Mac's office at four o'clock.

"I figured out the problem with Carol Landis as a suspect," I told Mac as he drove us to the jail. "If she had killed Cassandra and then faked the suicide note, she wouldn't be giving Ivanhoe an alibi and insisting he had no reason for killing himself."

Mac nodded. "A pity, too. Ms. Landis had a double motive—love *and* money. Her ex-husband either never got around to changing his will or he was still quite fond of her. She was Ivanhoe's heir, which means she has inherited a substantial royalty stream as well as his share of the Ellicott family money."

I gaped. "How do you know that?"

"Ms. Ellicott told me. She is the executrix of the Ivanhoe will, you will recall. I was also able to establish by subtle questioning that Ms. Landis can prove she was in Los Angeles negotiating a film contract when Ivanhoe was killed."

So the person with the strongest financial motive was ruled out. "There was one other thing that Ivanhoe left behind—leadership of the Ned Ludd Society," I pointed out. "I'm sure Abbott can tell us who inherits that."

"There is no Ned Ludd Society," Abbott snorted. "There never was. That was just a name Ivanhoe dreamed up. Do you have any idea how easy it is to establish yourself in the media as the leader of an organization that doesn't exist? They never ask how many members you have. If you really want to cover the bases you can pay a teenager to create an impressive website for you, but you don't even need that."

Abbott sounded like he was talking from experience.

"You should be proud of your jail, by the way," he added. "It's one of the nicest I've been in." Oscar tried not to look pleased. He failed. "And that chaplain, Sister Polly, she's a real crackerjack. She brought me a book." He held up a paperback *Star Trek* novel by Christopher L. Bennett.

"You read science fiction?" Mac said. "That seems a bit paradoxical."

"Not all science fiction. I'm a Trekkie."

"Fascinating," I said in my best Mr. Spock voice. "But how can there be no Ned Ludd Society? What about all of Ivanhoe's followers?"

"Define 'followers.'"

"I take your point," Mac said. "The late Mr. Ivanhoe was something of a leader in a nascent movement, but not truly *the* leader because he had built no organizational structure. That being the case, he had allies rather than followers. Ergo, he has no heir apparent."

Abbott paused. "I'd never thought about it that deeply, but I suppose all that is true. I'd certainly consider myself an ally because our interests intersected, although I'd actually only met him once."

"But you got thousands of names on a petition supporting the Ned Ludd Society!" I protested.

"People will sign anything, thank God. But don't quote me on that."

Quote him? I wanted to strangle him.

"Don't you think Ivanhoe's death will bring new attention to the downside of technology?" I said.

"I certainly hope so! But it's not like he was some kind of a martyr. He didn't die for the cause."

"That's not the impression you gave at the news conference when you talked about picking up his fallen banner."

"Did I say that? Well, sometimes I get carried away."

Chapter Twenty-Five
Col. Teal Tells a Tale

"I'm not convinced," I told Mac as he drove us back to campus, where I had left my bike. "Abbott was trying too hard. Did you notice how he threw in the part about how he'd only met Ivanhoe once? It was like he was holding up a flashing neon sign that said 'Not a Suspect.'"

"Of course I noticed, old boy. However, as Freud once observed, sometimes a cigar is only a cigar."

"What's that supposed to mean?"

"Perhaps Abbott only told us that because it is a fact. He himself does not appear to benefit in any way from Ivanhoe's death. His interests are allied with Ivanhoe's, as he acknowledged, but they are not identical. Abbott's obsession is Artificial Intelligence, not all digital technology. Nor were the two men rivals for leadership of the same movement."

"Who *does* benefit from Ivanhoe's death—other than his well-alibied ex-wife?"

"That is the crux of the matter, is it not?"

Thanks for nothing.

So I was already in no fine mood when I walked into the family room of Chez Cody that evening. My frame of mind wasn't improved any by finding a handsome baby-boomer with gray-streaked hair holding my daughter in his muscular arms. He made strange faces accompanied by even stranger noises.

"Look who's here!" Lynda gushed.

Like I could avoid it.

"Hello, Colonel," I said. "Jake," I amended.

"I'd shake but my hands are full."

"That's okay." *I'm shaking enough for the both of us.*

It's not that I was exactly afraid of Col. Jacob Andrew Teal, U.S. Army, retired. After all, he's my father-in-law, even if he does pack a gun. But four years into my blissful marriage to his daughter, I felt like I remained on probation with him. I also still have to fight the urge to salute him, even though I was never in the military.

"Daddy's come for a visit," Lynda said.

Oh, joy.

"To what do we owe the pleasure?"

"I stopped fighting the urge to play with my newest grandchild." He had three others, courtesy of Lynda's librarian sister, Emma.

"Sorry you didn't make the baptism," I said.

"So am I, Jeff. Press of business." He tickled Donata's cheek with his finger. She smiled. "She reminds me of her namesake, God rest her soul."

For a minute I got lost in a reverie about the Colonel and what he'd missed by having a life of adventure and marriage to a famous beauty. He and Lynda's mother, Lucia, had been divorced since before Emma was born— which didn't stop them from producing Emma. They often got together again whenever Lucia was between husbands. But apparently they were both too passionate in ways other than the romantic sense for the liaison to last more than a couple of weeks at a stretch.

My thoughts jumped and I wondered briefly what it was like between Ivanhoe and Cassandra. Their romance relationship, too, had begun years ago and resumed after a hiatus.

"How about a drink, Jake?" I said, shaking off the pointless musing.

"Bourbon?"

"I think I can find some," Lynda said dryly.

"Hold the rocks."

"And while she does that, Colonel, you can tell us why you're really here."

My wife, who should have known better, made question marks out of her eyebrows. But her father smiled, managing to look hardly at all like a crazed killer in a Quentin Tarantino flick. The Colonel is a straight-talking man who appreciates straight talk (although he did briefly look like he wanted to play basketball with my head).

"I would have come to see the baby anyway, trust me on that, son, but I did have a secondary reason for coming to Erin. It's a freelance assignment."

"Who do you have to kill?" I joshed. At least, I think I was kidding. I've never completely accepted Jake's assurance that his former job as editor of *Stars & Stripes Europe* wasn't a cover for something else. He's the second toughest-looking person I've ever known, right behind Sister Benedict Marie, one of my fifth-grade teachers at St. Polycarp elementary school back in Virginia. (In reality, Sister was about as tough as chocolate pudding. Unlike Jake.)

Jake chuckled as Lynda handed him a manly portion of Knob Creek, matching the one she'd poured herself. I had a feeling I would need a drink of my own before dinner.

"Ever hear of an online newsletter called *The Third Rail*?" Jake began.

That didn't ring any bells for me. Lynda looked equally blank. "Is it about Social Security reform?" she asked. She'd actually been paying attention to my lectures on the subject!

But her father ignored the humorous sally. "It's a Washington-based site run by two former Navy SEALs, dedicated to exposing graft, corruption, fraud, waste, abuse, and crimes in high places."

"Must keep them busy," I said.

"They especially like poking their fingers in the eyes of the military-industrial complex, and not only in our country."

Hmmm. "Uh, Jake, don't you draw a comfortable pension from the military-industrial complex?" I said.

"No, just from the military. I've never worked for the industrial side. Besides, there's nothing wrong with hedging your bets, son. So I've done a few investigative stories for *The Third Rail* on commission. They like to hire retired military and the pay is decent."

"And they want you to do something in Erin," Lynda surmised.

Jake nodded. "I'm checking on a tip from a dead man—James Ivanhoe."

His low-key delivery—very matter of fact, no pause before the name or sinking into a whisper—did nothing to stop my skin from erupting into gander-sized goose bumps.

"Two days after he died, a letter from him arrived at the offices of *The Third Rail*. I have a high-resolution copy right here." He handed Donata over to me since I didn't have a drink in my hand.

The letter, written in what looked to me like the same typewriter font as Ivanhoe's suicide (?) note, was short, vague, but attention-getting. It was addressed to Richard Weigel, whom Jake identified as the editor of the online muckraking publication.

Dear Mr. Weigel,

I have information that a company in my hometown is violating federal law and putting the security of the United States at risk by the illicit sale of technology to a foreign power. If you are interested, I will be happy to tell what I know to one of your reporters. Please write back to me at the above address if you are interested. I am willing to travel to your offices in Washington.

Sincerely,
James Ellicott (Ivanhoe)

The first sentence had thirty-three words, I noticed. That should be long enough to satisfy Mac, who had complained that the short sentences in the suicide note were un-Ivanhoe-like.

"This looks like exactly what we've been looking for—motive with a capital 'M,'" I said. "Somebody killed Ivanhoe to keep him from telling what he knew."

"That thought had occurred to me, son." His drink half-gone, Jake took another swallow.

"Carol Landis has a motive," Lynda said.

"She also has an alibi." I hadn't had the opportunity to let Lynda down easily. "And I still say the murderer wouldn't undercut the murder-suicide scenario the way she's been doing."

Lynda stared at the letter. "I can see why he used the Ivanhoe name on the letter. That gave him some credibility because his latest book is doing so well. But I wonder why he signed his family name, too."

"It was still his name, so far as I know," I pointed out. "I never heard that he changed it legally. Ivanhoe was just a pen name."

"Or maybe there's another reason," Jake said, returning the photocopy to his shirt pocket. "The company he writes about could be the Altiora Corp.—they do a lot of defense work." Altiora, though not based in Erin, was our biggest employer. "But I'd bet big bucks that Mr. Ellicott-slash-Ivanhoe was offering to rat on his own family firm, Samson Microcircuits."

Chapter Twenty-Six
Proof Positive

"That is intriguing to say the least, and possibly even pivotal," Mac pronounced when I'd told him over the phone what we'd learned from Jake. I felt like he'd just patted me on the head. He asked me to meet him in his office at ten the next morning and bring Jake. But I decided that Jake could get himself there.

After my father-in-law left our house that evening, well fed and sober enough to drive to his hotel ("I wouldn't think of imposing on you lovebirds"), Lynda and I caught a few minutes of Bennington Lee on our bedroom TV. It was one of PNN's later programs, combining reporting with commentary from the host and the occasional verbal wrestling match between the host and a newsworthy victim.

"The mysterious death of best-selling novelist James Ivanhoe just keeps taking new twists and turns," Lee announced, standing in front of Ivanhoe's cabin. "Was it murder-suicide, as indicated by a note left behind, or"—hokey dramatic pause—"was it murder?"

Lee quoted Johanna's story, showed Mac's picture ("declined an interview for this broadcast"), interviewed a few people on the street, and gave some of the background on the contentious Ellicott family.

"He's treating it like a soap opera," Lynda complained.

"You can't blame PNN too much," I said, turning out the light on my side of the marital bed. "It *is* a soap opera. The only thing missing is amnesia."

"There's even a fight over a will! I'd forgotten about that particular mess. Why would Ivanhoe blow the whistle on a company he owned a big chunk of?"

It was a sensible question, to which I didn't have a sensible answer. I made a mental note to ask Karen. She seemed to know "Jamie" as well as anybody.

The next day, Tuesday, I drove to work in my vintage lime green New Beetle because it was raining. As I fired up the engine, the radio went on and I was so startled my foot slipped off the clutch. The voice coming out of the cracked speakers belonged to James Ivanhoe.

". . . always been interested in alternative history stories, but I've never actually written one. In a lot of my novels, characters have somehow found themselves back in time trying to change history to affect the present. Or they're doing just the opposite—trying to prevent something from happening in the past that would change our present. But my work in progress actually involves a timeline in which technology developed differently and the South won the Civil War. This is about the present, not the past, but it's a different present shaped by an alternate past."

I think I've got that, but don't ask me to repeat it.

"The Confederate flag stirs strong emotions even today," came the faux Oxford English voice of Tony Lampwicke, the mainstay of our campus radio station. "Are you deliberately seeking controversy in your next novel by positing a world in which the Confederate States of America won the Civil War?"

"That's a minor element of the book, Tony, and controversy wasn't my goal in plotting it. I just asked myself what would have happened if the nations of the world had developed solar energy instead of electricity and gasoline engines in earlier centuries. What would be the upsides? What would be the downsides? There are always downsides to any technology. One of them is that you get too dependent upon it. Another is that it always becomes a national security issue, as it does in *Sunbelt*.

"You could read this novel as a dose of reality for my naive techno-selective friends in the environmental movement. But my real hope is just that it will be a fun book, and maybe a little thought-provoking."

At this point Tony's voice returned, apparently live, to remind the listeners that this was a reprise of a *Crosscurrents* interview with the late James Ivanhoe from last January.

If there were any justice in the world, I thought as I walked from the parking lot to my office, that interview would have contained a clue to solve the case. *And if a frog had wings, it wouldn't bump its ass on the ground*, my grandfather would have added. The only thing I got out of the interview was that Carol Landis had told the truth about Ivanhoe's new book that he'd been working on, *Sunbelt*. The reference in the "suicide note" to his creative juices drying up was smoke and mirrors for sure.

Could some rabid solar power enthusiast, hearing this interview or another like it, have killed Ivanhoe to keep him from finishing the book? I barely had the question formulated in my head before I knew what it meant: This business was really getting to me.

Jake Teal made it to Mac's office before I did. He sat comfortably in front of the big guy's messy desk, decked out in gray slacks and a blue blazer. All he needed was an ascot.

"Good morning, Jefferson!" Mac greeted. His first cigar of the day was already half-smoked. "The Colonel and I were just discussing the implications of Ivanhoe's letter to *The Third Rail*."

Jake, Lynda, and I had worked that over pretty well the night before, I thought. What Ivanhoe alleged could, if true, result in serious prison time for somebody, maybe several somebodies. And that was bad for me because one of those somebodies could be St. Benignus board member Walter Ellicott. That would depend on how high up the corruption went, but as the company's general counsel he ought to know a thing or two.

"The consequences of discovery could certainly be severe enough to motivate murder," Mac said. "That would fit under the general category of 'fear'—fear of exposure."

"Killing Ivanhoe got rid of whatever was in his head," Jake said, "but that can't be the only place it was. He must have had some evidence tucked away somewhere."

"Perhaps that is what was burned up in his fireplace—extensive typed notes of what he had learned," Mac mused. "Or perhaps he even fictionalized it in the novel he was writing, like the dead man in 'The Adventure of the Three Gables.' Carol Landis might know whether the storyline of *Sunbelt* involved illegal sales of technology."

"I don't know about that," I said, "but I do have some new intel on the book." I filled them in on Ivanhoe's discussion of it on *Crosscurrents*, including his comments on its plot and themes.

"That could have been his greatest work," Mac said with a sad shake of his head. "Again I say, how unfortunate that he never finished it."

"I'm sure he thinks so, too," I quipped.

"Hello?" said a female voice.

Mac looked behind me. "Ah, Alexandra! Please join us."

Professor Alexandra Powers, Mac's typewriter geek from Bowling Green State University, didn't look old enough to get into a bar, much less graduate school. Strikingly pretty, with wide brown eyes, she stood maybe five-two. Her shiny black hair was cut chin length, parted in the middle. She carried a travel mug of coffee in one hand and an attaché case in the other. I'd been expecting somebody more like Professor McGonagall in the Harry Potter movies, who certainly never wore stone-washed jeans and a denim jacket. The bright pink glasses perched on her head did nothing to professor-ize her, either.

"I asked Alexandra here to tell you two what she has already told me," Mac informed Jake and me.

Setting down the mug and valise on a nearby table, she extended a firm handshake before sitting down and pulling two pieces of paper out of the attaché case.

"In my opinion, the person who typed the letter to Carol Landis did not type the letter purporting to be a suicide note from James Ivanhoe." Professor Powers held them up, Exhibits A and B.

"Mind telling us how you reached that conclusion?" Jake drawled.

"The letter from Mr. Ivanhoe to his agent shows uneven pressure. He wrote in bursts, as if he were thinking in between. Some of the words are typed firmly, others lightly. In the suicide letter, supposedly composed under circumstances where one might expect even more hesitation, all of the words are typed with even pressure."

"Wait a minute," I said. "Strictly speaking, we don't know that letter to Carol Landis came from Ivanhoe. For all we know, she could have typed it herself."

Mac raised an eyebrow. "To what end, Jefferson? We know that the work in progress described in the letter actually exists—or did."

I shrugged. "I can only say that Carol Landis seems determined to prove that Ivanhoe didn't kill himself. I can't think of any nefarious reason for that, but there it is."

"Surely any number of easily authenticated letters and manuscripts from Ivanhoe must exist. Any such deception would be easily uncovered."

"We don't even have to wait for that." Jake pulled a folded piece of paper out of an inside pocket of his blazer. "Here's a letter he signed, the one that brought me here. Maybe you can tell whether the same person wrote the letter to Ms. Landis." He handed it to Alexandra Powers.

She moved her glasses down to her nose, pulled out a small magnifying glass—really!—and studied the letter for a while. "They were written on the same typewriter. The worn-out *e* and the chipped *t* make that a no-brainer.[5] It was a Remington Noiseless Portable No. 7, by the way, a great little machine." Then she went back and forth between that and what I thought of as "the Landis letter."

"Normally, I wouldn't reach an opinion so quickly," she said after five minutes or so of this. "But I'm already well acquainted with Mr. Ivanhoe's typing style, presuming that's who wrote the letter to Carol Landis. I feel very comfortable saying that the author of this letter also wrote that one. I'm no expert on handwriting, but the signatures look the same, too."

"That seals it, then," Mac said. "There is no conceivable reason why someone other than James Ivanhoe would have written both the letter to Carol Landis and the letter to *The Third Rail*. That means that James Ivanhoe did not write the alleged suicide note found with his body. Ergo, he was almost certainly murdered."

---

[5] These distinctions in the letters are not discernable as reproduced but, for the record, Professor Powers had it right in all her conclusions.

Chapter Twenty-Seven
Up Against *The Third Rail*

"This is progress," I said after Mac had sent Alexandra Powers on her way with thanks (and a hearty "check will be forthcoming" promise). "If Ivanhoe didn't kill himself, then presumably he didn't kill Cassandra with the same gun. Somebody else killed both of them, and I vote for whoever has the third key."

"The problem with locked room mysteries in fiction," Mac mused, regarding his cigar, "is that the explanation is usually either too complicated or too simple. I prefer the simple. This would all be much simpler if Cassandra had killed Ivanhoe. Who better for him to have that key made for?"

"She wouldn't even need a key," I pointed out. "By the time Ivanhoe died, she was a ghost."

"There is that, old boy."

"So as I said, one murderer for both—probably somebody who was trying to cover up dirty doings at Samson Microcircuits. Cassandra must have known whatever Ivanhoe knew."

Jake stood up. "Let's not get ahead of ourselves, boys. As motives go, Ivanhoe's letter to *The Third Rail* looks like a dandy. But maybe not. We don't even know if what he wrote is true. I've been assuming that Ivanhoe had the goods, and he probably did, but I've gotten bad tips from credible sources once or twice."

"So you propose to investigate?" Mac said.

"Propose hell." He consulted his watch, which Mac apparently had left on his wrist in a fit of absent-mindedness. "I have an interview at Samson Microcircuits in twenty minutes."

I was impressed. "Somebody agreed to talk to you?"

Jake nodded. "They fobbed me off on their PR guy, name of Carboy. His title is vice president of public affairs, but he's the PR guy. He turned me down at first, but I used my southern charm. Also, I dropped your name, Jeff. I might have even mentioned that we were kin. Would you two care to go along for the ride? As long as you're just seen and not heard, I'm sure Carboy wouldn't mind."

He minded.

Neil Carboy's well-appointed office wasn't half the size of Trey Ellicott's. Also, his administrative assistant was no Ms. Najinski—she didn't even offer us coffee.

Carboy looked like he was wearing a three-piece suit even when he wasn't, but today he was. Was that a look of annoyance behind those Ray-Bans?

He put on a strained smile. "Mr. Teal? I know the other gentlemen by sight and by reputation, but I wasn't expecting a trio of inquisitors."

"Oh, they're just here to watch the journalist in action."

I inwardly winced. Watching a journalist in action ranked just below having my toenails pulled out on my list of favorite things to do. Having worked with journalists all my professional career, and now married to one for almost four years, the process of putting a news story together reminds me of that witty Otto von Bismarck line about laws and sausages—you don't want to see how either one is made. So it is with the news.

"Perhaps it's just as well that you're here, Mr. Cody," Carboy said, arousing my curiosity. He invited the three of us to sit, which we did.

"As you know, we're a private, family-owned company and we don't sell directly to the public. Consequently, we don't seek media attention. My job largely involves dealing with various levels of government and occasionally the trade press. In fact, my first impulse was to turn down the interview request. But Mr. Ellicott—Mr. *Walter* Ellicott—seems to have a lot of respect for your discretion, Mr. Cody. He urged me to talk to Mr. Teal, so I will. But I have to warn you, sir, that I may not be able to answer all of your questions for proprietary and/or national security reasons."

The Colonel nodded. "That goes without saying. I know a bit about national security."

"Yes, of course. You mentioned your military background in our phone conversation. I gather that you are now a freelance journalist."

"That's correct."

I noticed that Carboy didn't refer to the publication Jake was working for on this particular assignment. So my father-in-law hadn't mentioned *The Third Rail* to Carboy. Good thinking! If Carboy had taken one look at *The Third Rail*'s website, which I had, he would have run screaming in the other direction. Jake had told him the truth, but not the whole truth. The ethics of that were debatable, and I could argue either side. If I were a lawyer, I could probably argue both sides at the same time.

"What's the angle of your article?"

"Well, once we get started, who knows where it might go." Jake chuckled benignly. "But this all started with a tip from an Erin resident who thought there might be a story in your company."

Carboy nodded. "That's because we're an anomaly, I assume. Southern Ohio isn't exactly a Midwestern Silicon Valley. There aren't a lot of other high-tech companies in this area, except Altiora, of course. We've added four hundred jobs to the local economy in the past five years.

And Mr. Cody can tell you that we've been a very good corporate citizen."

I could, but I didn't. This wasn't my show.

"What exactly is it that you do?" Jake asked.

"As our name would indicate, Samson makes radiation-hardened microcircuits. Our founder, Mr. Ellicott—that's Mr. Samson I. Ellicott, Junior—was a brilliant engineer. He started the company in the 1980s to make and sell reaction wheels, also known as momentum wheels, for the space industry. That's a kind of flywheel that helps to stabilize satellites and spacecraft without firing rockets, thus saving energy. Do you follow me?"

"Yes," Jake and Mac said, nodding in tandem. I stayed mute.

"After Nine-One-One, we branched out into anti-terrorism devices."

"Such as what?"

Carboy smiled. "I'm sure you understand why I can't answer that in much detail, Mr. Teal. Suffice it to say that we produce devices to detect explosives, bio-chemical weapons, and narcotics in cargo containers, as well as a system to scan airline passengers for weapons."

"Those are handy gadgets to have in a post-Nine-One-One world. You must do well with them."

Carboy frowned, showing that he was a novice at being interviewed. I try to never let my emotions show. *Keep calm and carry on!*

"For several years we did. Candidly, it's no secret in the industry that the Great Recession hit us hard. Everything slowed up after 2008 and it's taken years for the world economy to claw its way back. Military budget cuts also had a significant negative impact on revenues and earnings. Mr. Ellicott Junior had to lend the company money from his personal funds to keep it afloat and save jobs." This was stirring stuff. I wish I'd known about this when I was writing the press release on Walter being added to the St. Benignus board. Clearly he came from noble stock.

"Apparently he did not impoverish himself in the process," Mac observed. "The enterprise seems flourishing today."

"It didn't happen automatically. As Mr. Ellicott Junior pulled away from day-to-day operations, his sons stepped up and took us into new markets."

"Can you give me an example?" Jake prodded.

"I'm afraid that's proprietary."

"Well, how about, for example, Iran or China or North Korea?"

Carboy blanched. "I'm sure you know there is a U.S. arms embargo against Iran and North Korea. I don't think we make any products that we could legally sell to them."

"Exactly."

The two men locked eyes for a while without saying anything. I would love to see those two play a game of poker. Carboy cracked first.

"What are you getting at?"

"The suggestion for a story about Samson Microcircuits came in the form of a letter to an online publication called *The Third Rail*. It accused your company of illicit technology sales to a foreign government."

"That's outrageous!" Carboy looked at Mac and me. *Hey, I'm just along for the ride.*

"Since he's dead I think it's ethical to tell you that letter came from James Ellicott, alias Ivanhoe," Jake continued. "He should know something of the workings of Samson Microcircuits. He inherited part of it from his father, didn't he?"

"The Ellicott brothers—the real Ellicott brothers—are challenging their father's will in court. Ivanhoe had nothing to do with this company."

"He had something to do with the general counsel's wife, it appears."

Carboy stood up. "That's it. This interview is at an end." That's never a winning tactic for dealing with journalists, by the way.

Jake didn't move. "I noticed you didn't actually deny that Samson has sold microcircuits to a country on the U.S. blacklist."

"I do deny it! That didn't happen." Apparently Carboy wasn't getting my "keep calm and carry on" vibes, because he was anything but calm.

"Neil, I—"

Karen Ellicott stood in the doorway, her pretty face clouded by a "what the hell?" look.

"What are you doing here?" She threw this at me in an accusatory tone. I immediately thought of an old joke that ends with "everybody gotta be someplace" uttered in a Yiddish accent. But this didn't seem the right time to tell it.

Her boyfriend-in-doubt answered before I could.

"These *gentlemen*"—I know sarcasm when I hear it— "have just made the ridiculous claim that the company is selling microcircuits to North Korea or some other banned country for military purposes."

"Probably China," Jake said. "Some technology sales to China are legal, but not all. The Chinese have been trying for years to ramp up their system of satellites in low-earth orbit as part of their goal to surpass the U.S. in military power. They need microcircuits for that. The military implications are very big because more satellites would help the Chinese communicate better with their fleets and bombers."

This sounded vaguely familiar. Hadn't I seen a few seconds of a story about a crackdown on illegal technology sales to the Chinese about a week and a half ago on PNN?

"You're making this up," Karen said. But I could tell that she didn't believe herself.

"No, I'm just extrapolating from a letter your younger brother wrote." Jake handed her the copy. She read it quickly.

"That bastard! He didn't tell me any of this."

"Maybe because it isn't true," Carboy snapped.

"You'd like to think that, Neil. I'd like to think it, too. But I bet it is true. I bet Trey made saps of the rest of us—Walter most of all. He must have told Walter what was going down because he had to. But Walter does whatever Trey tells him to, so that was no problem. That had to have been what happened. Why would Jamie risk his reputation on an accusation that wasn't true or that he wasn't sure of?"

Carboy made a visible effort to control himself before he responded. I was proud of him.

"That's a logical question, Karen, but I'm not sure that your favorite brother's actions were logic-driven."

"That reminds me," I said. Actually, it didn't remind me. I just thought this was a good time to finally jump in, beating Mac to the punch. "Why would Ivanhoe blow the whistle on a company that he owned a chunk of?"

Karen didn't even have to think about it. "Money didn't mean much to him, for one thing—not as much as his ideals meant. He had a very romantic view of himself as a knight in shining armor—an Ivanhoe with a typewriter. Talking to Carol over the past few days, I've come to realize that he probably cared about his ideals a lot more than he cared about real people. I bet he found out what was going on from Cassandra and didn't hesitate a second to use it."

"Karen, do you really think—"

"Yes, Neil, I really do. Maybe you ought to think, too."

Every romance has a few rough spots, I suppose, but not always in public. Maybe out of sensitivity and kindness, but probably not, the Colonel brought the subject back to the accusation and away from the accuser.

"This letter isn't very specific. It also isn't proof. If Ivanhoe had any evidence of what he alleged, he must have tucked it away somewhere safe but accessible. Where would he be most likely to do that?"

Not in a computer.

Karen shook her head. "If it's not in the cabin or a safety deposit box at his bank, then I don't know; I'd have to think about it some more. But we may not need any proof to get to the bottom of this. I bet if we push Walter hard enough he'll crack like an egg."

And all the king's horses and all the king's men . . .

Chapter Twenty-Eight
Confession

"Well, then," Mac said, "let us be about it."

Karen hesitated. "I really don't want to do this to Walter. He's just Trey's dupe."

"At some point," Jake said, "the FBI is going to come knocking on Walter's door. Maybe we can help him if we get there first."

The speed at which my father-in-law figured out the right button to press on Karen impressed me. But she responded with a side question:

"Why didn't Jamie just write to the Feds instead of to some third-rate website?"

Jake shrugged. "I didn't know the man, so I can't say for sure. But maybe I was wrong to assume that he had proof. Maybe he was counting on *The Third Rail* to get that. And don't put it past me. I'm pretty good at digging, especially where there's a cyber-trail to follow. But it would be easier for us and better for Walter if he would just come clean."

"All right," Karen snapped. "Let's get it over with."

Carboy followed us out of his office as we prepared to mount an assault on Walter's, talking as he walked. "You're making a mistake, Karen."

She spun around. "Maybe I am, Neil, but don't forget that I'm still an Ellicott and an owner of the company. Not even Trey can take that away from me. Whose side are you on? It's time to decide."

No more Ms. Nice Girl.

Carboy took longer to answer than I would have, given that boy-girl thing they had going. But he pulled it out in the end.

"I'm on your side, Karen. You should know that."

"All right, then," she said, with a Mona Lisa smile. "Let's go."

Once we got past an easily intimidated administrative assistant—presumably Fred Gaffe's niece, Betty—we found Walter playing at his computer. It hit me how much more gray-streaked his mustache was now than it had been the previous spring. He must have been losing a particularly vicious game of solitaire, because he looked over as soon we entered, as if in relief.

"What's this—a posse?" he said with an unconvincing chuckle.

Close enough.

"How long have we been selling microcircuits to the bad guys?" Karen said.

"What are you talking about?" He got the words right, but the delivery failed. He sounded scared, not puzzled.

"Meet my father-in-law, Colonel Jake Teal," I said. "He has some bad news for you, Walter."

Jake ran with it. "Your late brother, James, several days before his death, wrote a letter to an online magazine I write for called *The Third Rail.*"

"Oh, no."

"You've heard of the *Rail*, I see. That's nice. His letter makes very serious allegations that Samson Microcircuits sold technology to a foreign government in violation of U.S. arms embargo laws. I'm betting the government in question was China."

Walter's watery blue eyes darted. He saw an out. "How would Jamie know anything about what the company was doing? He hadn't lived in town for years until recently, and he barely knew what a microcircuit is."

"I'm just going to make an informed guess about that," Jake said. "Did you tell your wife?"

The lawyer's face colored. "Don't bring Cassandra into this, you heartless bastard!"

"Walter." Karen channeled her normally dominant softer side, lowering her voice. "Cassandra brought herself into it if she passed Jamie information. Did you tell her about what the company's been doing?"

Walter sank back. "The pressure was getting to me, looking over my shoulder for the FBI 24/7. I had to tell somebody. I just can't believe Cassie betrayed me like this. The physical infidelity was one thing, but this . . ." Out of words, he stared straight ahead.

Carboy put in his two cents. "Maybe you should get a lawyer before you say anything more, Mr. Ellicott."

Karen gave her beau a withering look, but Walter spoke for himself:

"I *am* a lawyer, Neil, and a damned good one." Carboy's attempt to help him seemed to have brought Walter back to the moment and put some steel in his spine.

"Then you know that if you cooperate with the authorities you might get a break," Jake said. "That's no small matter, considering that this rap could fetch a one-way ticket to one of our less luxurious federal prisons."

"That may be true. It's worth a try. But I get no time off for spilling to the press, and I'll be damned if I talk to that online rag you work for!"

Jake spread his hands, a pleading gesture. "I'm just a freelancer."

"Still."

"All right, all right." Jake closed his notebook and put it in his breast pocket. "I am no longer a reporter, but I'm still curious as hell. I promise that I won't use anything you say until you give me permission, if ever. It's all going to come out in court anyway, and *The Third Rail* would like to have it first. Maybe we can work out a deal after you lawyer-up. I'm sure you're not the brains behind this criminal conspiracy. No offense. I want to hear how you got sucked into this. So please talk."

Walter hesitated.

"Confession is good for the soul, Walter," Mac platitudinized. If anybody else had said that, he'd have lambasted the cliché to heck and back. "As a Catholic, I believe that quite literally."

"Oh, hell, it doesn't matter now. What's the use? Cassie . . ." Walter's voice sounded dead. "Samson Microcircuits was losing money big time after the stock market crash and Great Recession. Dad propped up the company with personal loans for a while, but he couldn't do that forever. I think seeing what was happening to Samson ruined his health. He wasn't really that old when he withdrew from day-to-day operations. Not long after Trey took charge as CEO, we acquired a big new customer."

"He went to the Chinese?" Jake speculated.

"They came to us. We had a product they wanted. That seemed like an answer to a prayer. A couple of orders, no big deal, and we'd be on our feet again. Four years later, we're doing millions of dollars in business with China. We report the sales as momentum wheels for income tax purposes. We didn't cheat on the taxes." Walter shook his head. "I blame myself. I should have put my foot down and told Trey it was wrong from the get-go."

"I gather you had no hint that your prodigal brother was on to your misdeeds," Mac said.

"No, I had no idea."

"What about Trey?"

"Why do you ask?"

"If Trey was aware that Cassandra and James knew about Samson's illegal sales to China, then he had a golden motive to kill both of them."

Karen gasped.

"But Jamie killed himself," Carboy said.

"No, he didn't," Karen said.

"We have virtually proved as much," Mac said. He gave the *Reader's Digest* version of the evidence, starting with the expert opinion that the suicide note was phony and moving on to Carol Landis's alibi for her client and ex-husband.

I had a sudden flash of memory that I shared with Walter when Mac had finished talking.

"Ivanhoe practically told you he had something on you," I said. "I heard him at Cassandra's funeral."

"You heard no such thing!" Walter protested. "You're making that up."

"I'm not the only one who heard it. It was the last thing Ivanhoe said after your argument almost came to blows and before he stalked out of the funeral home: 'You're going to wish I'd never come back to town.' I'm pretty sure those were the exact words."

If I'd punched him he couldn't have looked more surprised. "I thought that was just Jamie being full of himself as usual."

"The meaning seems clear in retrospect," Mac said. "Ivanhoe was hinting at his intention to expose the criminality at Samson Microcircuits. However, one could hardly say that his intention was explicitly stated."

Walter shook his head. "Like I said, I didn't know and Trey didn't know that Jamie had any idea what we were up to. And we wanted to make damned sure that he didn't find out. That's the real reason we filed a lawsuit to block him from inheriting a share of the company. It wasn't just the money, like I said before. If Jamie got his hooks into Samson, he'd be pouring over the books looking for a way to take us down. He wouldn't be happy just taking a decent profit."

Shouldn't that be "an indecent profit" in this case?

"You mean he wouldn't be a patsy like me," Karen said bitterly.

Walter winced. "It's not your fault that you never suspected we were into shady dealings. With the Chinese, for God's sake! You were too nice, too honest to guess. And I wouldn't let Trey bring you into it because I knew you wouldn't go along. You'd have turned us in—like I should have."

"Oh, Walter." I couldn't tell for sure whether that was a "what a crock" sigh or a "you poor sap" sigh.

"The bottom line here is that Trey had a solid gold motive for killing your wife and your other brother," Jake told Walter. He's not one to sugar coat.

Walter was shaking his head before Jake had even finished. "No, no, no. Kill Cassandra and Jamie? No way."

For reasons unclear to me at the time, Mac ignored his protestations.

"At this point everyone in this room has definite knowledge of a federal crime," Mac pointed out. "I believe that puts us all under a legal obligation to report it to the proper authorities."

"Not yet," Karen said in a tone of voice that brooked no argument. "I want a few words with Trey first."

She didn't look so nice.

Chapter Twenty-Nine
Confrontation

Ms. Najinski didn't have time to offer us coffee as Karen led us past her desk.

"But Ms. Ellicott—"

"I'll take the blame, Tamara. He can yell at me."

Without stopping to knock, Karen opened the door to Trey's private office and we all piled in after her.

Samson I. Ellicott, III, captain of industry, was stretched out for a snooze on his leather couch.

"Trey, you scum-bucket!"

His eyes popped open.

"Wha'?"

Karen stood over him like one of the Furies. "I always knew you were a weasel, but I never thought you'd stoop this low. You've blackened our father's name. I hope you rot in prison."

"Prison." Wide awake now, he sat up and regarded what must have seemed to him a room full of villagers with pitchforks and torches. His jaw dropped. "Walter! What have you done?"

"He manned up," Karen said.

"Jamie wrote a letter to *The Third Rail* about the Chinese deals," Walter said. "Cassandra must have told him."

Trey jumped up. "Cassandra! I explicitly told you not to tell that tramp. You fool!"

Walter's face flushed. "You just crossed the line, brother." Walter punched Trey so hard that the older man fell back on the well-padded couch. Blood trickled out of the side of his mouth.

"Damn, that felt good," Walter announced brightly. "It's been a long time coming."

A pitcher of water and some tissues stood at a credenza behind the couch. Jake gave Trey both for his bloody mouth.

"Who the hell are you?" Trey mumbled as he applied the tissue.

"Colonel Jacob Teal, U.S. Army, retired. I'm on assignment for *The Third Rail.*"

"Oh, shit. *The Third Rail?* Oh, shit. I want to talk to my lawyer."

"I'm your lawyer," Walter said with a grim smile.

"Not you, you Judas."

"Indeed," Mac said. "You will certainly require the services of an experienced criminal defense lawyer rather than a corporate one."

"For what it's worth, Trey," Walter said, "I don't believe you killed Cassandra and Jamie."

"Are you nuts? Who would think I did that?"

"Anyone who knows what a strong motive you had for silencing both of them," I said.

"I want a lawyer."

"Maybe Trey and Walter could get a discount if they went to the same attorney," I told Mac later as we sat in his man cave with Jake. "But I suppose Walter wouldn't like that."

"He does seem to have emerged definitively from his brother's shadow," Mac allowed.

In fact, Walter had said he planned to hire an attorney specifically to contact the Feds to strike a deal.

Mac's phone erupted into his "Ride of the Valkyries" ringtone. He answered. "McCabe here. Oh, yes Ms. Landis. Thank you for returning my call. I merely wondered whether, as far as you know, Mr. Ivanhoe's novel in progress was to include a subplot involving illegal technology sales to another country—perhaps to the Confederate States of America. Oh, just a notion I had. Well, not all of my notions work out. Thank you. Have a safe trip home." He disconnected.

"So Trey didn't burn the manuscript to hide his secret," I said.

"No, Jefferson. And that is exactly what I expected to confirm."

Then it must have been facts, and not fiction, that had been reduced to ashes in the fireplace of the murder cabin—Ivanhoe's notes about the corporate crimes of Samson Microcircuits. Or maybe Ivanhoe had simply gotten fed up with a novel that wasn't working out, never mind his optimistic reports to his agent/ex-wife. We'd never know for sure, I thought. But not all of my notions work out either.

"In the end the whole thing was the prodigal son story gone wrong, wasn't it?" I said. "Trey was trying to save his hide, sure. But he probably would have found a less drastic way of dealing with Ivanhoe if he hadn't already hated him for dancing back into town after thirteen years and worming his way into their father's will."

"Oh, I don't know," Jake said between sips of Jameson's Black Barrel. "He killed his sister-in-law, too, didn't he?"

"On what basis do you conclude that Trey killed anyone?" Mac asked mildly. He hoisted his glass of Mt. Carmel Coffee Brown Ale, freshly drawn from the tap at his bar.

"What the hell!" I exploded. "You said so yourself—when you found out about Samson's illegal sales to China."

"I said no such thing, old boy. I merely noted that the consequences of discovery could certainly be severe enough to motivate murder. And then later I noted that if Trey were aware that Cassandra and James knew about those illicit sales, then he had a golden motive to kill both of them. In both instances I was simply making observations of fact, not reaching a conclusion of guilt."

Jake looked at me. "Is he just playing word games?"

Am I my brother-in-law's keeper? (He could certainly use one.)

Mac didn't give me a chance to answer.

"Colonel, I assure you that I am not. My 'if' to Walter Ellicott was highly speculative. There is not a scintilla of evidence that Samson the Third knew of his younger brother's perfidy—or of his sister-in-law's. How would he know?"

"Ivanhoe probably told him, just to rub it in," I said. "That would be in keeping with his romantic self-image as brave whistleblower."

"And did he also tell Trey about his relationship with Cassandra? The killer had to know about that, too, in order to write the pseudo-suicide note."

"Sure, why not?"

"On the other hand, why? And if Ivanhoe told Trey these things, then why not tell Walter, whom he held in such contempt that he cuckolded him? Ivanhoe could have told both simultaneously at the funeral home, at least about the whistle blowing. That would have been the perfect time to lay it all out in front of an audience, if he had chosen to do so, instead of making a veiled threat.

"I ask you, Colonel"—Mac set down his beer and spread his hands—"did Trey Ellicott appear to be completely taken aback when he learned that James Ivanhoe had reported his crime to *The Third Rail?*"

"Yes," Jake admitted. "But maybe he's a good actor."

Mac cleared his throat. "I know something of acting, having dabbled in that line myself. I do not believe that he was acting." He waved away an objection that neither Jake nor I had made. "Yes, he was used to dissembling. However, he would have had to do more than that. He would have had to pretend shock immediately upon being awakened from a sound sleep."

I suddenly realized that Mac wasn't just fencing. "You think you know what happened, don't you?"

"Yes, Jefferson, I believe I do." Strangely, there wasn't a hint of triumphalism in his tone.

"And the hanky-panky at Samson Microcircuits had nothing to do with the murders?"

"*Au contraire*, old boy! Our adventures this afternoon have convinced me that the criminal behavior directed by Trey Ellicott had everything to do with the deaths of his brother and sister-in-law. But there was only one murder."

Chapter Thirty
A Matter of Justice

Mac told us the whole story as he had it doped out.

"I'll be damned." Jake helped himself to another glass of Jameson's. "That's a hell of a yarn. Can you prove any of that?"

"The case is admittedly circumstantial at this point."

"Oscar won't like that," I said.

And he didn't. Mac and I laid it out for him the next morning in his office.

"I can't just test-drive a hairball accusation like that against a solid citizen," he said.

"Perhaps you cannot," Mac conceded. "However, as a private citizen, I have much more liberty than you do. I believe that we should confront him with my suspicions."

"What about slander?" I objected.

"In order to be slanderous, a statement must be both false and damaging to a person's reputation. Since this will be a private conversation among four people, I hardly think that will damage his reputation even if my deductions should prove to be in error."

That last phrase was just a nod in the direction of humility. He really didn't think there was a snowball's chance in hell that he was wrong.

Oscar stood up and put on his official hat. "This town would have been a lot better off if Ivanhoe had never come back."

"I'm sure Lincoln Todd would agree," I said.

Todd had aged about ten years since his daughter's death, the lines in his face looking more like crevasses. He must have lost ten pounds.

"All right, what did you want to tell me about Cassie?" he said after he'd shut the door. We had assembled in the conference room where we'd held meetings of the parade committee. Oscar, Mac, and I sat across the table from Todd.

"We know how she died," Mac said.

Todd snorted. "So does everybody who watches that awful Prime News Network."

Mac waved that away. "Not the fairy tale; the truth."

Todd got up and poured himself a cup of coffee. His hand quivered. "Go on."

"We learned yesterday that the two remaining Ellicott brothers had good reason to want James Ivanhoe out of the way, a motive beyond mere umbrage. They made inviting suspects in his murder. However, that scenario had fatal flaws. So I mentally stepped back to look at the big picture. And what did I see? I saw that someone did not merely wish to kill Ivanhoe but to destroy him—to blacken his memory by presenting him as a killer and a failed writer. That suggested a very personal motive."

"What does this have to do with Cassie?"

"That was the question I asked myself. Hers was a most curious murder. It did not appear to be a robbery gone wrong, and yet her purse was evidently ransacked. Whatever the killer was looking for, and perhaps found, had to be a small item—small enough to fit into that purse. What was it and where did it go?

"There was something curious about the Ivanhoe murder scene as well. The door was dead-bolted. We initially assumed, as we were intended to assume, that Ivanhoe did that from the inside before killing himself. But we have established to our satisfaction that he did not fire that fatal shot. That left us with a locked room mystery.

"There would be no mystery, of course, if a credible suspect had a key to the Ivanhoe cabin. Amos Yoder did not fit the criterion of credibility. Jefferson learned that Phil Oakland had made another key, but its location was unknown. Neither Ivanhoe's sister nor his agent had it, and efforts to find it hidden outside the cabin proved fruitless. Jefferson set me to thinking, however, when he referred to Ms. Ellicott and Ms. Landis as the two women in his life 'who are still alive.' Who was more likely to have that third key than a woman who was no longer alive—the one woman in Erin with whom we know that Ivanhoe had had an intimate relationship?"

"Cassie," Todd said softly.

"As a thought experiment, I posited that the killer took the key from Cassandra's purse and used it to get into Ivanhoe's cabin—or, at least, to lock up after the murder. Since Ivanhoe's killer used the same gun that killed Cassandra, that made perfect sense."

"And who was this person who killed both Cassandra and Jamie?" Todd spoke in a cold, emotionless voice.

Mac shook his head slowly. "I said my thought experiment made perfect sense, not that it was correct in every particular. In reality, the same person did not kill both. And yet there was only one killer as the term is conventionally understood."

At this point I would have been ready to strangle Mac for not cutting to the chase if he hadn't already explained it to Oscar and me. But I knew what he was doing—ratcheting up the pressure turn by turn. Todd had to know where this was going as well as the rest of us. He looked angry.

"Why don't you cut out the double talk and just come out with it?"

"I would prefer to take you through my thought process so that you understand that my conviction about the identity of the killer is well founded. My mind turned to the murder weapon. The gun belonged to Walter Ellicott. Obviously, he was Chief Hummel's first suspect, as he should have been."

"Obviously," Oscar grunted.

"The gun fired in the heat of anger during a domestic dispute is almost a cliché, it happens so often. However, Walter had an indisputable alibi. Assuming premeditation, he could have hired someone to kill a wife who had given her affections to another. But surely no one, however dense, would provide the hit man with the gun and then later identify it as his own."

"My son-in-law is a good man," Todd said. "I never would have let him take the fall for something he didn't do. That's why I kept asking about the investigation—to make sure he wasn't on the hook. But Walter seemed to fade pretty quickly as a suspect."

Mac nodded, apparently buying Todd's assurances of his concern for Walter. I'd like to think that Todd meant it, but who knows for sure? Maybe not even Todd.

"Who besides Walter would have had access to the gun and knowledge of where it was?" Mac continued. "I knew that there was no maid or cleaning person. I also knew that one should never overlook the obvious answer, which in this case was Cassandra. She either came across the gun or always knew where it was. She used it to kill herself. And you found her body, Mr. Todd."

Todd sat back into his chair, as if Mac's words had delivered a physical blow.

"No wonder you were such a basket case the day of the committee meeting here in this office," I said. "Mary Landfair said you'd just gotten back in the office. That must have been right after you came back from Skylark Lane."

"She called me to say goodbye," Todd said slowly. "She told me what she was going to do and why. She said that she'd made a disastrous mistake and she didn't see any other way out—that Walter could never forgive her and she could never forgive herself."

"She had told Ivanhoe about Samson Microcircuits' illegal sales to China," Mac said.

Todd nodded almost imperceptibly. "Jamie told her that he was going to take the company down. She said the worst part was that he'd used her. She'd been a fool to fall for him again. Walter was going to be so hurt. I told her that I could help, that we could find a way out, but she didn't listen to me. She said good-bye and hung up. I flew out of here, ran to her house, and let myself in with a key that she'd given me in case there was a problem when they went on vacation. And there she was."

He put his head in his hands and cried.

"Why did you take the gun?" Oscar asked softly after a few moments.

"I didn't want anybody to know that she'd killed herself because of the reason. I didn't want her to be embarrassed in death."

"Surely there was more to it than that," Mac said. "Jefferson tells me that you are well known to be a quick thinker and one who makes decisions quickly. You must have decided on the spot to kill Ivanhoe with the same gun."

Todd sat up straight, back in the game. Confession time was over. "Kill? What makes you think I did that?"

"Whoever killed Ivanhoe did so for highly personal reasons that made him want to not only take the man's life but also destroy his reputation as a writer. The spurious suicide note indicated that Ivanhoe could no longer write. To bolster that claim—and perhaps also for the shear enjoyment of it—the killer burned the novel in progress. The manuscript of *Sunbelt* must have been in the fireplace, reduced to ashes, because it is nowhere else. And we know from Ivanhoe's agent that the novel had nothing to do with the unlawful activities of his family's company, so that is not why it was burned.

"Most significantly, though, the killer had Ivanhoe confess responsibility for Cassandra's death. That person must have known that no other candidate would emerge because Cassandra took her own life. Who else knew that but you, Mr. Todd? Once I realized that, I saw a few other indications.

"In a conversation after your daughter's death, you professed to not know about Ivanhoe's cabin in the woods, even though the whole town seemed to. And yet, later, in an interview with PNN's Bennington Lee, you referred to its interior, noting the presence of a refrigerator. I verified my memory of that by watching the video on PNN's website."

"I must have read that somewhere."

"That was a possibility that I could not discount, so I did a search of newspaper and magazine stories written about Ivanhoe since he built the cabin. A few alluded to it, but none described it.

"Then there was the matter of Cassandra's key to that cabin. There was no killer to take it from her purse—I realized quickly that I was wrong about that. However, you took it as part of your quickly formulated plan to kill Ivanhoe, make his death look like a suicide, and blame him for Cassandra's death. Perhaps using her key to get into her house gave you the idea. You also took the gun to bolster the murder-suicide scenario. Perhaps you also considered it poetic justice that Ivanhoe should die with the same gun that killed Cassandra, given that you blamed her death on him, and that he be thought a suicide."

There was a silence.

"That's it?" Todd said to Mac at last. "That's all you have?"

"It is the truth, is it not?"

"Wait a minute," Oscar said. "Before you say anything, Mr. Todd, you have the right to remain silent and to not answer questions. Do you understand?"

"Of course I do."

Oscar went through the whole Miranda ritual.

"Now I have a question for you, Chief," Todd said at the end. "You don't seriously expect the prosecutor to go to court on McCabe's theory without any real evidence, do you? I'm a respected man in this town."

Oscar squirmed. "We'll be searching the cabin for your fingerprints. That would put you on the scene. And you've already established a motive by telling us why Cassandra killed herself. But if you'd like to confess, that would be helpful and I'd be much obliged."

Maybe a look of concern passed over Todd's face, quickly replaced by one of determination. More likely, I just remember it that way because of what happened later.

"I'd like to help you out, Chief, but that's not going to happen."

"Capital punishment in the twenty-first century is not only immoral," Mac rumbled, "it is also unnecessary for the protection of society. I cannot accept it when applied by the state, and still less when imposed by a private individual in the form of murder. Therefore, I do not condone your actions, Mr. Todd. However, as a father, I understand why you felt that you needed retribution—"

Todd cut him off. "Retribution? I—*whoever* killed Jamie Ellicott acted as an agent of justice. That suicide note told the moral truth: He was responsible for Cassandra's death as much as if he'd pulled the trigger. But he was never going to be held to account for it in a court of law."

"Cassandra was responsible for her own actions, as are we all," Mac corrected him. "However, set that to one side. Whether you accept free will or not, vigilante 'justice' is no justice. That is why we have a hallowed system of due process and trial by one's peers in this nation. Be thankful that you will someday have the day in court that you denied to James Ivanhoe."

"Don't count on that. I admit my foolish actions in concealing Cassie's suicide, but I can't believe that Marvin Slade will want to prosecute a grieving father for that, and still less for your unproven murder accusation." Todd looked at his watch. "Well, the sun is over the yardarm." He opened the credenza behind him and pulled out a bottle of Maker's Mark. "How about a drink, gentlemen? You must be off duty by now, Chief."

Oscar stood up. "I'll never be that off duty."

Chapter Thirty-One
Fire!

"Jeff! Wake up! Ivanhoe's cabin's burning down."

My eyes popped open. "What?"

Lynda stood over me, baby at her bosom. "The place is engulfed in flames. I just saw it on TV4. A report, not the fire. They don't have a reporter at the scene yet."

The fingerprints! No cabin, no fingerprints.

"Damn that Oscar!" I muttered as I pulled on a pair of pants.

"What did he do?"

"It's what he didn't do. Mac was afraid Todd would destroy any evidence against him that might still be in the cabin, so he told Oscar to have the place watched all night. But Oscar said he's already over-budget for the month because of the parade. Apparently the mayor's after him to reign it in."

Quickly dressed, I took off in my aging but trusty New Beetle without even thinking to call Mac.

Smoke from the blaze was visible miles away. I pulled off to the road a quarter-mile or so from the cabin, right behind Oscar's car. Eb Schonert and his crew of firefighters were still at it, but clearly losing the battle. I pulled out my phone. It was almost six o'clock. Mac would be eating breakfast by now. I punched his name on my Contacts list.

"Good morning, old boy!" *How can he sound so cheerful at this time of day?*

"Not exactly. There's quite a bonfire going at Ivanhoe's place."

After a pause, Mac said, "Well, Mr. Todd is not one to take half-measures, is he? One has to almost admire his boldness."

I'm not there yet.

As we talked, I got out of the car for a better look. I saw Oscar standing next to Eb. Walking toward them . . .

"I don't believe this, Mac. Todd's here! I'll call you back."

I ran to catch up to the trio, struggling not to inhale too much smoke in the process.

". . . a tragedy, Chief," I heard Todd say. It was too dark to see the expression on his face an hour before sunrise, but he wasn't a good enough actor to keep the irony out of his voice.

"In the neighborhood, were you?" Oscar asked in a dangerously mild voice.

"I was having breakfast when I saw a report of the fire on television." He had dressed carefully, but in older clothes that he didn't have to worry about being smoke-damaged. "With the fire, the smoke, and the water, I'm afraid you won't be getting any evidence out of that cabin."

Oscar offered a reassuring smile. "Oh, you don't need to worry about that, Mr. Todd. You see, Mac was worried about securing the crime scene. I couldn't buy his idea of having somebody guard the place all night. Too expensive. But I did spend some overtime having my troops go over every inch of the place for fingerprints. Gibbons also picked up a sword that looked out of place."

"You're lying, Hummel."

Oddly enough, he wasn't.

Chapter Thirty-Two
Life Goes On

"The great irony," Mac mused, "is that this was a case of murder-suicide, just as we were intended to believe. However, the apparent murder was a suicide and the apparent suicide was a murder."

Lynda, Jake, and I stood with him at the bar of his study (AKA man cave) that evening. A party was underway downstairs to mark the actual feast of St. Patrick, but we were having a side celebration of our own. It was Jake's last day in Erin. Nelson Abbott had already left town, having served his time, to look for headlines elsewhere. Kate was in the kitchen, cutting a green velvet layer cake for those who didn't care about what that would do to their Body Mass Index. (Who am I to judge?)

Music from an Irish band called The Banshees, performing in the basement below us, made the floors vibrate. Still, we spoke in relatively low voices. Most of the revelers were in blissful ignorance that Lincoln Todd, pillar of the Erin business community, was facing a murder rap.

"No one will ever know how often murder and suicide have been confused," my brother-in-law went on. "Doubtless, murder most foul passed off as self-destruction is the more common instance. But suicide either made to look like or assumed to be murder is far from unknown."

"That happened in a Sherlock Holmes story," Lynda said. *Spoiler alert!* "In 'The Problem of Thor Bridge,' a wife crazy with jealousy stands at a bridge and shoots herself with a gun tied to a stone by a rope. Right according to plan, she falls dead, the weight of the stone pulls the gun into the water, and the governess who she thinks her husband is fooling around with winds up accused of murder."

"Brava, Lynda!" Mac said. "You have become quite the Sherlockian. 'Thor Bridge' is an excellent detective story, belying the old canard that all of the later Holmes tales are inferior to the earlier ones."

Whatever.

Lynda favored me with her gold-flecked baby browns. "And didn't you say that suicide made to look like murder was one of the solutions to a locked room mystery that Carr mentioned in that book Mac gave you?"

"But Cassandra's murder wasn't the locked room!"

Totally confused, I turned to Jake for a change of subject. "You've been poking around this story. Do you think Ivanhoe re-ignited his former flame just to get dirt on the family firm?"

He shrugged without spilling the amber beverage in his rocks glass. "I could roll the dice on that one. His sister said she didn't know what to believe about him anymore. Maybe he really cared about the woman, or wanted to recapture his lost youth, and the dirt about the company was just a gift that came out in pillow talk. Or maybe that's what he was after all along. From what Todd said before he clammed up, Cassandra felt used. But that's no proof. She also felt guilty about what she'd done, too, and that colored everything."

Mac quaffed his brew. Can one quaff meditatively?

"When we realized that Ivanhoe's death was murder," he said, "I speculated whether the motive was love or money or fear. It turned out to be love in an unexpected way, a distorted manifestation of parental love."

"Since Todd thought Ivanhoe was responsible for Cassandra's death, and he even framed him for the supposed murder," Lynda said, twirling her second

Manhattan, "why didn't he just plant the gun in Ivanhoe's cabin and leave it up to the legal authorities to take care of him? If he'd done that, he wouldn't be facing a murder charge now."

"Killers are not known for expecting that they will be caught. That is one answer. Another is that Todd set himself up above the law as judge, jury, and executioner."

"Didn't Sherlock Holmes do that a few times?" I poked.

Mac steamed on: "And yet a third answer—perhaps the most convincing—is that there could be no certainty that a living James Ivanhoe would be tried and convicted of murdering his paramour. Lincoln Todd, I am given to understand, is not one to take chances."

So risk-averse was Todd, in fact, that a week later he cut a plea deal with Marvin Slade when he realized that Oscar had the goods on him. Fingerprints on the underside of a light switch in the murder room put Todd at a location in which he, unwisely, claimed to have never been.

Less significantly, Lt. Col. Gibbons also was able to establish Todd as the owner of the broadsword he'd removed from the room, which fit Mac's theory that the killer had distracted Ivanhoe by showing him a potential addition to his weapons collection before he shot him. The Scottish sword came from a store in Georgetown, in nearby Brown County, which specializes in replica medieval weapons.

Erica Slade, the prosecutor's bitter ex-wife and frequent *bête noir* in the courtroom, publicly snorted at this purely circumstantial evidence. She tried to convince Todd that Marvin couldn't convict Jack the Ripper on proof like that, but he overruled her and insisted on copping a plea. Or so I hear. Apparently the possibility of lethal injection, however remote, didn't appeal to him. Or maybe he just didn't have the will to go through a long and expensive trial.

Samson I. Ellicott III, on the other hand, chose not to roll over. The day Walter began singing to the Feds, his big brother lawyered up with a D.C.-based attorney experienced in such matters.

"Walter will have to do some time, but not a lot of it," Karen told Mac and me when we ran into her on the street one day at lunchtime. "I promised I'd visit him. We're closer now than we've ever been. He did the right thing in the end."

"I assume that you are cooperating with the federal authorities," Mac said.

"What could I tell them? I didn't know anything."

"As the executrix of Ivanhoe's estate, surely you found whatever evidence he had tucked away against Samson Microcircuits."

"Not really. All I found was a reference in his journal to what Cassandra had told him. That's third-hand information, and unnecessary at this point."

Of course, she *would* say that if there were evidence that also implicated somebody else dear to her, such as her boyfriend. But I believed her.

Mac shrugged his massive shoulders. "Well, that is that, then. Colonel Teal was in error in his very natural assumption that Ivanhoe had proof of his accusation about the company. At any rate, Karen, may I take this opportunity to congratulate you?"

"On what?"

Mac pointed to a ring on the third finger of her left hand, studded with small diamonds but a lot of them. "On your engagement to Mr. Carboy."

She was too old to blush, so I won't say she blushed. But her cheeks changed color. "Oh, thanks. Our immediate prospects are not exactly bright. We both work for a company in big trouble, and I own part of it. But we'll be okay. Neil's shorts are a little tight, but he's a good man. Some other company will snap him up—and me, too, I hope. We're both willing to relocate. Maybe under totally new management Samson can survive and thrive. I hope so for the sake of our workers and for the town."

Change was in the air in Erin, and St. Benignus was not immune from the *Zeitgeist*. That hit home late one afternoon that April when the always-irritating Ralph Pendergast stopped by my office.

"I suppose you know that a search has been underway for Linc's replacement at the Convention & Visitors Bureau."

I'd gone out of my way not to mention Todd to Ralph, knowing that the two had been good friends. I'm not one to rub a sore spot if I can help it. Honest. "I hope you don't blame me that Todd's going to spend the rest of his life in prison," I said with a forced chuckle.

"What? Don't be absurd. I blame him."

"So, did you apply for his job?"

The wish is father to the thought. I couldn't be that lucky. How many times over the past six years had I daydreamed that Ralph, who hated McCabe's Department of Popular Culture and was none too fond of me, would move on?

"As a matter of fact, Cody, I did. The search committee recommended me and the directors of the association hired me. I'm here to tell you that I'm leaving St. Benignus at the end of the academic year. You might want to send out a press release about that."

"Leaving, as in gone?" *But not forgotten!*

"Yes, but only from here. I'm sure that you and I will have a chance to work together again on civic matters. The next St. Patrick's Day parade is only eleven months away."

A Few Words of Thanks

Once again Jeff Cody and Dan Andriacco both need to thank all the people whose talented work helped to made this latest Sebastian McCabe—Jeff Cody adventure see the light of day:

Ann Brauer Andriacco, for her constant assistance and encouragement, as well as her readership;

Kieran McMullen, my sometime co-author, for always being on call to answer questions about police procedure, for reading the first draft, and for suggesting the fire;

Jeff Suess, for proofreading and final preparation of the manuscript; and

Steve Winter, for applying his engineering eye to the text.

Special thanks, as always, must go to Steve Emecz for being the world's most easy-to-work-with publisher.

About the Author

Dan Andriacco has been reading mysteries since he discovered Sherlock Holmes at the age of nine, and writing them almost as long. The first six books in his popular Sebastian McCabe — Jeff Cody series are *No Police Like Holmes*, *Holmes Sweet Holmes*, *The* 1895 *Murder*, *The Disappearance of Mr. James Phillimore*, *Rogues Gallery*, and *Bookmarked for Murder*. He is also the co-author, with Kieran McMullen, of *The Amateur Executioner*, *The Poisoned Penman*, and *The Egyptian Curse* mysteries solved by Enoch Hale with Sherlock Holmes.

A member of the Tankerville Club, the Illustrious Clients, the Vatican Cameos, and the John H. Watson Society, and an associate member of the Diogenes Club of Washington, D.C., Dan is also the author of *Baker Street Beat: An Eclectic Collection of Sherlockian Scribblings*. Follow his blog at www.danandriacco.com, his tweets at @*DanAndriacco*, and his Facebook Fan Page at: www.facebook.com/DanAndriaccoMysteries.

Dr. Dan and his wife, Ann, have three grown children and six grandchildren. They live in Cincinnati, Ohio, USA, about forty miles downriver from Erin.

Praise for the earlier
Sebastian McCabe—Jeff Cody mysteries

"The ingenious twist at the end is an example of Andriacco's masterful ability to pen a page-turner. *Bookmarked for Murder* is a must-read for anyone who loves a classic who-done-it." —Mystery writer Kathleen Kaska

"You're in the hands of a master of mystery plotting here. *Rogues Gallery* is a delightful read, hard to put down, and highly recommended. And did I say fun?" —Hollywood screenwriter Bonnie MacBird

"The villain is hard to discern and the motives involved are even more obscure. All-in-all, this (*The Disappearance of Mr. James Phillimore*) is a fun read in a series that keeps getting better with each new tale." —Philip K. Jones

"*The* 1895 *Murder* is the most smoothly-plotted and written Cody/McCabe mystery yet. Mr. Andriacco plays fair with the reader, but his clues are deftly hidden, much as Sebastian McCabe hides the secrets to his magic tricks under an entertaining run of palaver." —*The Well-Read Sherlockian*

"I loved Dan Andriacco's first novel about Sebastian McCabe and Jeff Cody, and I'm delighted to recommend (*Holmes Sweet Holmes*), which has a curiously topical touch." —Roger Johnson, *The Sherlock Holmes Society of London*

"*No Police Like Holmes* is a chocolate bar of a novel— delicious, addictive, and leaves a craving for more." —*Girl Meets Sherlock*

Also from MX Publishing

Visit www.mxpublishing.com for dozens of other Sherlock Holmes novels, novellas, short story collections, Conan Doyle biographies, Holmes travel books, and more.

MX Publishing is the award-winning, world's largest independent Sherlock Holmes Book publishers with over 100 new authors and 200 new Sherlock Holmes stories in print.

Join us at Facebook at the largest Sherlock Holmes books page: www.facebook.com/BooksSherlockHolmes/

Also from MX Publishing

The Sherlock Holmes and Enoch Hale Series

The Amateur Executioner
The Poisoned Penman
The Egyptian Curse

"The Amateur Executioner: Enoch Hale Meets Sherlock Holmes", the first collaboration between Dan Andriacco and Kieran McMullen, concerns the possibility of a Fenian attack in London. Hale, a native Bostonian, is a reporter for London's Central News Syndicate - where, in 1920, Horace Harker is still a familiar figure, though far from revered. "The Amateur Executioner" takes us into an ambiguous and murky world where right and wrong aren't always distinguishable. I look forward to reading more about Enoch Hale."
Sherlock Holmes Society of London